The
Mongol Reply

The Mongol Reply

Benjamin M. Schutz

Five Star • Waterville, Maine

Copyright © 2004 by Benjamin M. Schutz

Quote from *A Man for All Seasons*, Random House, 1960.
Reprinted by courtesy of the publisher.

First Edition
First Printing: October 2004

Published in 2004 in conjunction with Tekno Books
and Ed Gorman.

Set in 11 pt. Plantin by Al Chase.

Printed in the United States on permanent paper.

Library of Congress Cataloging-in-Publication Data

Schutz, Benjamin M.
    The Mongol reply / Benjamin M. Schutz.—1st ed.
      p. cm.
    ISBN 1-4104-0200-2 (hc : alk. paper)
    1. Custody of children—Fiction.   2. Separated people—Fiction.
I. Title.
PS3569.C5556M66 2004
    813'.54—dc22   2004053346

DEDICATION

In memory of my mother
Rhoda K. Schutz (1926–2002)

All the leaves are gone—
Forever there will be a
Tiger in Paris.

And with heartfelt thanks to
"Swifty" Myers, Jr. and his
Lazarus Literary Agency.
It's great to be alive.

ACKNOWLEDGEMENTS

I would like to thank the following people for the gift of their friendship and expertise: Dawn Temple, typist; Tara Fajens, rock climber; Joe Condo and Glenn Lewis, whose skill and integrity bring honor to the practice of family law. Any errors are entirely my responsibility.

PROLOGUE

The rocking chair creaked rhythmically, rising in pitch as he rode it forward and then falling away with him. He clung to that sound, an anchor outside the storm in his head. He listened carefully. The sound was always the same. He would settle for that. Let everything stay the same. He looked out the window. No one had come yet. But they would. He would hear them before he saw them, drowning out the rocker, ending this respite.

The breeze caressed his face. He had opened the window to hear better. So he wouldn't be surprised. He didn't want to be surprised anymore.

He stroked the head pressed into his shoulder and rocked on, awaiting the announcement that once again his life had changed beyond return.

ROPER: So Now you'd give the Devil benefit of Law!

MORE: Yes. What would you do? Cut a great road through the Law to get after the Devil?

ROPER: I'd cut down every Law in England to do that!

MORE: Oh? And when the last Law was down, and the Devil turned round on you—where would you hide, Roper, the Laws all being flat? This country's planted thick with Laws from coast to coast—man's Laws, not God's—and if you cut them down—and you're just the man to do it—d'you really think you could stand upright in the winds that would blow then? Yes, I'd give the Devil benefit of Law, for my own safety's sake.

Robert Bolt
A Man for All Seasons
Act 1

CHAPTER ONE

Morgan Reece took a seat on the Metro facing the door. After the morning rush hour, the trains from Vienna to D.C. were empty. He took the chapter he was working on out of his briefcase, flipped to the last page he'd edited and began to read. The car would be pretty empty until it went underground in East Falls Church and began to burrow under Arlington towards the Potomac. By Foggy Bottom it would be packed, and he'd have to quit working. Thirty minutes in, thirty minutes out. An hour's worth of work on the paper beat fighting the traffic on I-66, he thought.

At each stop, Reece looked up at the doors for a moment to see who was coming aboard and, satisfied that his life would not be enriched or endangered, went back to work. By the Court House stop, Reece was sharing his seat with a construction worker who alternated one unlaced work boot over the other while he glanced nervously up and down the car. Reece leaned a bit away from the man and slid his papers towards one end of the briefcase. At least he could still stretch out his legs. As soon as someone took the seat perpendicular to him, that would end. He decided he'd stop work then and just count the stops and watch the faces.

A pair of ankle boots and leggings slid in and Reece withdrew to let them get settled. When they stayed tucked back along the edge of their seat, he reclaimed his position. He glanced up and saw hands shuffling papers in a lap. The woman had very short brown hair that stuck straight out like the first feathers on a baby bird. She was looking down at her papers while she rearranged their order. She had a long neck, Reece thought, like a Modigliani, and found himself surprised that he'd noticed.

Reece returned to the section on children's drawings as indicators of sexual abuse and how they compared with their use of anatomically detailed dolls. The train slammed to a halt and Reece's papers spilled over the end of his briefcase and littered the floor of the car.

"Shit." He muttered and bent forward to pick them up before the standing passengers adjusted themselves back into place and stood on them. Bending down, he saw something dark out of the corner of his eye and pulled back just before butting heads with the short-haired woman.

"Sorry," she said and then slid off the chair and nimbly squatted down to scoop up her papers from the floor.

Reece waited for her to finish, but when she was done, she twisted around to pick up his papers and handed them to him.

"Here," she said, and took her seat as the car began to move.

"Thanks." Reece smiled briefly, but she was looking down and shuffling the pages in her lap.

Reece tapped the edges of his papers on his briefcase and began to check the numbers. The car slowed, then stopped and the conductor called out "Rosslyn." The young woman stood up, adjusted her waist pack and strode out of the car. Reece glanced up for a moment, decided that indeed her neck was long, but not too long, and went back to his paper.

Satisfied that the pages were all there, he slipped them back into his briefcase and crossed under the Potomac into Washington D.C.

CHAPTER TWO

High above the steel worm that Morgan Reece rode, above the street-side scramble, in the pastel and Muzak calm on the sixteenth floor of the Hungerford Tower, two men met to preserve family values.

"I want that bitch dead," Tom Tully said.

"I don't think we can help you with that, Mr. Tully, we're just divorce lawyers," Albert Olen Garfield said.

"That's not what I've heard. A friend of mine, he calls you 'Agent Orange.' He says your shadow can kill. That's what I want." The big man jabbed his finger into space to emphasize his point. "I want that bitch to beg for death. I want her left with nothing, absolutely fucking nothing. Do her like these guys would."

Tom "The Bomb" Tully, special teams coach of the Virginia Squires and one-time scourge of NFL wide receivers, quarterbacks, runners, anyone unwary or unprotected, rapped a lumpy knuckle against the glass that covered Albert Garfield's copy of the letter from Subutai to Genghis Khan concerning his visit to the Persians.

Contemptuous of the barbarians, the Persians had taken the Khan's gifts, killed his emissaries and not once looked to the east. Subutai and 50,000 horsemen rode in reply. Stopping briefly in his pursuit of the Shah, (whom he would ultimately catch, and, before decapitating, pour molten silver into his eyes, ears, nose and throat), Subutai wrote this:

We have come to Persia. Where we found them we killed them all, man, woman and child. Villages we burn, towns we raze. We have sown salt in their fields, fouled their rivers, slaughtered their sheep, cattle and chickens, burned their crops, leveled their forests. There is a great shrieking before us and an even greater silence behind. Rejoice, the birds have all left Persia for there is nowhere to roost.

Twenty-five years after first reading that letter, Albert Garfield was still thrilled by each word. Ornately framed, it hung on the wall near the chair for prospective clients. Every once in a while one of them would invoke the Mongol reply and Albert imagined himself on horseback leading the hordes between the shrieking and the silence.

"Mr. Tully, is there any particular reason that you'd like us to visit all this misery on your wife?"

"Goddamn right there is. Somebody else is irrigating her trench, that's why! Nobody does that to me. Nobody." Tully shook his head in disbelief.

Ten years past his prime, he was still an impressive specimen. Six-feet-one and two hundred and five pounds, bowlegged, a wedge for a torso and arms down to his knees. All this commanded by a goateed skull with gun port eyes.

"This somebody who's 'irrigating' your wife, does he have a name?"

"If he did, I wouldn't be here. I'd be needing a defense attorney."

"How do you know your wife's having an affair?"

"I caught the bitch, that's how. I came back early from a practice and saw her playing tonsil hockey out in front of the house."

"Did you approach her?"

"No. I was in my car at the end of the block. They didn't

see me. I hung back waiting to see if the bastard was going to come into my house. Boy, did I want that. Please Lord, please let him come into my house and do this. Boom." Tully slammed a fist into a palm. "One dead motherfucker. No, two dead motherfuckers."

"Was the man driving his own car?"

"I guess. I decided not to get too close. I'd seen all that I needed to anyway. I let him drive off."

"Did you get a license tag?"

"No. It was a Toyota though, a Camry maybe, burgundy color."

"Have you talked about this with your wife?"

"No. I thought about going in, grabbing her by the throat and tossing her out the door. You want your dicking elsewhere, then park your sorry ass elsewhere. Then I decided her not knowing that I know was a good thing. Allow me to do it right, set her up, get on her blindside and tee off on her. I'm gonna go right through her, just like I did Conway. Boom. Lights out."

Cisco Conway, the Eagles wideout, had been tackled by the cornerback, who had both of Conway's legs around the ankles. He was trying to hop free when "The Bomb" exploded after a twenty-five-yard cross-field dash. He hit him chest high, helmet and forearm. Conway snapped over like a slinky. His head slammed into the turf and shuddered inside his helmet like a recoiling springboard. After two years in a coma, Cisco Conway died.

"And that's what you'd like our help with?"

"Yeah. I want to blow this bitch right out of the water. I don't want her to see it coming. From what I hear, you do that better than anyone else around."

Garfield smiled, "We'll take your case, Mr. Tully." He came around his desk, hand extended, and shook Tully's.

"I'm going to ask you to fill out a questionnaire now and leave a retainer with us." Tully was steered towards the door.

"How much?" Tully asked anxiously.

"Ten thousand dollars. Is that a problem?"

"Uh, no. I can cover that." Tully patted the breast of his jacket and removed an envelope. Garfield saw a thick wad of hundreds.

"Good. After we look at this initial information we'll be able to plan your strategy. One other thing, if we're going to use adultery as the grounds for divorce, you can't sleep with her. Once you've found out about it, that can be construed as forgiveness."

"No problem there. The bitch won't let me anywhere near her. My money's good enough for her, but not me."

"Don't do anything differently. Treat her just as you always have. We don't want her to have any idea about what we have in store for her. Okay?"

"Sure. No problem."

"Good. Looks like you came to the right place after all, Mr. Tully." Garfield clapped him on the shoulder and pulled the door open.

As Tully stepped through the doorway, Garfield said, "Why settle for dead though? We can do so much more."

CHAPTER THREE

"Why are we here this morning, Mr. Garfield?"

"Your Honor, we have a motion for emergency removal and exclusion from the marital residence and temporary custody of the minor children of my client, Mr. Thomas Tully."

Judge Harold Kenniston frowned at Albert Garfield. Such a motion was hardly ever granted in an *ex parte* hearing.

"And why should I grant this motion, Mr. Garfield?"

"Because my client fears for his safety and the safety of his children. We come before the court with an affidavit signed by my client, that his wife threatened to do a . . ." Garfield leaned down and flipped through the papers on the table before him. "Here it is, to do a 'Manassas' on him."

"A what?"

"A 'Manassas,' Your Honor. It is, I believe, a term of art among women these days. It means to cut off a man's penis while he sleeps, in retaliation for an imagined injury."

"And when did this occur?"

"Last night, Your Honor. My client was terrified. He spent the night in his bedroom with the door locked and barricaded. When he thought his wife had gone to sleep, he called me and I told him I would come right into court to get protection for him and his children."

"So that's why this hearing is an emergency. Why isn't Mrs. Tully here to respond to this?"

"We couldn't locate her to tell her of this hearing."

"You couldn't locate her?" Kenniston scowled at this development.

"Yes, Your Honor. She apparently left the house early this morning and Mr. Tully doesn't know where she went."

"Did she pack her clothes? Has she left the family?"

"No, Your Honor, we don't believe that's the case. We just don't know why or where she's gone, or when she'll be back."

"Has Mrs. Tully ever attempted to 'do a Manassas' or any other kind of bodily harm to her husband?"

"We have the children's nanny here who will testify to a fight between Mr. and Mrs. Tully where she attempted to scratch his face and kicked him."

"Mr. Garfield, you're going to have to do better than that. An affidavit alleging a threat, signed by one of the parties, and a fight where she 'attempted to scratch his face.' I am not moved."

"Your Honor, we have a number of other witnesses prepared to testify in this matter."

"Mr. Garfield, this is an emergency hearing and you have a number of witnesses ready to appear? When were they contacted?"

"Last night and this morning, Your Honor. Their availability attests to the seriousness of the matter and the long build-up of Mrs. Tully's profound emotional problems. Mr. Tully has sought help from friends, family and professionals to try to salvage his marriage and family. It wasn't until this last event that he sought legal protection. Your Honor, you will hear about her extensive psychiatric history."

"Wait a minute, Mr. Garfield, are you proposing to put on expert testimony?"

"Yes, Your Honor. Dr. Stanley Pecorino is here today. He has evaluated the children and is ready to opine on . . ."

"Wait just a minute, has he seen their mother?"

"No, Your Honor, but . . ."

"But nothing, Mr. Garfield. If you think that Dr. Pecorino is going to come into my court and tell me that these children should live with their father when he's never even seen their mother, you are sadly mistaken."

"Of course not, Your Honor." Garfield absorbed and redirected this assault on his battle plan. "Dr. Pecorino is here to give testimony about the children's perception of their mother. About the caretaking deficits that exist based upon their play in his office."

"Is he going to testify about her mental health?"

"Yes, Your Honor."

"And how does he propose to do that? What is his foundation going to be?"

"Well, the children's play, his interviews with them and the history he was given by their father."

"That's it?"

"Yes, Your Honor."

"I am telling you, Mr. Garfield, that I will not give such testimony much weight at all. I am still not inclined to grant your motion. Who are your other witnesses?"

Garfield was watching his carefully choreographed blitzkrieg turn into a self-inflicted gunshot wound. That was the problem with the system, he thought. You never knew what judge you'd get. Why couldn't he have drawn "Sleepy" Duncan, a man with no respect for the law or the facts? Good old Sleepy ruled entirely on his biases, carefully concealed under the comforter of judicial discretion. Old Sleepy would have heard all this and issued a bench warrant for Serena Tully's involuntary commitment. No, he had to get that prick Kenniston, Mr. Continuing Education.

"We have Mrs. Tully's sister, Amber McKinley, here,

Your Honor. She will testify to her sister's long history of mental illness and her deteriorating marital state."

"All right, Mr. Garfield, let me hear what she has to say."

Amber McKinley looked like a third generation Xerox copy of her sister and that fact dominated their relationship. The crisp clean lines of Serena's features, the fragile perfection of their proportions, was almost duplicated, but not quite. The taut jaw line was smudged and rounded. The nose a tad broader. The eyes a shade less blue. Being not quite beautiful was a blow she had never recovered from. Her sister's existence was a daily reminder.

After she was sworn in Albert Garfield asked, "Were you contacted by your brother-in-law Thomas Tully yesterday evening?"

"Yes, I was."

"What was the substance of the conversation?"

"He called to tell me what my sister had threatened to do. He was real upset. He asked me if she'd ever acted like this before."

"And what did you say?"

"Well, not exactly. I mean, she never threatened to cut off a man's penis before. Not that I know of. But she'd done other things." Amber stopped, unaccustomed to being asked what she knew or having anyone listen to her answer. Garfield led her on.

"What other things, Mrs. McKinley?"

"Well, there were the suicides. Not suicides actually, but attempts."

"Tell us about these."

"The first one was, let me see, she was in high school. Her boyfriend broke up with her. He was never really that serious about her, anyway. She took a bunch of pills. Our dad found her and took her to the hospital. She had to have her stomach pumped. Mom and Dad wanted her to go to therapy. She went but the doctor said she didn't talk about anything, so he put her on pills. Antidepressants, but they didn't help. She got fat and that made her more depressed. So she stopped taking them. Then she started taking diet pills and doing that thing, eating and then throwing up, until she lost the weight. It was pretty awful. I remember Mom finding plastic bags of vomit hidden in her room when she couldn't get to the bathroom fast enough. We tried to get her to talk to our minister but she wouldn't do that either. Nothing much helped until she went away to junior college. Then she got discovered by this modeling agency and things seemed to straighten out for a while. She was happy for a few years. But, you know, she didn't really make it as a model. I mean she worked as a model, she made pretty good money, but she didn't make it really big, the way she wanted to. I don't really know why, neither did she. I mean my sister's really beautiful. You should see her, Your Honor."

Kenniston nodded and smiled. "Please go on, Mrs. Mc-Kinley."

"Well, she never made it to the cover girl level or as the model for a line of cosmetics. She did local magazine work and a lot of specialty and runway work. Serena started to get depressed again. Things weren't working out like she wanted. She started missing shows and showing up late or unprepared. People stopped using her. She couldn't handle the rejection. That's when she made her second attempt. She cut her wrists after she got fired by her agent. I was pretty worried about her. Everybody knew that she didn't handle stress very well. So I went over to be with her as soon as I found out she'd been fired.

"I was the one who found her. The doctors said she was very lucky, cutting as deep as she did and not calling for help.

After that one she was hospitalized. First for her wrists, then the doctors put her in the psychiatric unit."

Judge Kenniston cut in, "Do you remember if she was committed or did she go in voluntarily?"

"I'm not sure, Your Honor. I think she was committed, but I'm not really sure."

"Thank you. Go on."

"Well, I guess this time they had medications that didn't make you gain weight. So Serena stayed on them for a while after she got out. She never went back to modeling. She got a job as a secretary in Tysons Corner. Everything calmed down for a while again. We didn't see much of her for a few years until she married Tom. I think she felt pretty bad about everything she'd put the family through so she stayed away. None of us felt that way about it, of course.

"Things seemed to go well after she got married. The wedding was so beautiful. Then I heard that she'd started seeing a psychiatrist again. This was about a year ago. We weren't sure if that was good news or not. I mean, she'd never gone to one before unless she had to, so maybe something was wrong in the marriage. You know, it wasn't working out like she wanted it to and she was getting depressed again. So when things started to go bad again it wasn't a surprise."

"What do you mean, 'go bad,' Mrs. McKinley?"

"Serena started to miss things. Like when she was a model and she wouldn't show up for things. She'd call and make plans to get together, or watch my kids and then she wouldn't be home. That was rough. My kids were really looking forward to seeing their cousins. You know when something like that happens, when an adult says things that gets their hopes up and then is irresponsible, you don't know what to say. Do you lie? How much of the truth do you tell them? You don't want them to think badly about their Aunt Serena, but you don't want their feelings hurt. The last straw was when she invited everybody over for dinner. We all got there and she hadn't made a thing. She acted like she didn't know what we were talking about. Everybody just shook their heads. We all felt real bad for Tom. We know what he had to be going through with her. We'd all been through it before. When he called last night and told us what she'd said, I mean it sent a chill up my back, but it didn't seem impossible for her. There were times before when she was really depressed she'd say terrible things to people. I mean she didn't do them and you tried to remember that it was the depression talking, not her. But to tell you the truth, I wasn't real surprised. Sad about it, but not surprised. I don't know if my sister's ever going to find any peace."

"Thank you Mrs. McKinley, you may step down."

She nodded deferentially to the judge and left the courtroom.

"Your Honor, I'd like to call Dr. Pecorino to talk about the connections between suicidal and homicidal impulses. These are not opposites Your Honor, but rather very closely related. Only the thinnest of margins can separate the victims."

"No need to convince me of that, Mr. Garfield. I am well aware of the risk in this particular situation. I am inclined to grant you emergency relief. At least until this woman's mental status can be assessed by a professional. Has your client spoken to her therapist?"

Garfield looked at his client then back to the judge. "Would you like him to take the stand, Your Honor?"

"Yes."

Tom Tully pushed his chair back and walked to the witness stand. Seated, he began to massage his left knee. Prolonged sitting and it began to stiffen up on him.

"Do you want the judge to repeat the question, Mr. Tully?"

"No sir. I asked Serena many times to let me talk to her therapist. Or come in for a session with her, but she wouldn't hear of it. Said it was her space for herself alone and she wasn't going to share it. I was afraid that this guy wasn't getting the real story from her. You know, about what things were like at home. There was no talking to her about this. I was so afraid of what would happen without her being in therapy that I didn't push it. So no, Your Honor, I didn't ever get to talk to her doctor."

"Thank you, Mr. Tully. You may step down. Mr. Garfield, I will grant your motion for exclusion of Mrs. Tully from the residence and for *pendente lite* custody of the children based on the testimony of Mrs. Tully's sister as to her history of emotional disturbance and suicide attempts. However, I am ordering a full evaluation of this family to assess the mental status of the parties and make recommendations in the best interest of these children as contemplated by Statute 20-107.2. That evaluation is to commence as soon as possible. Have your office prepare that order immediately, Mr. Garfield, and deliver it to my chambers for my signature before the lunch recess. Mr. Tully, you are to inform your wife as soon as possible about this morning's events so that she can seek legal counsel in this matter. That is not to be done in the presence of the children, is that understood, Mr. Tully?"

"Absolutely, Your Honor."

"Your Honor, about the evaluation. Since speed is of the essence, may I suggest that Dr. Pecorino continue with the work that he's already begun. He's established a level of rapport with the children that the evaluator may not be able to reach very quickly."

"No, Mr. Garfield. His level of rapport with the children may be substantial but I believe that Mrs. Tully and her counsel will have grave concerns about Dr. Pecorino's objectivity considering his willingness to testify in this *ex parte* hearing. Rapport with both of the parties is at least as important a consideration. As this order comes from the bench, I will appoint the evaluator. Have the order identify Dr. Morgan Reece as the evaluator."

"Your Honor, I object to Dr. Reece's appointment."

"On what grounds, Mr. Garfield?"

"He and I have an antagonistic relationship, Your Honor. I fear that it will affect his perception of my client."

"Mr. Garfield, I have no doubt that Dr. Reece will keep his feelings about you, whatever they are, separate from his opinion about your client. He is well known and highly regarded by this court."

"Your Honor, I must object most vehemently."

"Mr. Garfield, the more you object the more certain I become of the rightness of my decision. Am I understood, counselor?"

"Yes, Your Honor."

"Very good. Call Dr. Reece's office to confirm that he can perform the evaluation in a timely manner. If not, I shall appoint another evaluator."

Albert Garfield packed up the case file and slipped it into his briefcase. All in all, a very good morning. Not perfect, but very good indeed.

In the hall outside the courtrooms Tom Tully asked, "What was that all about, with this guy Reece? Is this a problem?"

"Dr. Reece and I don't like each other, Tom. We don't like each other one bit. But it's no problem. I can handle him and you will, too. Let's go back to the office. We have things to do."

CHAPTER FOUR

Tom Tully checked his watch. His wife should be home any minute now. Asking her to go to BWI to pick up his brother had worked out perfectly. She had to go straight from the health club. That kept her away from the house for most of the day. Long enough for Tom to arrange her welcome home. The private eye tailing her had called and given Tully updates on her emotional state and estimated time of arrival. She'd badgered the airlines people for a copy of the passenger list until a supervisor came out and told her that no R. J. Tully had purchased a ticket for that flight or any other from Memphis. He also told her that if she didn't calm down, he'd call the police. Tully chuckled when he heard that. She'd called R.J.'s home and got no answer, as planned. Three phones away from her, the p.i. kept his line to Tully open. After twenty minutes of trying to get through, she swore so that everyone in the concourse could hear her, slammed the receiver down, got into her car and sped out of the lot.

Tully sat in his recliner, swiveled to face the front door. Between phone calls he'd sip Jack Daniels, trying to get the right saturation rate so that he was able to do everything but fantasize about her on her back getting slammed into by some grunting no-faced son of a bitch or down on her knees rubbing her nose against his pubic hair while she sucked on his cock.

He hadn't been doing very well. As soon as he thought he

was in control, these images stormed through the barricades of distraction and alcohol, like the Huns on holiday.

The detective called to tell Tom that his wife was minutes from home. He pulled himself out of the chair, took his lawyer's letter from the hallway table and locked the front door behind him. Sitting on the front steps, he watched his wife pull into the driveway. She slammed the car door and stalked up the steps.

"Damnit, Tom, what's going on? I spent all day at the airport. They had no record of R.J. being booked on any of the flights. I tried to call you and the line was always busy."

Tully pulled the letter out of his pocket and handed it to her. "This is what it's all about, Serena." He knew the words on that paper would hurt her as much as any blow from him, but it wasn't very satisfying. He needed his forearm slamming into and through her teeth, the whispered groan in his ears as he knocked her out of her shoes and bounced her head off the concrete.

"Where are the children?" she yelled.

"They're safe. And they're in a place where you can't get at them."

"Tom, I want the children. Where are they? Tell me."

She pounded her fists into her husband's chest. He ignored that, reached down and grabbed her right hand hard enough to press all her knuckles together. A white-hot jolt of pain raced up her arm and she rose up on her toes to try to escape it.

Tully leaned down over her. "Listen good, you slut. You're out of here. No money, no house, no kids, nothing. I ain't putting up with your shit for one more minute. You try to fight me on this and I will fucking destroy you." He pulled her so close he could see her eyes dilate trying to take him in. "You know what I'm like, Serena. I'll burn everything to the fucking ground rather than let you have it. Be smart, kill yourself now."

She gasped as Tully kept squeezing her hand. "Tom, please. You're breaking my hand. My God."

Tully relaxed his grip. "Just let me into the house for a minute. I'll pack a bag and go. Let me see the kids and talk to them. Please, Tom."

"No way. There's nothing in the house that's yours. I took your clothes, and the rest of your shit and put it out by the side of the house. It's in a couple of garbage bags. The only reason you're getting that is I can't sell it to someone else. As for the kids, get used to it. You have no kids. See what that says. You're ordered out of the house. I get the kids and you have to get your head examined. I have custody. The kids are mine, not yours.

"Don't get any bright ideas about trying to get them at school. I've already called and faxed them a copy of the court order. They won't turn them over to you. I've also talked to all the neighbors. I've asked them to call me if they see you hanging around the house. I've told the police about your mental problems. They'll pick you up and throw your ass in a mental hospital. Remember what that was like? I remember what you told me. Want to go back? It can be arranged."

"Tom, why are you doing this? If you hate me so much, then let's get a divorce. But why hurt the kids? What did they do to you? You never spent that much time with them. They're going to be frightened if I don't come home. Let me talk to them. Try to explain to them what's going on."

"No way, Serena. This isn't going to hurt the kids one bit. You think having you for a mother is good for the kids? Yeah, let's all grow up to be a crazy slut like Mom. Now get off my property before I call the police and have them put you in jail." She backed away from him, left her belongings where they were, and drove away shaking and sobbing.

CHAPTER FIVE

Watching her car disappear, Tully muttered, "Oh yeah, the judge says you should get a lawyer. Fuck that, you're gonna need an undertaker."

Chester Polansky ambled across the front lawn to his client. He put up his hand to calm Tully down. "Relax, one of my men has picked her up from here. Interesting conversation you had."

"Yeah? How do you know?"

"Parabolic microphone in the van. I got it all. You were lucky there."

"What do you mean?"

"You called her a slut. Twice. I don't think she noticed. She didn't ask why you said that. Nothing. Didn't skip a beat. If she knows she's been made, she's gonna cool this relationship. We're gonna have a much harder time catching her out. You've just got a suspicion right now, what with her swapping spit out front with some guy. You're gonna need more than that."

"I know my wife. She's never been without a man. She wouldn't know what to do on her own. She's gonna crack. I'm gonna keep leaning on her until she breaks. She'll run to her new fool asking him to protect her.

"It won't take that long either. She hasn't got the stomach for a fight. She may fold up just so she can save her relationship. That's what I'm betting on. Either way I win. That's all that counts."

Polansky shrugged. "Maybe she was just in shock. You hit her pretty good there. I don't know. I like to watch people when they're unprepared. You get a real natural response. She didn't try to defend herself. You could be right."

"I know I'm right. Just stay after her. That's what you're getting paid for. You think she got hit here, let me tell you, she's got some real surprises in store for her."

Polansky nodded at his client and walked back to his van.

Twenty minutes after escaping her husband, Serena Tully pulled into her best friend's driveway. She had met Denise Fargo at an aerobics class six years ago after each woman's first child. She rapped at the door. Her hand pounded a faster and louder beat. Serena imagined the glass breaking and her arm stabbing itself again and again on the shards until she finally was calm and floating into the darkness she knew was always there.

Denise yanked the door open. "Jesus, Serena, what's . . ." One look at her friend's ashen face and she slipped an arm around her and pulled her inside. "Happened? You look awful."

Snatched back to reality, she said, "Tommy's trying to kill me, Denise. He went to court today, and got an order that says I can't come into the house. I can't see the kids."

"Why? For what reason?"

"I don't know."

"That doesn't make sense, Serena. This order, did you see it?" She walked Serena to the kitchen table.

"Yeah, Tommy gave it to me to read."

"Where is it? Did you take it with you?"

"I don't know. I don't remember if I did. Maybe it's in the car."

"Look, you just sit here. I'll go out and look for it." Denise poured a large glass of water for her friend and handed it to her. "Drink this. All of it. Slowly. I'll be right back."

She found the paper on the front seat of the car, picked it up and read it on her way back into the house.

"Serena, this says, 'It being found that Mrs. Serena Tully poses an immediate danger to her husband and children, she is ordered excluded from the marital residence.' What danger? This is crazy."

"I don't know, Denise. I don't know anything."

"Were you in court when this happened?"

"No. He did it behind my back. I didn't find out about this until it was all over."

"You need a lawyer. And a good one. Do you know any divorce lawyers?"

"No, Denise."

"How about a lawyer of any kind?"

"I can't think of one right now, Denise. My head is spinning. I've got to get back there and find the kids."

Denise fought the impulse to take one of her husband's cigarettes. Thank God the kids were out getting haircuts with their grandmother, she thought. That's all Serena needs to see right now is me sitting in my kitchen with my children.

"Let's call Simone. Ask her who handled her divorce. Her husband had plenty of money for lawyers and she made out okay."

Denise found Simone Nelson's number, called her and got her the name of Travis Pruitt III.

Pruitt's first question to Serena was, "Whose name is on that order representing your husband?"

"Albert Olen Garfield."

"Ah, yes. I know him well. Your husband has retained very effective counsel. You'll need an experienced attorney to deal with Albert."

"What are you saying, Mr. Pruitt? Isn't this your area of expertise? You come very highly recommended."

"Mrs. Tully, this is my area of practice. However, I can't represent you."

"Why not?"

"Because your husband consulted with me last week. He revealed personal information to me. I cannot turn around and represent you in this matter. If you'd like, I'll give you the names of some attorneys who might be able to help you."

"Please, I need help . . . badly."

"Try these attorneys. They are all topnotch: Joe Anthony, Carole-Ann Polan, Leslie DeSouza, R. J. Corman."

Four calls later, Serena Tully dropped the receiver into the cradle and stared dully at her best friend. "He called them all. They all say the same thing. Sorry, we can't represent you. Try these names. Then they give me the same names. I've called them all. Tom's been there first. He cut out all the competition." She laid her head across her forearms.

"There can't be only six divorce lawyers in Fairfax County. That doesn't make any sense."

"I know, Denise, but they keep saying the same things. Your husband has retained very effective counsel. You need somebody experienced to deal with Albert. What does that mean?"

"I don't know, Serena. Let's get out the yellow pages and see who's listed."

They found "Lawyers." All sixty-nine pages of them. First came the full page, multi-color ads with the disaster logos: handcuffs, smashed cars, covered gurneys. Then the smorgasbord ads, you name it we do it: criminal law, immigration, personal injury, family law. Half-page; quarter-page; dwindling down to the simple listings.

"This is insane, Denise. There are a million of them. What

am I going to do? Close my eyes and pick whoever my finger lands on?"

"Let's see what kind of ad the big names have," Denise said and took the book.

The names Serena had been given all had simple two-line entries. Name and address. No boldface, no proclamations. Finally, there was a listing by area of legal practice. Only one of the five names she had been given was listed there.

"These people do divorces. Let's find one nearby and see if we can get you an appointment."

"Fine. Fine."

Denise scanned the columns. "There are three nearby. Two women and a man. Do you care about that?"

"Yes. What's the man's name?"

"Gerald Stuart."

"Let's hope he's as 'effective' as Tom's is."

Her call to Stuart's office got her a five o'clock appointment.

"Denise, thank you. I didn't know where to go. I know I've made a mess of your afternoon. I'm sorry."

"Serena, please. What's happening to you is terrible. This is what friends are for." She walked over and put her arm around her friend, whose cheek pressed against her hip in the same place her oldest son's did. "This is the first thing you have to do. One step at a time."

"Thanks." She looked at her watch. "I have a little time before the appointment. I need to find a place to stay tonight."

"Don't be silly. You can stay here tonight or even over the weekend if you have to. I'll deal with Bill."

Serena took a deep breath. The first one that hadn't been in the steel corset that slipped over her as she read the Order of the Circuit Court of the County of Fairfax, the

Commonwealth of Virginia.

"I'm going to freshen up. I must look awful."

Serena Louise Tully, once Serena Louise Dilworth, put her hands on the sink and leaned forward until the mirror betrayed every blemish. The tiny creases around her eyes, laugh lines that made you cry. How long would her good genes hold time at bay? Being beautiful had sustained her for a long time. But the ride was fast, wild and short and it was slowing down more each day. Why hadn't she learned to rely on other things, things that didn't fade so fast? She knew the answer. It was easy and it was instant power. Therapy had taught her that much. How would she make her way without being beautiful? The thought terrified her and she felt her stomach clench.

This was as far as she ever got. The wish and the fear bedded down and produced twin offspring: good intentions and bad ends.

Serena sat her purse on the edge of the sink and set about to repair the damage her tears had wrought. Fresh mascara and eyeliner, a little concealer under the eyes and on her nose. God forbid Gerald Stuart should see her any other way.

CHAPTER SIX

Gerald Stuart greeted Serena at the door to the office he sublet from another lawyer. Only three weeks earlier had he been allowed to put his nameplate on the front of the building. He showed her into a seat, remembered that the coffee pot was unplugged and didn't offer her any, went behind his desk and asked how he could help her.

"I saw that you do divorce work. Is that a specialty of yours, Mr. Stuart?"

"It's not a specialty Mrs. Tully, but I have handled quite a number of domestic matters in my fifteen years as a trial attorney."

A sliver of truth lurked in the murk of that response. When he wasn't pleading out drunk drivers, he did some name changes, drew up wills, some uncontested divorces, or adoptions and a few custody disputes.

"My husband went into court today and got this order against me." She handed it to Stuart. He read it, put it down on the desk and patted it as if he expected it to burp.

"Now, this order says you're a danger to your children and husband. And it orders you to be evaluated by some doctor." He checked the still silent order. "A Doctor Reece. What could this be referring to?"

"I have no idea. This is insane. My husband is Tom Tully. He was a pro football player. He once hit a man so hard that the poor guy died. Look at me. I'm all of a hundred and ten pounds. How could I be a danger to him? And my kids? I've never done anything to hurt them. Ever. I don't know what lies he told the judge."

"Well whatever it was, it worked. The judge believed him. I'll call this attorney, this Mr. Garfield, and see what he has to say about the evidence he presented. Obviously you want back into the house and custody of your children restored. Is there anything else you'd like me to press for at this time?"

"I don't know. I don't want to go back into the house with Tom. He's the one who's dangerous. Can we make him leave?"

"Has he ever been abusive to you? Ever beaten you up?"

"Are you kidding? If he hit me once I'd be dead. I never let things go that far. Once Tom'd lose his temper, I'd just give up, agree, whatever. So no, he never beat me up. He didn't have to."

"Okay, Mrs. Tully, I'll see what I can do. Why don't you fill out this information sheet? I'll need a retainer check for two thousand dollars from you at this time. That's ten hours at my rate of two hundred dollars an hour." His new rate. Computed by taking the distance to the end of her rope and multiplying that by her Baume & Mercier watch. "While you do that, I'll call Mr. Garfield and see if we can discuss this."

Serena Tully filled out the forms and her check while Stuart held the line. Eventually he found that Mr. Garfield was out of the office and not expected back. Stuart left his number and said that he represented Serena Tully.

"That's all I can do right now, Mrs. Tully. First thing Monday morning I'll get with Mr. Garfield and we'll come to an understanding about this matter."

"Can't you do anything until then? I want to see my children."

"I wouldn't do that, Mrs. Tully. Your husband has a legal

order barring you from the home. If you go by the house and he calls the police it won't look good for you. He might claim that you're stalking him. That won't help. Please be patient, Mrs. Tully. First thing Monday morning we'll see about getting you access to your children."

Serena Tully found herself out in the parking lot, staring over the top of her car. She realized that she was drifting more and more frequently into reveries where she carefully analyzed everything that had happened for the clues that it wasn't real, it wasn't her life. Somehow she had gotten lost and wandered away from her life into this one. If she could only retrace her steps, find that wrong turn she'd made, she'd go back to her life with the familiar miseries she desperately longed for.

These thoughts led her back to her house. She sat in the driveway. The house was dark. She was back in her life, but everyone else was gone. Getting out of the car, she walked slowly towards the house, staring up as if it was a castle, and she a peasant girl without an offering. She fumbled in her purse for her keys and found that they did not work. Not on the front door, the garage, the back door or the patio. She stumbled over her belongings in bags alongside the garage wall. She dragged them back to her car and drove away.

On her way back to Denise's, she made a phone call that left her vomiting in despair.

CHAPTER SEVEN

Morgan Reece woke up, sat on the edge of the bed, rubbed his eyes and went to the bathroom to wash his face. He brushed his teeth, replaced the brush and considered eating.

In the kitchen he surveyed the contents of the refrigerator. While he did this, he groomed his mustache with his left hand. Another self-soothing habit he'd developed, like waking up with his penis in his hand. He had noted that his depression had lifted. A change he could not account for, nor was he entirely happy about it. Depression had its comforts. He had always been an anxious, obsessive man. Caring too much about everything. Depression relaxed him. He hadn't a care in the world. There was nothing bad left to fear. For almost five years the fertile void of that truth had produced nothing. For the first time, he thought it might.

Morgan Reece was forty-five years old. His sandy blond hair and beard and recent weight loss knocked a few years off that, but only at a distance.

Reece put the remains of a pizza in the microwave and made a pot of coffee. He read the newspaper while he ate. An average night in D.C. left three dead and two wounded. Today, with the temperature in the nineties, a severe bullet storm warning was in effect from eight p.m. on. Reece scanned the bad news from the rest of the country, then the world, and wondered why he bothered.

Reece showered, dressed and checked his voice mail. The

first message was from Albert Garfield. "Dr. Reece, Judge Kenniston has appointed you to conduct a custody evaluation. I represent the father in this matter. Please call my office to confirm your availability to do the evaluation." He wrote down the number, erased the message and played the second one. . . .

"Dr. Reece, my name is Lindsay Brinkman. I was riding on Metro a few weeks ago and some papers of mine fell on the floor. I'm missing a couple of pages and I have one of yours. I guess they got mixed up on the floor. I'd like to arrange to get my papers back. Would you please call me at (703) 555-1964? Thank you."

The bird. Morgan Reece went to his briefcase, unsnapped the locks and took out his chapter. He arranged the pages by number. As he did that, he found two five-by-seven cards stuck to the pages. He pulled them loose and felt their backs. They were slightly tacky. He held one up to look at. It looked like a copy of a black and white photograph. The mass in the center was vaguely rectangular, and shaded, suggesting depth, but with indefinite edges. Each picture had a series of circled numbers connected by dotted lines on them. Reece held them up side by side and could not detect a pattern in the numbers or the lines. In fact he had never seen anything like them before.

Reece dialed the number she had given.

"Rocky Mountain High. Lindsay Brinkman speaking."

"This is Dr. Morgan Reece. I got your message and I have two pages of yours. Is that all you're missing?"

"Yes. I have one page of yours."

Reece flipped through the chapter. "Is it page thirty-eight?"

"Yes."

The last one, he thought. That's why I didn't catch it right away. "How did you figure out that I had your papers?" he asked.

"Your page ends with a note that says, 'File: Reece Ch6 CSA.' I read the page. It's all about child sexual abuse. I figured that was CSA. I hoped your name was Reece. You were on the Metro in Virginia. So I looked up psychologists, psychiatrists and social workers in Virginia. You're the only Reece."

"How can I get the pages back to you? Do you want me to mail them to you?"

"No. I don't want to trust them to the mail. Can I come by to get them at your office?"

"I'm with patients straight through today until nine p.m."

"How about tomorrow? Are you done earlier?"

"Yes. I'm done at six. Then I have to go to the Borders in Tysons Corner."

"That's very close to where I work."

"I have to pick up some books they've ordered for me. I'll be there at around seven. Look for me in the coffee bar."

"Fine. Thanks very much. See you there."

CHAPTER EIGHT

Gerald Stuart got through to Albert Garfield around eleven o'clock.

"Mr. Garfield, my name is Gerald Stuart. I represent Mrs. Serena Tully. I'd like to talk with you about this unfortunate matter. This poor woman is just grief-stricken over this turn of events."

Garfield hated listening to posture-speak, the unnecessary sprinkling of self-serving adjectives over a recitation of the facts. He did it himself to impress the gullible client that he believed in the rightness of their every word and deed. He also did it with new judges who might confuse his pious bleatings with a truly just cause. But, one attorney to another, this was a colossal bore.

While Stuart talked, he flipped through his directory of the family law section of the Virginia Bar. No Gerald Stuart. Wonderful. Worst case, this guy was a general practice civil litigator, competent in court, but ignorant of the subtleties of case law and a novice about the particular tactics in this area of the law. Best case, he was a yellow pages pick, pin the tail on the lawyer.

"Look Mr. Stuart. The court has excluded the woman from the home. Do you know what kind of evidence it takes to get that, on an *ex parte* basis? Your client is a seriously disturbed woman. I'm not going to agree to visitation of any sort. Not until Dr. Reece's evaluation is complete."

"What about supervised visitation? Let her see the children. What harm can it do, with a supervisor there?"

"Isn't that a little out of your field? I think that's the purpose of the evaluation. To answer questions like that. If you move for supervised visitation, I'll oppose it. If you win, I'll ask for your client to pay for the supervisor, and the supervisor has to be acceptable to my client. No family or friends. A trained professional. Do you think your client has the resources to pay for that and to litigate every issue? I'm sure that you'll be sending me interrogatories and a request for documents. Why don't you wait until you get our responses? I think you'll see that this is a family without a lot of resources. Why piss them away on you and me? You want to do what's right for these kids; let's not stand in the way of the evaluation. I know Dr. Reece. He's going to want half of his fee from each of the parents. I didn't go in and ask for child support from your client. Instead of us spending more of these people's money arguing over spousal support, I'll talk to my client about guaranteeing the expert's fees in an effort to get this settled as quickly as possible. You know that once custody is determined, the money issues fall out pretty easily. Let's put the money where it'll do some good."

"All right. I'll wait for your answer to my interrogatories and request for documents. I'll discuss your offer of expert fees in lieu of spousal support with my client."

"Fine. We'll await your requests."

Garfield ran his hands around the waist of his pants. A habit he hoped would alert him to any extra pounds. Stuart was a putz. He didn't want to fight for his client. He wanted the easy way out. As long as it came with a rationale. He'd spin this guy around like one of those Jewish toys—a dreidel, was that it?

Each additional day without her kids or any money to live

on would sap her will. Her husband said she was a quitter. Never fought for anything. When this was over she'd have all the nothing she could stand.

Getting Tully to cold-call his competition was an excellent investment. For a couple of thousand dollars he'd cleared out the people who made him work every inning, every batter.

"Dr. Reece on line one, Mr. Garfield," came over his intercom. He leaned forward and depressed the speakerphone button.

"Good morning, Doctor, you received my message?"

"Yes. Do you have a court date for this evaluation?"

"No. Judge Kenniston will hear this on special docketing. He wants to maintain responsibility for this one."

"That's unusual. Why did he do that?"

"He issued an *ex parte* exclusionary order. He takes that seriously. It was entirely appropriate in this case. The mother's mental condition . . ."

"Is not something that we're going to discuss on the phone. At least not without her attorney on the line. Who represents the mother?"

"Guy named Gerald Stuart. You ever work with him?"

"No. I haven't."

"Well, he's a fine lawyer. You won't have any problems with him."

"Since I don't know him, and you and I are not a mutual admiration society, how did I get appointed to do this evaluation?"

"Over my strongest objections, Doctor, that's how."

"Do you want to call Stuart's office? See if we can do a conference call. Lay out the parameters of the evaluation and get this going."

Garfield paused. Getting this going before Stuart had any facts to work with was fine by him. Besides, if they forced her

41

to surrender before the evaluation was complete, whatever Reece found out would be moot.

"Hold on. I'll have my secretary try to get him."

"Gerald Stuart here," popped onto the line a moment later.

"Mr. Stuart, my name is Morgan Reece. I've been appointed to conduct an evaluation of the family that you and Mr. Garfield represent. Since I've never worked with you, I thought I'd go over my format for these evaluations, answer any questions you have and get started."

"Fine, go right ahead." Stuart said.

"I understand that there is no court date set on this."

Garfield jumped in, "That's correct."

"How long do you expect this to take?" Stuart asked.

"That depends. Let me get some information about this family. How many children and their ages?"

"Tom Tully, Jr. age six, and Tina Tully, age four," Garfield said.

"Any special needs? Learning disabilities? Emotional problems?"

"No. I think you'll find that these are normal children, Doctor."

"Are the parents involved with other parties? Any other *de facto* caretakers?"

"No, Doctor. They were just separated this weekend."

"Are there any special questions that need to be evaluated?"

This time it was Stuart. "What does that mean, Doctor?"

"Beyond looking at parenting skills and 'goodness of fit' with these children, are there allegations about things such as domestic violence, child abuse, drug or alcohol abuse, a history of mental illness, suicide risk, unusual sexual practices, religious cults?"

"Most definitely, Doctor," Garfield intoned. "The basis for our emergency hearing was a combination of these factors. Mrs. Tully is a seriously disturbed woman. She's been hospitalized before and made numerous suicide attempts. Her illness has affected her ability to bond and care for her children. As for drug or alcohol abuse, my client suspects that she is self-medicating at this time and has for quite a while. Her deteriorating condition led her to threaten her husband with castration, so yes, domestic violence is also an issue."

Reece shook his head. "Any other issues? Sexual or religious?"

"My client has not enjoyed a sexual relationship with his wife for quite some time. The reason for that he believes lies in her emotional condition. There's also a rift between the parties about religion. He's Baptist. She is a non-practicing Catholic who has refused to allow the children to go to any church."

All four horsemen of the Marital Apocalypse, thought Reece: sex, God, money and children.

"How about you, Mr. Stuart, is your client making any allegations in these areas?"

"Dr. Reece my client vigorously denies any of these allegations." He tried to remember what she'd said about her husband. "She denies any threats of violence to her husband, in fact she has lived in constant fear of the man, who has been verbally abusive to her and intimidated her throughout the marriage. She denies any problems in her care of her children. I have not yet seen the records of her psychiatric care, but I am sure she poses no harm to anyone and that her husband is blowing this entirely out of proportion."

"Let me interject here, Dr. Reece. I'll have a copy of the transcript of the hearing sent to you. The testimony of Mrs. Tully's psychiatric problems came from her sister—not my client. He has downplayed her problems. If he's erred in any fashion, it's in staying with her this long."

Stuart scrambled around for a rebuttal and settled for, "Obviously, sorting all this out is going to be your job, Dr. Reece. I don't think what we tell you is going to carry much weight, am I right?"

"Not in my conclusions. It just helps me figure out the scope of the evaluation that needs to be done."

"Time and money, Doctor," Garfield said. "Do you have an idea of the cost of this evaluation? Money is tight for these people."

Reece looked at his notes. Not a simple evaluation, but not the most complex either.

"I'm asking for eight thousand dollars as an initial retainer, to be split equally by the parties."

"And how long will the evaluation take?" they both asked.

"I estimate it will take four or five weeks to complete. Then I'll arrange for a meeting with both of you to present my conclusions, and then I'll see your clients to tell them what my findings are."

"Will that include a written report?" Garfield asked.

"No. I usually ask that a court reporter be there to transcribe my presentation. Their appearance fee is much less than the time for me to prepare a formal report. A transcript can be made if this matter doesn't settle and that can be entered into the record as my report. I do it this way because the vast majority of cases I do get settled, not litigated. This saves your clients money."

Reece's last comments were aimed at Albert Garfield who would litigate whether the sun would rise, and if he lost that, he'd be back the next day to argue about the direction.

"While I'm working I'll accept no *ex parte* communications. If either of you wants to tell me something, we do it by a conference call. Same thing if I need to get in touch with you."

"Why would you need to do that?" Stuart said.

"I may require your assistance in getting copies of records. Subpoenas, court orders, etcetera. If Mrs. Tully's mental health history is extensive, that may be the biggest delay. It can be difficult getting records, particularly if they're old and not local."

"I don't have any questions, Dr. Reece," Albert Garfield said.

"We've got a problem with this fee of yours, Dr. Reece. I don't think my client has access to that kind of money. Do you accept any other kind of arrangement?"

"I'll accept other arrangements provided that they are acceptable to both of the parties. If one side wants to advance all the money against reimbursement later out of the property settlement, that's fine. If either of you has a concern about my knowing where the money comes from, you can send it to a third party who sends me the check. That shields the origin of the money. I just need to know before I begin working."

"There's no need for Dr. Reece to endure our deliberations on this matter, Mr. Stuart. We'll call as soon as we've reached an agreement."

"Fine. All I need are your clients' phone numbers so I can contact them and start the process." When Reece scribbled down the numbers they gave him, he hung up.

CHAPTER NINE

Gerald Stuart went to the library he shared with all the other sublettors and found the continuing legal education pamphlet entitled, "Sample Forms for Interrogatories and Production of Documents in Domestic Relations Cases." He copied them, filled in the appropriate blanks, sealed them up and set them out for the mailman.

That done, he called his client, who waited by the phone tapping out Morse code in caffeinated agitation.

"When can I see my children?" she asked.

"That's something the evaluator will have to decide. He's going to call you today to set up a first meeting. You can ask him directly."

Serena's heart sank and she steadied herself against the kitchen counter as she lowered herself into a chair.

When she said nothing, Stuart went on. "We have to discuss money, Mrs. Tully. Dr. Reece has asked for an initial retainer of four thousand dollars from each party. Can you get that kind of money together?"

Four thousand more? This in the space of seventy-two hours. Did Tom have that kind of money in the accounts? She'd been offered money like that once before. She did a runway job at a fundraiser for some Arab-American group and a man in sunglasses and a *djelleba* offered her that for a weekend underneath one of the visiting dignitaries. Something about her hair being as golden, soft and fine as sunlight.

"I don't know. I'll have to check. I'll call the bank and see what we have in our account. Tom took care of the money. If there isn't enough there, I have a gold card with cash advance. I can use that to write a check. Let me find out and I'll call you back."

"Okay. We should also make an appointment to go over some things that your husband's attorney raised today."

"What things?"

"He claims that you have an extensive history of psychiatric treatment and that because of that you've threatened him with harm, neglected your children, abused drugs and abandoned the marital bed. If there's truth to these matters, Mrs. Tully, I can only say that regaining custody of your children may prove difficult."

"Oh my God. That was years ago. Yes, I've had problems but it never affected my children. Tom doesn't even know which one's the girl!"

"Why don't we make that appointment now and I'll let you call your bank. How about four o'clock today? Can you make that?"

Serena Tully fought the impulse to shriek. Unreality was seeping into every segment of her life. First her present disappeared. Gone were her home, husband and children. She was living in someone else's house, barred from seeing her children, forbidden to reach out and tousle their hair, kiss the tops of their heads and feel the strength of their love flow back through the arms that squeezed her legs. Her future had evaporated into a hole followed by cascading dollar bills. Now her past was being rewritten, inverted and perverted. She looked down at her hands, turning them over and then back again. Only the shiny ridges that ended her career as a hand model seemed real to her now.

"Mrs. Tully, four o'clock. Can you make it?"

"I have an appointment. How about five or five-thirty, actually?"

"All right. I'll see you then."

Serena pulled the telephone into her lap. She dialed information for the bank's phone number. When she was connected, she asked for the balance in their account. The teller told her nine dollars and sixty-three cents.

"That's not possible. That account never gets that low. How long has it been like that?"

"Let me switch to another screen. Since Friday. There was a withdrawal that day of two thousand and twelve dollars."

There was more money there. Where? Tom used to joke about it. Overdraft. An overdraft line of credit.

"What about the overdraft line of credit? How much is left on that?"

"Let me check for you. That's been cancelled, ma'am."

"As of when?"

"Friday, also."

"Thank you."

Panic began to take hold. Serena saw the firestorm of her husband's rage roll out in shining waves and incinerate everything in its path. Convinced of the answer, she pulled out her wallet and began to dial 800 numbers for all of her credit cards. Her credit cards, that was a laugh. They were all in his name, with her as an approved user. Tom said she could get higher credit limits using him as the income source. Anyway, he said, it was only fair since she didn't work.

One after another she dropped the cards onto the floor. On Friday she had been cancelled as a user on all of them. All the store cards, the ATM machines, the gasoline company cards, the phone cards. Even the grocery stores had been contacted and advised that she had no money in her account against which to write checks.

While Serena Tully sat there feeling each side of the coffin her husband had built for her, Gerald Stuart, answering a silent alarm about the negotiability of her retainer check, was taking it down the street to his bank. He asked the teller to call the bank it was drawn on to verify that there were sufficient funds to cover it. The teller put the phone down and handed the check back to Gerald Stuart.

"Well?"

"I'm sorry sir. The bank says there is no money in that account."

"Why am I not surprised?" Stuart said as he pocketed the check and hurried back to his office. Maybe Garfield's client would cover his fees.

CHAPTER TEN

Albert Garfield adjusted his notepad and pen, then took the phone out of the hollow of his shoulder and reviewed the morning's developments with his client.

"He's going to be sending over interrogatories. Those are written questions that you have to answer in writing. Don't worry. I'll go over your answers before you send them out. These are sworn to as truthful. He's also requesting a lot of documents about the marital assets. When we see them, you'll have to produce copies for him. That'll show him what property there is to fight over. We've already sent ours over to him. We'll see what her position is on all this."

"She gets nothing. Not a fucking thing."

"And that's what we'll try to do. I'm only interested in her position to see what it tells me about what's important to her. Not that I have any intention of giving it to her. It tells me what she cares about, where she's weakest. Think of it as a look at the other side's game plan."

"Pretty stupid thing to let you see."

"Part of the rules of discovery. That's the way this game is played. Puts a premium on planning and surprise."

"Any news from the p.i.?"

"Nothing yet. He says she looks pretty bad. She's either spacing out or looks like she's gonna pass out. If we keep the heat on her, she may not even make it into the evaluation."

"What about this evaluation? Do I have to go talk to this clown too?"

"Yes, that's what the judge ordered. Don't worry about it. The evaluator, Dr. Reece, wrote a book about what he does. I have a copy here in my office. Come by, read it before you go in to see him. It's like looking at his game plan. He's got copies of his questionnaires in there. Practice filling them out. In fact, let me see about something. I'll call you right back. Where are you right now?"

"I'm at the weight room. Just call the front desk number I gave you. They'll page me."

"Okay, be right back."

Garfield dialed the number of his own in-house expert, Dr. Henry Pecorino.

"Henry, Al Garfield. How'd you like a shot at Morgan Reece?"

"Where and when?"

"He's been appointed in the Tully case. I was thinking of having you do a shadow evaluation of the father and the kids in case Reece comes up bad. But that's a lot of money, particularly if we front all of Reece's fee. How about if I send Mr. Tully over to you for a consultation? I'm going to give him Reece's book and those others you told me about on the Rorschach and the MMPI. If he has any questions, how about he comes to you? We'll call it parent counseling. He's learning how to take care of these kids all by himself now."

"No problem, I'll be glad to talk to him. If you want the shadow evaluation, just give me enough notice. I'll be glad to second opinion that S.O.B.; I've waited a long time for a shot at him."

"Enjoy. If he doesn't come out one hundred percent for my client, he's all yours."

"Have your client call me when he's read the books."

Albert Garfield dialed his client back. "Tom. I've spoken with Dr. Henry Pecorino. He's an expert in the area of child custody. After you read the books I have at my office, I want you to call Dr. Pecorino and set up an appointment to consult with him."

"What for? I already have to talk to one shrink."

"So that you can get guidance on how to best take care of the children, Tom. That way when Dr. Reece asks you questions about them, you'll know exactly what to say. Do you understand what I'm saying?"

Tully laughed. "Loud and clear."

"We also have to talk about money for the evaluations. If you've been successful in cutting her off from any assets, your wife won't be able to pay her half of Dr. Reece's retainer."

"How much are we talking about here?" Tully demanded.

"His retainer is eight thousand dollars. Half from each parent."

"What the fuck! Eight grand!"

"This is what I recommend. Reece won't work without his fee. The court wants him to do it. If she goes in and says she can't pay, the court will direct you to do it and then seek reimbursement at the property settlement. I'd rather offer it to Stuart in trade for spousal support. I want to know where her money is committed. I don't want her to have money to use in ways we can't anticipate and control. I also don't want her to have any to live on. Without it, she's got to rely on handouts and gifts that'll dry up pretty soon. The more pressure she's under, the quicker she cracks and you get what you want. In addition, if she cracks in the evaluation, it'll go against her in the custody dispute. Consider it an insurance policy. We want her to fold under professional scrutiny. You just have to pay for it."

"What if she folds before the evaluation is done? Do we get the money back?"

"Absolutely. So there's a premium on keeping the pressure on her."

"I don't know. Another eight grand is pretty stiff. Let me talk to some people about a loan. When do you need an answer?"

"As soon as possible. I want to get her in front of Reece before she can regroup and pull herself together. By the way, where is she staying?"

"I don't know."

"I have a number for her. Stuart gave it to Reece. Do you recognize it?"

Garfield read off the number from his notepad.

"Yeah, that's Denise's phone number. One of her friends from the health club. Another bitch."

"Any way to force her out of there? Make it too uncomfortable for her to stay there?"

"I could arrange to call her all the time from public telephones. I could . . ."

"Don't say anything. I'm just thinking out loud. If for some reason Denise came to feel that harboring your wife was not a good idea, it would be to your advantage to have her without food and shelter. Can you come by tomorrow to pick up these books on custody evaluations?"

"Sure. I'll have an answer for you about the money, too."

"Good."

"Any word from the p.i. yet?"

"Nothing so far. If we can't catch her with this guy, we may have to change our pleadings."

"What does that mean?"

"It means we ask for the divorce on grounds other than adultery. I wish you hadn't let it slip that you suspected her, no matter how angry you were. She's probably cooled it."

"Not for long. She wasn't putting out at home, so she was getting boned somewhere. I know my wife. Two days without a dicking and she started to worry that her looks were going. She won't be able to go through all this without a man by her side. She'll crack and go running straight to him."

"Let's hope so."

"Mr. Garfield, Mr. Polansky calling on line two. He says it's urgent." Sandra, his secretary cut in on the intercom.

"Tom, hold on a minute. It's Polansky now. Maybe he has some good news for us."

Garfield depressed the hold button and put Polansky through.

"Yeah, Chet. What's up?"

"Where's your client, Al?"

"Out at the weight room, why?"

"Well, he'd better get his ass over here right now."

"Where's here? What's going on?"

"Wifey-poo just pulled up in front of the school. I think she's gonna try to snatch the kids."

"Great. Get photos. Don't call the police until she actually takes the kids out of school. I'll get my client over there immediately. Boy, has she shot herself in the foot."

Garfield switched lines. "Tom. Serena has shown up at school. Polansky thinks she's going to try to snatch the kids."

"I'll call the school. They know not to let her have them."

"No, don't do that. Just get over there right away. If she convinces them to let her have the kids, that's good for us. Let her get out of the building, then stop her."

"Any suggestions?"

"Any way you have to. Those are your children she's trying to steal."

CHAPTER ELEVEN

Serena Tully sat in her car across the street from the school. She still hadn't decided what she wanted to do. Or what she dared to do. She wanted to race into the school, sweep Tommy up in her arms and disappear with him. Tina was at home with Felicia, the nanny. By the time she left here, they'd call Tom. He'd call the police. Then she'd be in jail. Not a step forward, she concluded. Every time she tried to call the house she got the damned answering machine. Tom had changed the message so that it was in the children's voices. Every time she heard them it hurt.

Tom was legal custodian. She guessed that meant that she couldn't do anything with the children without his permission. Maybe she could just go in and ask to sit in Tommy's class. Just to watch. Not to say anything. Just watch him play or work. He was learning to do so much. Addition and subtraction. Reading. Making his letters. Serena found herself walking into the school, although it felt more like floating. She drifted past the sign that read: "ALL VISITORS MUST CHECK IN AT THE MAIN OFFICE." Tommy's class was on the right at the end of the hall. The playground was just outside. Maybe they'd go there to talk.

Chester Polansky watched her walk into the school. This was going to be one short case. If there was anything judges had no tolerance for, it was child snatching, especially in violation of a court order. Showed you had no respect for the law, or the child's relationship with the other parent. A parent like that couldn't be trusted. Couldn't control their own feelings well enough to think about the impact on the child. He'd heard all the arguments. This lady was digging her own grave. Custody my ass, by tomorrow she'd be lucky to qualify for supervised visitation.

He looked into the rearview mirror as the Cherokee pulled up behind him. Tom Tully bounded out.

"Where is she?"

"She just walked into the school. They may turn her away without the kid. It's the boy, right?"

"Where's the girl?"

"She's home with the nanny."

"What took her so long? You called about twenty minutes ago?"

"I don't know. She just sat there staring at the school. Like she was trying to make her mind up or something."

"That's her. A fucking space cadet. You talk to her and she doesn't hear a word you say. Used to drive me crazy. I'd have to tell her everything twice. I think they closed her up before they finished putting all the wiring in."

Polansky listened. Thirty years of listening to other people betray themselves more than their worst enemies had taught him the virtue of silence.

"Why don't you wait a couple more minutes? She comes out with him and we've got her," Polansky suggested to Tully's receding back. "Well, make sure you check in at the office."

Serena stood outside the door to Mrs. Nash's first grade class. She searched for Tommy's blond head. There he was in the corner. Coloring with another child, a dark haired girl with long braids and a very serious look on her face. Staying inside the lines was hard work.

Tommy stretched and looked her way. She smiled and his face radiated joy and relief. Serena pulled the door back and stepped into the room. All heads turned toward her.

Mrs. Nash, reading to a circle of children, followed their distraction to its source. As soon as she saw Serena, she cringed. Another civil war was being fought in her classroom. Tommy had been alternately morose and frantic all day. Coloring finally had calmed him down for a while.

Tommy scooted out of his seat and dashed into his mother's arms. She picked him up and pressed him against her chest while she whispered in his ear. "It's all right Tommy. Mommy's here."

Serena looked past Tommy's head and met Mrs. Nash's stare. She thought about saying she was only going outside to talk to Tommy for a minute but she didn't. She knew she wasn't. She was going to run with Tommy and Tina as fast and as far as she could. She knew she couldn't let go of her son, and he had now locked his legs around her waist. Whatever happened, it would happen to them together. Love's promise to us all.

Serena Tully spun around and stepped out into the hall. Then she saw her husband and the principal walking toward her. Holding Tommy around the waist, she pushed open the door and began to run toward her car.

Tom Tully reacted on instinct, like a dog with a mailman, a lion and an antelope. Accelerating rapidly, he closed the distance in seconds. Out the door, he skidded, trying to change direction, and then came up on his wife. He raised his arm to slam through the back of her head when he saw his son's open-mouthed terror. Pulling up alongside his wife, he grabbed a fistful of her hair and yanked her off her feet. She staggered backward. Tully slipped an arm around his son's waist and pried him loose. By her hair he threw her away from him. His son kicked and screamed, "Mommy, Mommy." She saw her son, tears running down his cheeks, imploring her with outstretched arms not to leave him again. Tom Tully walked away without a backward glance just as he had done after he hit Cisco Conway. His son flailed and wriggled, trying to escape. Tom Tully just increased the pressure until the boy's cries were of physical pain not grief. He relaxed his grip a bit and the boy fell silent, gasping for air.

Serena Tully scrambled back to her feet and swept her hair out of her face. This time she didn't think about all the things that could go wrong. She sprinted after her husband. Grabbing the arm that held her son, she pulled with all her might. Tom Tully shook his head in disbelief as if Cisco Conway had come back to life. He reached out and grabbed his wife's face in his hand and prepared to hurl her away. She slipped her face loose from his grip and bit down hard on his forearm. Tully yelled, dropped his son and punched his wife in the side of the head. Her head snapped back and she released his arm. Serena Tully was out before she crashed.

Tom Tully looked around for his son, now trying to burrow underneath her crumpled body. He reached down and pulled his son out by an arm. Staring down at her, all the rage he had been titrating burst through. He looked at her pale white skin, blue eyes and blonde hair and saw a doll, a fragile china doll whose pretty little head would shatter as soon as he kicked it. Tully stepped forward, shifted his weight and Chester Polansky stepped between him and his wife's body.

"You don't want to do that."

"Get out of my way, fat man."

"Not a chance. You don't kick someone who's down. Not on my watch. You got the kid, I got the photos. She's in a lot of trouble. Go home, call your attorney. See if he wants you to press charges. Things like this, the first one to the magistrate wins. Leave now before you fuck this up. I'll call the police."

Tom Tully was amazed at the fat man. He had twenty years on him. He could kill him, but the guy was not afraid.

He turned away, tucked his sobbing son under his arm and walked back to his car.

Chester Polansky knelt and felt for a pulse.

CHAPTER TWELVE

While Chester Polansky put the finishing touches on the immolation of Serena Tully, her husband drove home, dropped his son with the nanny and left a message for Albert Garfield. Then he called some friends about money for the evaluation. Garfield might be right. Getting her in front of a shrink right now might be a good idea. Trying to fight him. Man, the bitch had lost her mind.

As Tully drove up I-95 to Baltimore, Chester Polansky was telling the police that he had pictures of Serena Tully running with her child away from the father who had legal custody and that he had pictures of her assaulting him and that Mr. Tully's response was entirely in self-defense. It was unfortunate that Mrs. Tully had some loosened teeth and an apparent concussion. However, her husband panicked when she bit him because he had asked her to take an AIDS test and she'd refused. The police and paramedics standing there with their latex gloves on all nodded in understanding. The principal confirmed that they had received notice that she wasn't to take the child and that she hadn't checked in with the office. He also confirmed Polansky's story from his vantage point in his office. The officers asked Polansky where the father was. He said he told him to take the child home to spare him any more trauma and get his arm looked at. He wasn't sure whether Mr. Tully would want to press charges but they should call his attorney, Albert Garfield.

Realizing that she probably was no longer on her husband's health insurance, Serena Tully refused to be taken to the hospital for observation. The police wouldn't let her drive and she had to be picked up by Denise Fargo. After some deliberation with the watch commander the officers let her leave, but warned her that if Mr. Tully chose to press charges she would be arrested and that she might want to consult a criminal defense attorney.

Tom Tully took 395 through South Baltimore, past Camden Yards Baseball Stadium, right on Conway to the inner harbor, around the shopping pavilions, the tall ships, the submarine tours and then up Calvert Street. Just north of Pratt, Tully parked and walked down Baltimore Street to "The Block." These days it's shrunk to two blocks of peep shows, pornographic video stores, latex love enhancers and topless and bottomless clubs.

Tom Tully made his way down the street, gliding past the hallucinating homeless, dodging the dancers late for work jumping out of cabs wearing buckskin jackets and nothing else and ignored the doormen touting the delights of each club.

He stopped in front of the door to the Passion Pit. Its name was painted in pink letters over the black paint that covered the glass door. He stepped inside and let his eyes adjust to the darkness. The cigarette smoke was so thick you could chew it. He walked down the aisle between the tables and the raised dance floor and eyed the girl on the stage. She was arched in a bridge with her heels touching her wrists. Tilting her head back, she attempted to slide an entire long neck down her throat. For her efforts the patron whose beer she'd just engulfed held up a five-dollar bill. Once she righted herself she smiled and slipped it into her garter.

The man who sat by the door marked "Office" was so big

he ordered his clothes in latitude and longitude. His hair was combed straight forward and cut short in a straight line across his brow. Thick down-turned lips and a permanent frown made him look like he was pondering an especially difficult math problem. His egg-shaped head was repeated in his slope-shouldered torso. When his hands weren't in use he wrung them constantly. He always wore black from his ortho-pedic shoes to his sausage skin turtlenecks.

"Hey, Carmine. How ya doin'? Vinnie in?" Tully asked from a respectful distance.

"He's busy."

"When will he be free?"

"When he's done."

"I called. He said I should meet him here. We've got things to discuss."

Carmine swiveled slowly. "He's busy."

Tully had seen him wrap his hands around another man's and break fourteen bones, all the while calmly telling him he should leave the club before he really got hurt. Tully decided to wait.

Twenty minutes later a young girl with thick shiny black hair like a mink's pelt staggered out of the office. Her eyes were out of focus and her lipstick was smeared from her chin to her nose.

Vinnie, "The Bat" Colabucci stepped into the doorway. He saw Tully and smiled. "That was an audition." He laughed, "She passed. Come on in."

Tully stepped past Carmine and entered the office. Vinnie closed the door behind them and went back behind his desk.

"You should'a seen the look on her face when I pulled it out. She looked like a python trying to figure out how to eat a twelve-point buck. She did okay though. Started to cry after a while, so I let her catch her breath. But she finished strong.

So what's this evaluation you need the money for?"

"I've been ordered by the court to be evaluated by some shrink so I can get my kids. I'm getting a divorce."

"Nah. Really? You're dumping your old lady? She's a prime piece of ass. What the fuck, you been running around on her as long as I've known you. What's a matter, she frigid?"

"Yeah, but now she's running around on me. No way I'm going to stand for that."

Vinnie nodded in silent agreement. "So why do you need an evaluation? You just tell her to get the fuck out of the house and don't ever come back or you'll kill her."

Talks like this reminded Tom Tully that as hard as he was, he'd only killed a man by accident. Vinnie Colabucci talked about killing people like he was ordering carryout.

"Yeah, well, my attorney says this is the best way to go. Get it done with real quick. If I get the kids she doesn't get any support. We're going to prove the adultery and a bunch of other stuff. That way she doesn't get any alimony either. No kids, no money, no nothing."

"So this evaluation is going to show that you should get the kids."

"Yeah."

"Who's doing this evaluation?"

"Some shrink. His name is Morgan Reece. I need to front the money for the whole thing. We've cut Serena off from any dough. We're trying to strangle her and get her to quit."

"How much are we talking about?"

"Eight grand up front. We'll probably get most of it back. Serena really fucked herself up today. She tried to snatch Junior and we got the whole thing on tape."

"This evaluation, what's the guy looking at?"

"I don't know. He wrote a book about what he does. My

lawyer wants me to pick it up tomorrow and study it so I'll know what to say when he asks me questions."

"Any way that he's gonna be looking into your job and where your money comes from?"

"No way. Why should he? That doesn't have anything to do with me being a father."

"Eight grand. That's four weeks' salary I'm advancing you. The interest on the first one's on me. You get paid on Friday. The interest on the other three is a thousand a week. Next week instead of two, it's three."

Tully figured he'd just hold onto the next few paychecks and return them to Vinnie. In a month he'd be clear.

"No problem. This isn't going to last that long."

"Hey, I know you're good for it, Tommy."

"This is a done deal. A mortal lock. No way my wife's not going to fold under the pressure."

"You should know. You married the broad. Keep me posted."

"Sure, Vinnie. No problem."

That said, Vinnie turned to the safe behind him and withdrew eight bundles of ten one-hundred-dollar bills each, handed them to Tully and the meeting was over.

After Tully walked out, Vinnie shook his head. "A mortal lock. You putz. If you could pick winners, we wouldn't own you now." He made a note to follow up on this evaluation nonsense.

On the way out of the club, Tully stopped in the bathroom and wrote, "For a good time call Serena or Denise. Trains leave every hour on the hour." Then he scrawled the phone number. He repeated the message in the bathrooms of every bar on the block.

64

CHAPTER THIRTEEN

At Denise's, Serena lay on the sofa with a large ice pack against the side of her face. She was rapidly going chromatic, heavy in the blue-purple end of the spectrum. All the aspirins in the world would not keep her teeth from aching.

Denise had given up trying to get Serena to go for X-rays. She sat nursing a drink and stared at her friend. The last few days had left her secretly reassessing her own marriage. "If that bastard presses charges, don't worry, I'll post bond," she told Serena. "You won't go to jail."

"Thanks." Serena mumbled behind her icepack. "I can't seem to do anything right. Every move I make, Tom has anticipated and cut me off. When I *do* do something, it's the wrong thing. I'm beginning to wonder if I shouldn't accept whatever Tom wants and put an end to all this. You should have seen Tommy's face when his dad took him away from me. I can't let him go through that again. If I agree to stop fighting, at least I'll have some time with the kids. When Tom gets over his anger, he'll realize that he never wanted to take care of the children. Maybe it'll take awhile, but I could get them back that way."

"Serena, you're dreaming. You woke up to the man Tom Tully was years ago and from what you've told me, you tried everything under the sun to make him happy. It didn't work. What makes you think he'll get over his anger? Everything I've ever seen tells me that Tom Tully *is* his anger. Without it,

I don't know what else there is. I think you should hold on until this Dr. Reece starts to see you and Tom. If he's any good, he'll see the truth. You could do a lot better, a lot quicker."

"But I don't have any money for this. The guy wants four thousand dollars just to start."

"How about your parents? I know you aren't close, but if you tell them what's been going on, I'm sure they'll lend you some money."

"I hate to ask them for anything. I've never been anything but trouble to them."

"Serena, cut the 'poor me' crap. Your parents weren't Ma and Pa Walton, not if half of what you told me is true. Those scars on your wrist aren't proof of a perfect childhood. Give them a chance to do the right thing."

Serena sat up and waited for her head to stop throbbing. Denise pushed the phone over to her, daring her not to pick it up. Serena pulled it into her lap, dialed her parents and prayed for a busy signal.

When her mother answered the phone, she asked to speak immediately to her father. First, he controlled the money. Second her mother would embalm her with questions she didn't really want answers to and saccharine comments about how wonderful things were. A conversation with her mother was just an exercise in endorsing her desperate wish that everything was fine with everyone, everywhere.

"Hi, Dad. It's me, Serena."

"I know who it is. What's going on?"

Serena's sensitivity to her father's disapproval reacted immediately. "Going on? What makes you say that, Dad?"

"Don't fool around with me, Serena. We've been through too much. Tom called me. He said you and he were having troubles. Your depression again."

"It's not my depression again, Dad. It's Tom. He's the one who wants out and he's trying to destroy me. I can't see the children."

"That's not what he says, Serena. He wants to work this thing out between you two. Go to some kind of psychologist. Get some help. I think that's a good idea. Serena, they've helped you before."

"Okay, Dad. Fine. Whatever. But this good idea costs money. Four thousand dollars to be exact, Dad. I don't have that kind of money. Tom has completely cut me off."

"Serena, he told me he'd pay for the whole thing. I don't see what the problem is."

"The problem is, I have no money, Dad. He's thrown me out of the house, emptied the bank accounts, cut off my credit cards. I'm a bag lady now, Dad. If I wasn't staying with a friend, I couldn't feed myself."

"That's not what Tom says, Serena. He said he'd be glad to give you whatever money you need, just so long as it isn't for an attorney. He said he's not going to pay for a war."

"Dad, why is it that you believe anything Tom Tully tells you and you won't believe anything I say?"

"I believe him, Serena, because he hasn't ever lied to me. There wasn't hardly ever a time I could say that about you."

Serena felt her will to fight evaporate and then transform itself into a lacerating self-loathing.

"I understand, Dad. I'm sorry I troubled you with all this. I'll just wait for Tom to tell me what he wants me to do and I'm sure it'll all work out just fine. Don't bother to get Mom, she'll just worry about all this and she's done too much of that already."

Before her father could reply, Serena hung up the phone.

"You know, I never feel so bad that talking to my parents can't make it worse. Shine their little light of love and support my way and there's nothing that can't happen." Serena laughed hollowly.

Denise had listened to the conversation deteriorate from the outset. She wondered how long she and Bill could afford to keep Serena. Short-term was no problem, but what if it dragged on for months? She wasn't going to raise that with Serena now.

The phone rang, pulling them out of their funk. Denise picked it up, listened and handed it to Serena. Doing that, she mouthed "your attorney." Serena winced. She'd forgotten her appointment.

"Mr. Stuart, I'm really sorry about this afternoon. Something came up at the last minute. You see . . ."

"I know all about it, Mrs. Tully. I got a call from Albert Garfield. I don't know how I can represent you when you go off and do things like this without asking for my guidance. You're in a huge mess of trouble now."

"I know, Mr. Stuart, I know." Serena struggled not to cry. As a little girl she cried over everything. At thirty she resolved never to cry again. That lasted three weeks. These days she tried to cry alone.

"Well, I may be able to get you out of some of it." Those were the first positive words she'd heard since her free-fall began on Friday.

"Mr. Garfield has suggested that in the spirit of conciliation, he might be able to get his client to waive pressing charges against you. He also has a motion to show cause ready to go. When you took your son, you were in violation of a court order. That's a jailable offense. He thinks that a reciprocal act of good faith would be appropriate. He suggested that an agreement to waive spousal support would be well thought of. His client would agree to pay for the evaluation, to keep the process moving, but nothing else. I attempted to deposit your retainer check this afternoon, Mrs. Tully. It was not covered and this case has grown more complicated by the minute."

Serena was embarrassed by the check bouncing and sought to make amends by deferring to Stuart's wishes. "What do you think, is it a good idea?"

"You can't even afford to pay me, Mrs. Tully. You'd have to get a legal aid lawyer to defend you on the child snatching charges and represent yourself against Mr. Garfield on the domestic matters. Are you up to that, Mrs. Tully?"

Serena was awestruck at the speed and comprehensiveness of Tom's attack on her. If Garfield had been the architect of that, she knew she was way overmatched.

"No, Mr. Stuart, I'm not." That admission of defeat magnified her dependence on Gilbert Stuart, who hadn't managed to anticipate, outwit, or blunt any of Albert Garfield's plans. Contemplating that she had placed her life and those of her children entirely in the hands of an incompetent was too terrifying, and so like her mother before her, she chose not to.

"Are you authorizing me to accept that offer, Mrs. Tully?"

"Yes, Mr. Stuart, I am."

"Very good. Now that we've got that settled, you should hear from the psychologist, a Doctor Morgan Reece, any day."

"Fine, Mr. Stuart. Thanks."

When Stuart hung up, Serena couldn't shake the feeling that Tom's apparent generosity only masked a larger theft, but she didn't know what else she had to lose.

CHAPTER FOURTEEN

Morgan Reece slipped into the water. He spit into his goggles, rinsed them and pulled them on. Grabbing the wall behind him, he flexed his legs and pushed off to begin his laps.

For almost two years he had done no exercise. Fortunately he'd lost his appetite at the same time, and so the cardiac risks of his inertia were not multiplied by obesity. He now swam three times a week at the local YMCA.

For the first few laps, he enjoyed the warmth of the water flowing past him. Then he focused on his hands pulling through the water, then his kick, first his feet, then his thighs. He moved smoothly down his lane. Taking a breath, he saw Mrs. Gerardi backstroking in the lane next to him. Her husband was next to her, his stroke having reduced him to dog paddling.

Reece tried imagining himself as a fish. A shark? Too sharp. All those serrated teeth and that flexible jaw bouncing below the snout. No, he was sleeker, rounded. A dolphin? No, they were too acrobatic and talkative. He felt steady and silent. A killer whale. Yes. And so he did his next quarter mile, clearing his blowhole every other stroke, his arm coming over like a long black dorsal fin.

Reece learned that counting laps made exercise into torture and had quickly given that up. Next he'd tried to use the time as a case conference with himself, but found that he needed to leave his work behind even more. Currently he played imaginary soccer matches in his mind. For today he chose Brazil 1970 vs. Germany 1972. Pele and "jogo bonito" against "Kaiser" Beckenbauer and "Der Bomber," Gerd Muller. Brazil won in extra time.

Only recently had Reece been able to relax for a few laps and let his mind wander or dare to be empty. For a long time he avoided being alone and undistracted whenever possible. He found those times as dangerous as tiger pits in high grass. One false step and he was hurtling downward, falling through the present to be impaled on a memory.

Reece swam on, his mouth open wide, then his left arm coming over like a side-wheeler. His mind was as clear as the water. Reece was simply a strainer, a net waiting for something, anything, to get stuck.

Numbers and lines emerged. The pages that that woman lost. Dotted lines, zigzagging between the numbers. Then the black background, shaded and edgeless. Reece tried to deduce what they were. Irregular, but sequential. The numbers went from bottom to top, and left to right, but no line connected a top number to the next number at the bottom. The two pictures were not connected. They both began at one and went until there was a number in the upper right quadrant. The lines took different paths to connect the same numbers. Two of the same kind of things. Unique in their totality, but orderly within.

Reece finished his mile and sagged over the lane divider. What were those diagrams? He spent another minute thinking about them and then shook his head, baffled at the things that floated up in his empty mind. Who cares what they are, he thought, and hauled himself out of the water.

CHAPTER FIFTEEN

That night, Tom Tully finally got around to doing his homework. Albert Garfield wanted him to search the house for any evidence of the affair: letters, gifts, pictures, souvenirs. He wanted him to check for long distance phone calls over the last six months.

When he went through her belongings he found no jewelry or perfumes he couldn't account for. No motel matchbooks in her empty purses. He'd tossed her bathroom pretty good and the medicine cabinet.

Tonight he went through the kitchen, her cookbooks and recipe files, the china cabinet, her sewing table, any space that was primarily hers. Nothing. He went through the things that were in storage. More kitchen stuff, food containers, Christmas things, gift-wrapping supplies. More nothing.

Tully poured himself some bourbon and sat with the long distance phone bills. Most of them were his and he recognized nearly all of the numbers. A couple of calls he wished he could have back now, especially if Serena's lawyer ever wanted to look at these logs. He'd say he misdialed. They were brief calls anyway.

Tully leaned back and sipped his drink. Where would he hide things if he were Serena? He'd assumed that anything she wanted kept private would be in space she used almost exclusively. That made sense if you wanted easy access for yourself and no accidental discovery. But what if the other person doesn't trust you any more? That's exactly where they'd go look. He'd stick something he wanted to hide from Serena right in her personal space. She'd never look there. Just not in a space where there would be an accidental discovery. Someplace you would never look except in a search. You wouldn't search yourself. Where had he first looked? Her closet and dresser. He went up to the bedroom and into the closet and looked at his side. He moved each suit and shirt, the belts, shoes, hats. He looked at the underside of each shelf.

Then he went to his dresser. He emptied each drawer, removed and checked the sides and back. First his underwear and socks, then this casual shirts. Then his athletic gear. Finally, his sweaters. Still nothing.

Tully sat on the bed. Maybe he'd given Serena too much credit. After all, he'd been cheating on her for years and she'd never caught on. He kept no reminders of his conquests. Most were forgotten before the sheets had cooled. Serena would keep things. Women were like that.

Tully frowned. One last place to try. He slid off the bed, turned onto his back, and lay on the floor and reached underneath the dresser. His hands swept over the bottom of the frame. A finger nicked something. He went back over that area slowly. There it was! He hooked a nail under an edge and began to pull it away from the wood.

He slid away from the dresser and pulled out his prize. It was a brown letter-size envelope. Tully sat on the bed and turned the envelope over. No writing. He wondered if he should open it. Garfield said not to. Just deliver it straight to him. He'd know best what to do with it.

What would be the worst thing inside? A letter to Serena from this guy telling her how much he loved her and what he'd do for her and how beautiful she was and what a great fuck she was.

Tully searched for a reaction to that. Nothing. If it was signed, then he'd have a focus for his rage. What about a photograph of them together? As long as it wasn't one of those in his head, he didn't have a reaction. Just a face for the name. More focus.

Tully peered into the envelope. There was a folded piece of paper. Tully took it out and unfolded it. A letter. That's all. Two pages. Centered on the first page was a poem. He read the first line and scanned to the signature, E. St. V. Millay. Nobody on the team, that was for sure. The second page was a letter, unsigned. The handwriting was terrible. Tully could hardly make it out.

St. V. Millay. What kind of a name was that? The guy had to be a complete fruit. Tully went over to his desk and opened the Northern Virginia phone book. No entry for the name. He tried D.C. and Maryland. Nothing. Okay, the guy had an unlisted phone number. Garfield would find him. But now we had a name.

Tom sat on the bed. The poem was typical romantic bullshit. What kind of man could write crap like that? He put the letter on top and tried to make out the words. It was slow going but Tully pieced it together.

I know you have doubts. Doubts about us, about yourself. It's always that way when you start a new relationship. Following your heart's own truth is always a difficult path. No one else can tell you what is right or wrong for you. Listen to your heart, to what it tells you, to your truest feelings.

Don't doubt me. I know what I feel. I know my truth. You are the most extraordinary woman I have ever met. I feel like I am truly alive for the first time. I loved you long before we ever got together. Holding you in my arms completed the circle, fin-ishing the arcs we had both been drawing.

We are at a vulnerable time. Love demands that we be to-gether at once and always. We must be careful. If your hus-band is half the monster you say, he could make things very difficult if he found out. For now, our love must beat its wings inside a cage. Patience sweetens desire.

Tully did not remember the top of his head exploding or the hot white light consuming him from the inside like he'd eaten a phosphorus grenade, only the image of his wife in an-other man's arms, conspiring against him, lying to him, be-traying him over and over.

Tully closed his eyes, raised his fists to the side of his head and bellowed. He opened his eyes. The pain inside was still there. He did the only thing he knew to free him-self.

Tully threw himself at the dresser as if it were a tackling dummy. His first attack caved in the drawer fronts. Tully slid down to his hands and knees. Crawling away, he turned and threw himself against the wall, forearm up, over and over until the plaster cracked and then his arm did.

"Daddy, what's wrong?" Tommy cried from the doorway. He stood there with his sister. She was blinking away tears and stifling sobs by sucking her thumb ferociously.

On all fours, Tully looked back at the door. The respite al-lowed the pain radiating up his arm to overtake the pain in his head.

"It's your mother, Junior. She's trying to kill me. Now go back to bed. That's an order."

Tommy stood there, trying to see where his mother was hiding. Maybe his father had fought her off, and she'd jumped out a window. He didn't understand how she could kill his dad. When they fought this afternoon, he beat her up pretty easy.

When neither child moved, Tully roared, "Go to fucking bed, goddamnit."

Tommy grabbed his little sister's free hand and raced off to his room with her. They fell asleep face to face. Once Tina was asleep, Tommy freed his hand and began to suck his own thumb.

Tully, cradling his broken forearm before him, went to the desk and called the team doctor. With all the security around injuries, they still made house calls.

"Hi, Jeff, sorry to call you at this time of night, but I've had an accident."

After three hours of tossing and turning, Serena got up off the family room sofa and went into the kitchen. She picked up the phone and dialed her therapist.

His message said that he was still out of town at a conference. It gave an emergency number for the therapist providing coverage. She thought about using it and then decided to just leave a message.

"Hello, Simon, this is Serena. I'm sorry to call you so late, but I really have to see you. So much has happened. My head is reeling. We really have to talk. I don't think I can wait for my regular appointment."

CHAPTER SIXTEEN

Morgan Reece set the newspaper aside and dialed Serena Tully's number on his cell phone.

"Fargo residence."

"Serena Tully, please."

"Who may I say is calling?"

"Dr. Reece, Morgan Reece."

"Hello," another voice said.

"Ms. Tully, my name is Morgan Reece. I'm the court appointed evaluator in the custody dispute with your husband, Thomas Tully. I'm calling to arrange the initial interview, tell you some things about the evaluation process and answer any questions you have."

"I'd like to start the process as soon as possible."

"How about tomorrow? We could do the initial interview in the morning, then let you take some psychological tests in the afternoon."

"I guess that would be okay. I'm trying to find a job. I doubt that I'll get one today, so okay."

"We'll start at nine o'clock. The first hour or so will be a joint interview with your husband. I'll be going over some of the groundrules for the evaluation in a fee-for-service agreement that I use, then we'll . . ."

"Do we have to meet together? I'd really rather not be anywhere near Tom Tully."

"I understand. However, I find that it's important in terms

of establishing my neutrality if I discuss the format of the evaluation with you both at the same time."

"I don't doubt your neutrality, Dr. Reece. I'm afraid of Tom, plain and simple."

"What are you afraid of, Ms. Tully?"

"I'm afraid of getting beat up again, that's what."

"You said beaten up again. When was the last time, Ms. Tully?"

"How about yesterday?"

"Yesterday? What happened?"

"Well, he threw me down on the ground by my hair. When I went after him to get my son back, he punched me in the side of the head, knocked me out cold. The entire side of my face is swollen and four of my teeth feel pretty loose."

"Why are we having this evaluation? If what you've just told me is true, he should be in jail on assault and battery charges."

"I wish. No, he has temporary custody of the children. I went to the school to see my son. My husband had me thrown out of the house. I couldn't see the children. He won't let them answer the phone. Anyway, when I tried to talk to my son, I saw Tom coming down the halls. I knew I wouldn't get a chance to tell him anything about what was going on with his father there, so I did something really dumb. I ran with Tommy and that's when he caught up with me and hit me."

"He still can't haul off and cold cock you, even if you've got the child. He can restrain you. This doesn't sound right."

After a pause, Serena Tully said, "I bit him. That's why he hit me. That's why he's not in jail. I would be, if he pressed charges. That's what my lawyer told me."

"I appreciate your candor, Ms. Tully. I'm going to have to hold to my request that the first part of the meeting be joint. I run a very tight ship. I won't tolerate any threats or insults. It won't get close to physical. If Mr. Tully doesn't accept that, I have no compunctions about calling the police."

"Okay."

"First, let me give you directions to my office, it's in Vienna." That done, Reece went on to confirm his understanding that the entire retainer was going to be paid by Mr. Tully. "After the joint interview, I'll ask you to fill out a questionnaire about yourself and the children. To do that you have to bring the names, addresses and phone numbers of the following individuals: any mental health professionals who have ever treated you . . ."

"Ever?"

"Yes."

"Isn't that a little unfair? I was in therapy and I was hospitalized years ago. What does that have to do with me now?"

"I don't know. Maybe a lot, maybe nothing at all. That's what looking at the records will tell me. That and your interviews and testing and my observations of you with your children. Just because you've been in therapy or had an emotional disturbance doesn't make you a bad parent. They're two separate domains. They may overlap, they may not. You could be pretty crazy and still be a good parent."

Serena Tully closed her eyes and felt the first wellspring of hope push up from her gut, fountain in her head and run down her cheeks. "Dr. Reece, that's the best news I've had all week. That may be the best news I've ever heard."

"Let me go on and tell you what other information I need. Names and addresses and phone numbers for any physicians currently treating you or the children, the kid's schools and day-care provider. By the way, what are the children's names and ages?"

"Thomas Drew Tully, Junior, he's six. I call him Tommy, his dad calls him Junior; and Tina Nicole Tully, she's four."

"Also any Department of Social Service agencies that have worked with the family?"

"What do you mean?"

"Child Protective Services. Any allegations of abuse or neglect filed against either parent?"

"There's nothing like that. At least not that I know of. I'll tell you, these days I don't know what's real anymore. Wait a minute. I don't mean that the way it sounds. It's just that when it comes to my marriage, what my husband and I think is real or right or true or fair seems to be very different."

"Are there any questions that I can answer at this time?"

"Just one. How good are you at spotting a fake, Dr. Reece? My husband hasn't had much time for the children. He's doing this just to punish me, because he knows it'll kill me to lose the kids. This is his way of killing me, by using them."

"Ms. Tully, I'm not infallible. I'm sure I can be fooled and probably have been. I do everything I know how to cut down on the chances of being fooled. If what you say is true, the recency of the separation is a factor that might work in your favor. The children won't change their attitudes and expectations that quickly and Mr. Tully will have to learn an awful lot in a short time."

"That's reassuring. Thank you, Dr. Reece."

"If you don't hear otherwise from me, I'll see you tomorrow at nine a.m."

Morgan Reece tried to reach Tom Tully at home but missed him. He was already on his way to his attorney's office to tighten the screws another turn.

CHAPTER SEVENTEEN

Tom Tully took a cup of coffee from the receptionist and watched her butt flex and relax as she walked back to her desk. Great legs in a black sheath dress, patterned stockings. The sound of nylons mating quickened his pulse.

"Come in, Tom. You said you found something useful. Sandra, hold my calls."

Albert Garfield followed Tom across the room, slid behind his desk and reached out for the envelope. He read the poem and the letter.

He looked up at Tully and nodded at his arm. "What happened?"

"Nothing. I was moving some furniture and a dresser fell over and fractured the arm. These new casts are amazing. No plaster. Just slip one on and pump it full of air. I have to wear it about a month."

"This is excellent. We'll go with adultery as the grounds for the divorce and we'll get the name in interrogatories."

"Don't we have the guy's name, St. V. Millay, right there on the poem he wrote her?"

Garfield pursed his lips to mute his mirth. "St. V. Millay is the name of the poet who wrote the poem. Edna St. Vincent Millay. Your wife's lover copied the sonnet and sent it to her as a gift. It gives us a sample of his handwriting, but that's about all."

"What else do we need?"

"You've got her kissing somebody else while you were supposed to be out of town and this letter. We're on our way, but this isn't enough. We need an admission from her, an eight-by-ten glossy of her sitting on somebody else's dick, or for Chester Polansky to put her in a motel for a couple of hours with somebody. We don't have that yet. We've got enough to go forward and put more pressure on her, but this isn't a done deal."

Garfield dropped the letter and handed Tully the interrogatories and request for documents from Gilbert Stuart. "Read these, write down your answers, not on these forms, and drop them at my office when you're done. I'll look them over and call you if I've got any questions and send them back to her lawyer. I'm sending him ones of our own. Once we've got the names and addresses of her therapists, we'll depose them all. She can sit in while we go over her pathetic past. Hear what the experts think about her. She'll find that pretty unnerving."

"Aren't all these depositions going to get pretty costly?"

"Yes, but they're worth it. Litigation is just like war. No, litigation is war. There are two ways to win a war. One is to prevail in a decisive battle. That's the courtroom. The other is to sap the will of your opponent to fight, so that they sue for peace. Everything we do between now and the court date will be geared to help us in either of those two ways. To position us to prevail before the judge or to crack your wife's will to fight. That's why we cut off her money, her supports, her family, the kids, the house. If she had money to fight us with, I'd bleed it out of her with as many motions and appearances as I could. From what you've told me about your wife, the two tools that will cause her to abandon the fight are isolation and shame. We've done the first, now we focus on the latter."

"Why don't we make her an offer now? I think she's been

softened up pretty good. Every day she makes it might give her confidence that she can go on."

"What do you want to offer her? You started out saying nothing."

"Can I get away with giving her nothing?"

"Absolutely nothing? No, not really. Her lawyer would never agree to it, just to protect himself from malpractice. We can probably get pretty close though. Her lawyer is an idiot. He's reacting to everything we do. He hasn't once attempted to put any pressure on us. If she agrees to something and it isn't absolutely indefensible, he'll sign off on it. As for making an offer, there really are only two things to consider: money and custody."

"What's the least we can give her on custody?"

"You get sole legal custody. You are the one to make all the decisions. You don't have to consult with her or get her approval. You get primary physical residence. The kids live with you. She gets supervised visitation. She pays for the supervisor. Say four hours every other weekend. Once you've got custody and control, there are lots of things that can affect how kids look at the parent that isn't there any more. You put the kids in therapy. You tell the therapist the kids are real upset when they have to visit, they don't want to go. You make it more attractive not to go. Pretty soon the kids start to control the issue. You go back and argue that it isn't in the kids' best interests to see their mother. It takes a while, but you can remove her completely from their lives and yours.

"Money. With you getting full custody, she's going to owe you child support. You may get tagged with alimony, since she's never worked and was home with the kids. That's likely to be a wash. From what you've told me, your assets are your pension, the equity in the house, the household belongings and the two cars. The cars are in your name. Get her car repossessed and sell it as soon as you can. If there are no insurance inventories on file, sell everything in the house you don't want. Let her prove what was there.

"She'll probably get a piece of the house. Let me work on that. We'll have to fight for your pension, argue that it predates the marriage, even though as a coach you continued to feed into that pension and you've been married for some of these years."

"Sounds like keeping custody of the kids is important to keeping her from getting money."

"That's absolutely right. Through the kids we argue for the house, and we claim child support. That cuts into whatever monetary claims she might make."

"Let's make her a deal. Let's get this over with. I want that bitch out of my life now."

"If that's what you want. We'll draw one up and send it to her attorney along with a letter stating the grounds for the divorce and a little warning about what she can look forward to if she fights this."

"I think this is a good time to do it. Thinking about how close she came to going to jail is still going to be fresh in her mind. That and how sore her face is. She won't be feeling too feisty right now."

"We'll get on it today. While you work on these interrogatories I want you to read these books to help prepare yourself for the evaluation. Here's Dr. Pecorino's card. Call him if you have any questions."

CHAPTER EIGHTEEN

Morgan Reece finally caught up with Tom Tully around three in the afternoon. After introducing himself he went through the same information that he covered with his wife.

"All these records, is there anything else you want?"

"Not at this time. Are there other things you think I should look at?"

"I don't know. I was just wondering about whether we could give you things if you didn't ask for them."

"Sure. If you send me a lot of stuff, I'll just ask you to consider how important it is, because it can get pretty expensive to read it all."

"Fair enough. When can we get started?"

"How about tomorrow? I've already spoken to your wife. She can come in at nine."

"You mean together?"

"Just for the first part where I go over the groundrules. After that, all your interviews will be individual."

"All right. I just hate being around her. It disgusts me to even look at her."

"After the joint interview, I'll ask you both to fill out some questionnaires, and sign consents for records. Then while I interview one of you, I'll set the other up with some psychological tests. You should expect to be in the office until five o'clock. I prefer to see people for large blocks of time. It's usually easier to get off from work that way. Do you have any questions I can answer at this time?"

"Yeah, how are you gonna deal with the fact that my wife is a real good actress? She's on trial here and she can put up a real good show in public. I'm the only one that ever saw her shit. And the kids, but they were too little to remember."

"Well, Mr. Tully, I'll look at your wife in as many ways as I can. Her report of things, the reports of others, what she actually does, psychological testing. If her act isn't perfect, she should slip up somewhere and hopefully I'll be there to see it. It isn't perfect and I can be fooled, but I do everything I can to try to prevent that."

"Well, I just wanted you to be aware. She can look pretty good, but it's just a show."

Morgan Reece drove home. He stopped at Bob Kinkead's Colvin Run Tavern in Tysons Corner for dinner.

Reece finished his meal, said goodnight and walked back to his car under a crisp, cloudless fall sky. It was six-thirty. He'd go over to Borders, pick up the books he had on order, browse, maybe have a coffee and dessert and return the pictures.

Reece wandered through the huge bookstore, browsing in his interest areas: architecture, psychology, literature, mysteries, sports. He went to the new release tables and then checked out the magazines. Empty handed, he went to the checkout registers and picked up his order: two recent polemics from each side of the repressed memory controversy.

Reece went back to the cafe and ordered a coffee. He looked around and found an empty table by the railing. When his coffee came, Reece sipped it and watched the people in the store.

"Hi, Dr. Reece, I'm Lindsay Brinkman," came a voice from his blindside.

Reece turned and saw the woman from the Metro. He extended his hand and said, "Hi, how are you?"

"Fine. Thanks. Do you have my route maps?"

"Yeah, here they are." Reece pulled them out of his jacket pocket and handed them to her.

"Great. You wouldn't believe how much work went into these."

"What are they? I looked at them for quite a while but I couldn't come up with anything."

"They're routes for climbs. For my next vacation. I went out and lead-climbed these faces to plan the routes. Next time I'm going to free-climb them. One of these has never been done. When I do it, I get to name it. So I didn't want to have to start over."

Reece glanced down at her hands, then quickly up her arms to her head. Short nails, venous hands, ropy muscular arms and short hair. It all made sense. Make yourself compact, functional. Don't carry anything you don't have to up that rock.

"That's fascinating. I'm terrified of heights. I can't even use a glass elevator. What's it like?"

Lindsay Brinkman looked around the store for a moment as she decided whether to sit or not. She did.

"It's what I live for. I love it. The challenge, the danger, the thrill of the peak. Just me and the cliff. No ropes. No harness. Just my hands."

"Whew," Reece said, shaking his head. "I could never do that."

"That's what I thought when I started. I saw these people going up the face like Spiderman. I wanted to be able to do that. It's very basic. You and the rock. You climb or you fall. The harder the climb, the sweeter the peak. I wish the rest of life could be like that. So clean, so simple."

"How'd you get into it?"

"My boyfriend was a climber. He got me started. I dropped the boyfriend, but kept the rocks."

Reece began to relax. Listening to other people talk, drawing them into the space he felt around himself was his life, first by preference, then by training.

"Oh," she said, and reached into her waist pack. "This is yours." She pulled out the page from Reece's manuscript. She winced at its creases and folds.

"Sorry." She shrugged and handed it to him. "I travel real light. Keep my hands free."

"That's okay. It's just a draft," Reece said, and slipped it into his jacket.

"Sexual abuse evaluations, pretty intense stuff, huh?" she asked.

"Yeah."

"Anything like rock climbing?"

"I think of it like bomb disposal work. The parents have wrapped themselves and the kids in dynamite and they each have their fingers on the detonator. Most of the time I can get everybody out of the building. Every once in the while I can't. It's the 'most of the times' that keep me going back. That's my peak, when everybody walks out of the building alive and they can get on with their lives, with better lives."

Lindsay Brinkman shuddered. "I think I'll stick to the rocks," she said, and stood to leave.

"Well, It's been nice talking to you. Good luck on your trip," Reece said.

Lindsay Brinkman started to go, then turned back and heard herself say, "If you ever want to work on your fear of heights, call me. You have the number at RMH. I know some real good instructors."

"Thanks. I'll think about that." Reece contemplated her

sculpted features, as taut and austere as the rocks she loved. She touched her short, spiky hair and wished it was softer. Reece smiled and wished he was younger.

CHAPTER NINETEEN

At nine o'clock the next morning, Reece arranged his case file, note pad and coffee mug and went out to the waiting room to meet the Tullys. Tom Tully popped up out of the chair, pumped Reece's hand briskly and, after a nod in greeting, walked into the office. Serena Tully stepped up, her face still lopsided and yellowing, shook hands and preceded Reece into the office.

They stood waiting for Reece to identify his seat, both wanting to sit as far away from the other as possible but not wanting to sit in his chair. Once he indicated where he'd sit, they retired to their corners.

"Good morning," Reece said. No one agreed. He handed out a three-page form to each parent. "Please read this carefully. It outlines the important parameters that govern the evaluation we're about to begin. It covers what you need to do for me, how long I estimate the process to take, financial matters, how my report will be distributed, privilege and confidentiality issues. If you understand and agree to these terms, we'll move on to the interviews."

While they read, Reece took a moment to size up each of the Tullys. Tom Tully radiated aggression as a lambent energy. Serena Tully was a striking woman, her white blonde hair, blunt cut, rippling with each movement like a curtain made of snow. Small dimples bracketed her full downswept mouth like parentheses. Her eyes were as large and bright as a pair of topaz stones.

"How long do you expect this to take, Doctor?" Tom asked.

"Depending on how many records have to be retrieved, I'd guess a few weeks. That's if things stay as they are. Right now this is the only evaluation I'm doing."

"This thing about the initial retainer being only an estimate. Do you mean this could cost even more?"

"That's possible, Mr. Tully. When I begin to investigate a family situation, I have no idea what I'll find. It's like exploratory surgery. Sometimes I come across things that are a problem that no one else has noticed before. Sometimes I may require a consultation with another expert, such as a learning disability specialist or someone to diagnose hyperactivity. I just don't know what I'll find."

"What if there isn't any more money?"

"Then the evaluation comes to a halt until funds can be located. I'll let you know how we're doing against the retainer. If it's exceeded, it won't be a surprise. There'll be time to make arrangements. I think my estimate is a good one. It should cover everything, but it is only an estimate, not a guaranteed ceiling."

"Tom, where did the money come from? We didn't have that much in the accounts. Have you sold anything?"

"Where I get my money from is none of your damn business. Nothing about my life is any of your damn business. You lost that right a long time ago, bitch."

"Whoa, let's hold it right there. Those kinds of questions can be asked by your attorneys. The purpose of this meeting is for me to give you information about what I'm going to be doing. You should be asking me the questions, not each other. Can we continue?"

Tully stared his wife down and she broke off her gaze. She

switched over to Reece and asked, "I have a question, Dr. Reece. All the stuff about confidentiality is pretty confusing. Could you go over it one piece at a time?"

"Okay, the first piece has to do with the children. Regardless of what happens in court, you two will continue to be these children's parents." Reece halted as he caught Tully sneering at that thought. "I want to protect those relationships if I can. I will explain to the children that I cannot guarantee that what they say to me can be kept secret. If they are concerned about either of you finding out what they said to my question, they can tell me that they are uncomfortable and would rather not answer. If they won't answer questions, knowing why might tell me just as much. I am the children's agent, not yours. What is best for them is my concern, not what is best for either of you."

"Thank God," Serena Tully whispered. Her husband looked at her balefully.

"As for you, there is no confidentiality here. Anything you tell me can and most likely will be discussed with the other side or third parties for corroboration. If it's relevant to the question of custody then it will find its way into my report which will be sent to the court. When I send out consents for information, I'll ask you both to sign them. It may not be legally necessary, but it alleviates anxiety on the part of the people we're asking to send records and will speed the process. You did bring the list of collaterals that I requested?" Both of them nodded.

The Tullys returned to reading the fee agreement. When they were done, Reece asked them each to sign one. He countersigned and gave them copies for their own records. He set Mr. Tully up in the waiting room with a lengthy questionnaire to fill out. An hour later, Tom Tully knocked on the open office door.

"Here's the questionnaire and the retainer," he said, handing Reece a fat envelope. Reece invited him in, counted the money and gave Tully a receipt. Then he directed him to another office to take some psychological tests.

Sitting in his office, he stared at the stack of bills and wondered where it had come from. He had never before been paid in cash.

CHAPTER TWENTY

There was a knock on the door. "Come in."

Serena Tully opened the door and stood there with the clipboard in her hands. "I've finished the questionnaire."

Reece stood up, took the clipboard and motioned her to a seat. Serena tucked her purse out of the way, crossed a nyloned leg over the other and sat at attention. Her heart was pounding in her chest. This man was the key to getting her children back. How to impress him? Serena knew this feeling well, the frantic search for clues to the mystery at hand, the mystery that occurred whenever she met someone new. How to be pleasing and get by on the gifts of others. She didn't think he was going to help her out. When was she going to stop this shit?

"Let me look over the questionnaire, use that as a start for the interview." Reece took a yellow marker and ran it through answers that interested him. He passed some blank consent forms over to her. "Sign and date these. One will be for the school, one for the nanny, one for the therapist who treated you as an adolescent, one for the one who saw you about ten years ago and one for your current therapist."

After she passed the consents back, Reece double-checked them and set them aside.

"Let me start by asking you to tell me your side of the events of the past week. Why do you think your husband had you excluded from the home and from seeing the children?"

"I don't know. He hasn't told me. He just yells at me, calls me names, threatens me and tells me I'm going to get mine."

"Why is he so angry?"

"I don't know."

"That's pretty extreme behavior and you have no idea where it's coming from?"

"It could be anything. You have to understand my husband. He's a bomb that doesn't tick. It'll go off, that's for sure. You just don't know when. He's always angry. He thinks that everyone is out to get him. That he's never treated fairly. He thought he should have been a Hall of Famer instead of a special teams player. He should have made the big money. Things never go the way Tom thinks they should and it's always somebody else's fault."

"That sounds pretty hard to live with. Why are you still in this marriage?"

"I could tell you it's for the children, but that wouldn't really be true. Well, not all of the truth. I'm still here because starting over and having to deal with Tom just seemed too hard and too scary. I've never done the hard things in my life, the scary things. I was always looking for someone else to do them for me. In the beginning, Tommy did that. He isn't afraid of anything. I think he got bored with me. Instead of rescuing me, he became my latest mistake. The older I get, the bigger my stack of regrets, the less energy I have to try to do anything about them. So here I am."

"You seem to understand yourself pretty well, but that hasn't helped you one bit."

"No. I had a therapist once who said, 'Insight changes nothing. It just tells you the name of the crossroads you're at. Change is courage, moving your feet in some direction.' "

"What about suicide? That's a move in a direction."

"I haven't tried that one in about ten years."

"Tell me about your attempts. The transcript of the hearing they held said you attempted suicide twice. I think it was your sister who talked about it."

Serena smiled and shook her head. "My sister. Did she say that I tried to commit suicide after I found out that my boyfriend was sleeping with her too? That blew me away. I was already in trouble, drinking and smoking dope. That's one way I learned not to be afraid all the time. Bobby liked me best when I was fucked up, so I got fucked up all the time. I was pretty rowdy when I was fucked up. There was nothing I wouldn't do if you dared me and I had enough shit in my system. I danced naked on the altar at St. Mary's. I'd have had sex with Bobby right there and then, only he was too afraid to get it up. My sister and I have never been close. It's a real jealousy thing. There's never been enough of anything for both of us to be happy. Bobby made me happy so she had to have him. When I found out I just took more pills than usual. Sleep the big sleep; stop feeling bad. Feel nothing at all."

"What about the second attempt?"

"I was working as a model. I'd been having a relationship with my agent. He was starting to pull out of it, getting interested in a younger girl, a fresh face, a new look. I pulled the same stunt. I cut my wrists and almost died. My sister found me and called the ambulance. I still wonder why she did that. That was the stupidest thing I ever did." She extended her hands in front of her and looked longingly at them.

"I had beautiful hands. Some of my best work was as a hand model for jewelers." She turned them over and looked at the slick rubbery scars across each wrist. "Now I look like Frankenstein." She looked up at Reece. "The second one was hard to do. I cut the first one so deep, I almost didn't have the strength to hold the razor."

"Why haven't you done it now? You seem to have lost just about everything."

"Have I lost it? It's been stolen from me, but I know who the thief is. You're the judge. I'm counting on you to get it back for me."

"And if I don't, what then?" Her candor was veering dangerously close to becoming self-destructive. Nothing new about that, Reece thought.

"I don't know. I won't kill myself. Not for myself, but for the kids. They'll need me even more if Tom has them. He hasn't a clue how to raise kids. I couldn't abandon them like that. I brought them into this world. I probably shouldn't have done that."

"Why?"

"Mistakes number two and three. Things with Tom were already bad. I thought being a family would make them better. I look back at that now and wonder what possessed me to think that. Maybe being a mother would make me feel better. It did. It was the first thing I felt good at. But I should have left Tom and had them on my own. I didn't, and now I can't leave them behind."

Morgan Reece put his pen down and stared out the window. The bullet train of grief was making another run through him. Roaring past every station. The wind that cored him left nothing standing. Reece searched for his voice. When the wind died down, he spoke.

"After each suicide attempt, you spent some time in therapy. What was your motivation for being in therapy at this time?"

"Things were getting worse with Tom. I asked him to get into therapy with me, try to turn things around. He wouldn't have any part of it. He thinks he has no problems. The world has problems, but not Thomas Drew Tully. I went anyway. I wouldn't have made it this far without it. It's been a lifesaver. When I need support or tips on how to deal with Tom, Doctor Tepper has always been there."

"Simon Tepper?"

"Yes. Do you know him?"

"Only by sight. We've been at a few of the same conferences." Simon Tepper was a psychiatrist who ran a treatment center in Fairfax.

"What attracted you to Tom Tully?"

"He wanted me. Bad. He was famous. Sort of. The way any professional athlete is. He knew what he wanted and he went for it. He had all the energy for life that I didn't have. I attached myself to that."

"Did it ever work?"

"For a while. I did everything I could to please him, but it wasn't possible. There was never enough of anything to please Tom, to live up to how he thought things should go for him. He turned his rage against me and then it all went bad. The baby delayed things, that's all. A son named after him, a fresh start. We were going to be the perfect family. Well, we weren't, we were just real. With the morning feedings and the shit and the vomit and the colic and the ear infections. It never got better again."

"Your husband got this emergency order on the basis of an affidavit that you had threatened to cut off his penis while he slept and that you had a fight with him where you tried to scratch his face. The nanny reported that."

Serena Tully looked at Morgan Reece as if he'd just sprouted a giant sunflower from his forehead. "He said I did what? Cut off his penis? I never said such a thing. I never even thought such as thing. And the nanny said I had a fight with Tom. This is rich. This shows you how well Tom has thought this all out.

"You asked me why is he doing all of this? Because he wants a divorce and he wants to hurt me and leave me with nothing. I think he's got a girlfriend and he's ready to switch and he doesn't want me to get anything. This is all choreographed.

"Let me tell you about our nanny. Felicia Hurtado. Tom comes home one day about three months ago and says we need a nanny for the kids. I need to get out of the house and get a job. We need to bring in more money. So why are we paying for a nanny? Let me get a part-time job, work while Tommy's in school. Put Tina in a daycare program. No, got to have this nanny. Now I see why he's got her in the house. She's my replacement after I'm locked out. That way Tom doesn't have to take care of the kids. You want to know about our 'fight'? Tom was after me for sex. I didn't want it. I was pissed off at him over the nanny thing. He got me in the kitchen. He grabbed my wrists and pulled them behind my back, then he was making gross noises while he told me what he wanted me to do. Felicia asked him something, he told her to come into the kitchen. I was furious that he wouldn't let me go, so I kicked him and told him I'd scratch his eyes out. Of course Felicia was in the doorway when that happened."

"What about your sister's report of an invitation to a dinner for the whole family? They show up and you haven't prepared anything."

"That's another part of Tom's plan to make me look like a nutcase. He wanted a big family dinner, so he suggested a date. I told him fine. I'd shop the week before, do all the cooking. He said he'd tell Amber and his parents. Only he told them a different date than he told me. So yes they all showed up and yes I looked like a complete fool. I didn't want to embarrass myself any more by accusing Tom of doing it on purpose, so I just apologized to everyone. When I confronted him afterwards, he denied that he'd told me the wrong date. I thought that I was going crazy, I'd misheard him and it was all my fault. I never suspected that he'd done it on purpose as part of a scheme to completely discredit me."

Reece had heard stories like this before. Gaslighting or paranoia? Would he know at the end of his tour of the funhouse?

"The whole idea of me being violent with 'Tom the Bomb' Tully is laughable. He's a guy who made his reputation as a completely nuts special teamer. The hardest hitter in the league. If there's anyone who's violent, it's Tom. He's never as happy as when he's hitting something."

"Has he ever been involved in any assaults on anyone? Bar fights? Traffic incidents? Has he ever used a weapon?"

"Tom has had so many run-ins, I couldn't begin to tell you."

"Has he ever been arrested?"

"No. Tom is a very scary guy when he's lost it. Most people back down. The couple of times people haven't backed down, he's goaded them into throwing the first punch. Both of those guys went to the hospital, but Tom got off on self-defense."

"As for a weapon, he's never used one. He has a couple of guns at home. Some huge revolver. He called it 'Dirty Harry!' "

"A .44 Magnum?"

"Yeah, that's it. He said he thought we should have something for self-protection. I was very uncomfortable having that gun in the house with two little children. I know there was a time that Tom slept with the gun under the mattress. He never talked about it. He'd get it and put it there after he thought I was asleep. I guess he pissed someone off and was worried about them coming after him. But that wasn't too long and he put the gun away."

"You said he had two guns."

"Yeah, the other was a gift from some fan. It was an automatic. The metalwork was all engraved with patterns, you know filigree—it was actually beautiful if you didn't think about what it was. The handles were made out of wood, really polished with a strong grain. Black walnut I think, and the wood was carved. One side was a football player and the other had Tom's name and number. He called it a presentation piece. It had a wood and velvet case. Tom kept it on the mantle. He never took that one out of the case."

"Tell me about your children. How would you describe them? What are their strengths? What is hard for them?"

Serena leaned forward and her eyes brightened for the first time all morning. "Tommy is a typical little boy. He's inquisitive, adventuresome, mischievous. He's not a troublemaker though. He has a good heart. He's affectionate and he's very protective of his little sister. He's got his father's genes for athletics. He's already playing up a year on the soccer team. He starts at forward. His father isn't too happy about that. He wants him to play football, period. He's a happy kid most of the time. What's hard for him? He has trouble sitting still. I think he might have problems with homework, but he doesn't get any yet. The teachers haven't commented on it as a problem but I watch it. When he's tired at night he loves being read to and he goes straight off to sleep.

"Tina's a lot like me. She's been a quiet, shy child ever since she was a baby. She used to startle easily and it took forever to breast feed her. She's very observant. I think she's very bright. She thinks about everything, but you won't hear about it for a while. Then out of nowhere, boom, she'll make a pronouncement. She's artistic. She loves to color and paint. Bright colors. She doesn't seem to be athletic, but it's too soon to tell. I think she's a happy kid too. She gets scared a lot more easily than her brother, even when he was her age."

"How would you describe yourself as a parent? What do you think you do best? What's the hardest thing for you to do? Tell me the same things about their father."

"I think I'm very involved in my children's lives. I'm very supportive of their efforts. I try to help them believe that they can do anything they want. I think I'm a good teacher to the kids. I'm patient. I think that what's hardest for me to do is keep after them when they don't do their chores or they break a rule. Sometimes it's just easier to do it myself, and I do. That just makes it harder to set a limit. I know that I'm just not real good at doing it all the time. I am getting better though.

"Their dad. What does he do best? When he remembers they're around, he will shower them with affection. Then he'll ignore them. Tom really hasn't taken care of them at all. That's why I know this is just an attempt to hurt me. He likes them when they do well. When Tina is cute or when Tommy scores a goal. But all the stuff that goes on before that, he has no time for. I don't know what he'd be good at if he put his mind to it. He just hasn't really tried to be a father. I think that probably answers what's hardest for him. Putting somebody else's needs before his own. He also gets really frustrated with the kids. When they don't behave, he starts yelling and threatening them. I think they're afraid of him, already. I did everything I could to keep the kids away from him unless they were showing him something they'd done at school and he was in a good mood."

"Your attempt to see Tommy at school, how do you feel about that now?"

"It was stupid. I know that. I hurt myself big time, by doing that. I look like I only care about myself, not the kids or the law. That's not true. I know I should have just put Tommy down and given him to his father. It was terrible for him to see me and his father like that, to put him in the middle of that. He was so frightened. I was just overcome with panic and desperation. Tom and his lawyer had thrown me out of my home, cut me off from my children, taken all the money. I just wanted to hold Tommy and tell him I loved him, and tell him it would be okay. It was wrong but I didn't know what else to do. My attorney was telling me to go along with everything they were suggesting. Do it their way. It was for the best. I didn't have any choice. Doing things their way was killing me."

Reece finished with his notes and looked at the asterisks in the margin. Items to pursue with Mr. Tully or by third-party informants. "Ms. Tully, that ends our interview for today. I'm going to discuss many of these things with Mr. Tully. Once I've heard his perspective on them, I may have you back in to address inconsistencies or contradictions in your perspectives. After Mr. Tully is interviewed, I'll be talking to the children. Before I do that, I'll discuss with you and Mr. Tully how I'm to be introduced to the children."

"Fine. I'll wait to hear from you then?"

"Yes. Right now I'm going to check and see if your husband has finished the testing. If so, he'll come in for his interview and I'll set you up with the tests."

"Can I ask you a question, Dr. Reece?"

"Sure."

"I'm starting to have second thoughts about my attorney. Tom seems to be getting everything his way. Everyone says that Tom's lawyer is very 'effective' and he's lived up to that reputation. Mine doesn't seem to be. Do you think I should change lawyers?"

"I'm sorry, I can't answer that question. I'm not a lawyer.

I don't know what your lawyer should be doing for you. If you're unhappy with your lawyer, it's always a good idea to get a second opinion. Call some experienced domestic relations attorneys who know Garfield and see what they say."

"I did. None of them can talk to me. My husband contacted them all first and now there's a conflict of interests if they talk to me."

Reece rattled off some names.

"I've talked to them all. Everybody gives me the same names."

"How about Lou Carlson?"

"No. Nobody ever mentioned him. Who is he?"

"He's a law professor downtown. He used to be one of the very best domestic relations lawyers in this town. He closed his practice up a couple of years ago. He'd had a heart attack and he was only in his mid-forties. Lou was a real hard charger. I'll bet your husband didn't call him because he's not practicing these days. Why don't you call him for a second opinion? He's extremely knowledgeable. If he thinks you aren't being well represented, he can probably find you some up-and-coming attorney who can deal with Garfield but who your husband missed."

"Do you think that was something my husband thought of, or did his attorney suggest that?"

"I'd rather not speculate, but Albert Garfield is 'effective.' How he does that leads to a lot of other descriptions. I'll let Lou Carlson give you his take on Albert Garfield. They've tangled many times."

Reece went to his desk, flipped through his Rolodex and copied Lou Carlson's phone number at Georgetown University Law School.

"Call him, today. Each day you're badly represented can

result in ground being lost that cannot be regained."

"Thanks."

Serena Tully's smile was a tentative thing.

Morgan Reece hoisted one up in response. It hung there for a moment, then slid away.

CHAPTER TWENTY-ONE

Tom Tully had just finished his testing when Morgan Reece and Serena concluded their interview. Reece had Mr. Tully go into the waiting room, then he motioned Mrs. Tully to come down the hall to the testing room. He gave her the instructions to the tests and closed the door to the room.

Tully preceded Reece into the office, went straight to one of the recliners and sat down. Reece went to his, took Tully's questionnaires, read through the answers and highlighted those of interest. He handed him the consent forms that his wife had already signed and had him co-sign.

"Those will go out today. Let's start with the history of the marriage. What attracted you to your wife?"

Tom grinned. "You've seen her. She's a beautiful woman. She was a lot of fun to be with. She loved to party, to dance. She and I just fit perfectly. She liked all the same things that I did. She was tremendous in bed. I thought I'd died and gone to heaven. What a laugh."

"Did you know about her suicide attempts?"

"Nah. She hid all of that from me. Until after the wedding."

Reece frowned. "What about her wrists? How did she explain those?"

Tully hesitated a moment. "Oh, yeah. Those. Yeah, I guess I knew about that attempt. I just figured, you know, she got dumped on by this guy. I wasn't gonna dump her so there'd be no call for that kind of thing."

"Why did your wife want to get into therapy? How did you feel about that?"

"I gotta tell you, Doc, I don't have a lotta use for this head-shrinking stuff. You gotta problem, you fix it yourself. I never saw the use of talking to somebody else about it. She was un-happy with the way things were going. She wasn't getting her needs met, we weren't being intimate. That's what she said. Hell, we were having sex as often as we ever did. There weren't any problems as far as I could see. So I told her no way was I going to see some shrink. She had a problem with her life, she could go. So she did. I don't know, I thought it was doing her some good. She wasn't unhappy all the time, complaining about everything. I figured, hey, it's a female thing. They're always talking about their problems. Now that I look back on it, I should'a figured everything wasn't right. She stopped being interested in sex. Man, it was like pulling teeth to get her in bed. After a while I gave up on it. I wasn't gonna beg for what I had a right to. All the therapy was doing was cooling her on being married. I could see it in lots of other ways, too."

"Such as?"

"The kids. She got obsessed about them. She devoted her whole life to them, but it wasn't healthy. Tina was turning into a little 'Nervous Nelly.' She couldn't discipline the kids. I was always having to step in and be the bad guy. That was the only way she let me be a part of their lives. She cut me out of everything else. That's why I started pushing for a nanny."

"Why was that?"

"To try to break that bond they had. She and the kids. It wasn't healthy. I hoped by her getting out of the house, get-ting a job, maybe she'd get a better balance to her life. You know the way she'd cut me out of her life and the kids, it was

107

like she was having an affair with them. I'll admit it, I was jealous. I loved my wife. I wanted her back. I thought this would help."

"You know, your wife believes you're having an affair. That's why she thinks you're doing all this."

"That's rich. She thinks I'm having an affair. Let me show you something." Tully opened his briefcase and handed two pieces of paper to Reece. "There's no harm in you seeing these. My attorney is filing for divorce right now on grounds of adultery. Hers. Not mine. She'll find out about it as soon as she talks to her attorney. Take a look. That's something to find, isn't it?"

Reece glanced down at the papers.

"I'm trying to win her back 'cause I think she's over-bonded to these kids and she's out doing the tubesteak boogie with some other guy. That other thing is some piece of poetry he sent her. I don't know who the guy is. She's pretty careful. Shopping, workout, therapy, that's about all she's doing these days, but I'll find out who it is and he's gonna pay too, believe it. I may look like I'm playing hard-ball here, but you gotta understand where I'm coming from. You find something like that, it undoes you. Everything you think you've known or believed about this other person who you've trusted more than anyone is all a lie. It's enough to make you crazy. You spend your life trying to make someone happy, trying to be there for them and this is how they repay you."

Reece read the poem and the letter. Bad things getting worse. Albert Garfield loved adultery cases. He'd have a shadow on her night and day. He handed the papers back.

"No, you can keep them. They're copies I made for you."

"So you're going to sue for divorce on grounds of adultery. You petitioned for custody on grounds that your wife was a danger to you and the children. I find that a bit incongruous, given your reputation."

"My wife wasn't threatening to punch me out. She said she'd cut off my dick while I was sleeping. I think to even threaten somebody with that is crazy. It just clued me in to how sick she was."

"Her history is one of suicide attempts, not violence directed at other people. Why do you think that's changed?"

"Because she's got some other guy. She's not interested in making our marriage work. She wants me out of the picture. I just beat her to the draw. Once I found out about the affair, lots of stuff began to make sense."

"It doesn't sound like you think your wife is crazy, just angry at you and no longer hiding it."

"No. I think she's crazy. She assaulted me after she violated a court order. She has no respect for the law. No thoughts about the kids, just herself. She tried to bite me. She was lucky I pulled my punch. Not only is she crazy, she's a terrible role model for the children. She's broken our marriage vows and the law. What kind of moral influence is she going to be on the children?"

"Your wife says you've had fights where you put people in the hospital. That for a while you slept with a gun under your bed. What was that about?"

"I had a reputation as a hard guy when I played. That was a game. It had rules. Everybody knew the risks. I'm sure you know I killed a guy, Cisco Conway. I hit him legally. I was never fined. He just landed badly. I'd hit plenty of guys harder than that. I felt real bad about that. In fact, I probably wasn't the same player after that happened. I was always holding back a little. Well, there are guys who always want to find out how bad you really are. I was just defending myself. I was never charged with anything. There were always plenty of witnesses. One of those guys threatened me after he got out of the hospital. Told me he'd shoot me. I bought a pistol to protect myself and my family. After nothing happened for a while, I put it away. That's all there is to that."

Reece went over the same detailed questions that he'd asked Serena Tully about school, preferences, daily activities and habits, rules and discipline. Based on her report of his lack of involvement, he expected him not to know many of these and he was surprised when he answered them exactly as his wife did. Reece would not have been surprised if he'd known that last night Tom Tully had sat down and gone over the answers to all the interview questions in Reece's book with the two children.

After discussing the possibility of a second interview and how to prepare the children for their interviews, Morgan Reece finished with Tom Tully. A little later Serena Tully finished her testing and told him that she had a four o'clock appointment with Lou Carlson.

When they had both gone, Morgan Reece went over his notes and planned the next step in the evaluation. In some cases one parent would come in and tell him that the glass was half full of water; the other would tell him that it was half empty. They'd both be right. Accurate but different. Some cases one parent would come in and tell him the glass was three quarters full and the other would say one quarter full, and he'd find that one was accurate and the other was not. Every once in awhile the parents would tell him what they saw in the glass and he'd find that there was no water at all. He wondered how this one would turn out.

CHAPTER TWENTY-TWO

Serena Tully stopped at the pebbled glass door and read G. Louis Carlson, Associate Professor of Law. She knocked on the door, heard a voice mumble something and opened the door.

The man sitting with his feet up on the desk smiled at her.

"Ms. Tully?"

"Yes."

"Have a seat." He pointed to the only chair not filled with books, papers or journals. Three of the walls of the office were shelves, filled with magazines and books, most vertical, some horizontal across their tops, and manila folders swollen with Xeroxed journal articles. The fourth wall was a blackboard. Carlson's desk was a compost heap. The bottom layers of paper were yellowing and on their way to mulch. The desk had a photo of his wife and children, a huge Rolodex, mail to be read, correspondence to be typed, and papers to be graded. Perpendicular to the desk was a computer with a work in progress on its screen, modem, fax and a phone with an answering machine.

Serena Tully expected the man in the middle of this paper maelstrom to look like Lieutenant Columbo. Lou Carlson was surprisingly thin and crisp in his charcoal gray pinstripe suit, gray shirt, and red silk tie. Prematurely graying at the temples, his badly mended nose was a reminder of his collegiate boxing career.

"So you want a second opinion on your case and Morgan

Reece recommended me, is that correct?"

"Yes."

"Did he tell you that I no longer practice?"

"Yes, he did. He said you'd had a heart attack."

"Yeah, about two years ago. I've got two little kids, three and five."

"What are they?"

"A boy and a girl."

"So are mine. They're four and six."

"And a wife who threatened to divorce and kill me, not in that order, if I didn't start to cut back on my practice. I found that I couldn't practice that way, so I retired and became a teacher. So I can't take your case. If I think you're being badly represented, I'll tell you and try to recommend some good people to you. Who's your husband's attorney?"

"Albert Garfield."

Carlson shook his head. "What does that mean, Mr. Carlson?"

"It means I'm sure you've been having a bumpy ride."

"Bumpy ride? I have no home, no money, I cannot see my children. I think that's more than a bumpy ride."

"You're right. I'm sorry. It sounds like Albert's been having his way so far."

"Everybody says he's very 'effective.' You can hear the quotation marks around that. Dr. Reece said you'd tell me what that really means. What am I up against, Mr. Carlson?"

Lou Carlson put his feet down and leaned forward. "Albert Olen Garfield, is known as 'Agent Orange.' What he puts his hand to withers and dies. He's a formidable foe. There are only a few really destructive attorneys in this town. Generally they're pompous blowhards who promise their clients things they can't deliver, or who give them bad advice that escalates conflict unnecessarily. They don't often prevail, but they create havoc that lasts long after they are gone. Garfield is something else. He's *sui generis,* one of a kind. He's a psychopath with a work ethic. The practice of law is perfect for someone like that. The job description reads: attack without restraint, demonize, and then destroy what you have made. That may work for some kinds of law, but not domestic. You're not sending people to jail for twenty years. You're sending them back out to raise a child together. It just doesn't work. There is very little that he would not do to beat a person down. Some of the things he does are probably unethical, but he's so cunning you can't prove them. You just know his handiwork when you see it, like the leaves falling off the trees. You cannot go up against him unless you are completely prepared and ready to do battle."

"Who can do that? My lawyer can't, I'm sure of it."

"Joe Anthony can do it. Joe prepares as well as Albert, and he's very good in court. Law is one half chess, one half poker. You've got to be able to play both."

"I don't understand."

"What you do outside of the courtroom is chess. Assessing strengths and weaknesses, devising strategy. It's mastering the known. Poker is what you do in negotiations and the courtroom. It's how you manipulate the unknowns, your anxiety, your client's, your opponent's. Sometimes you only need one to win a case. Not with Al Garfield. He can do it all."

"Joe Anthony is someone my husband already called. He can't help me. Who else is there?"

Predictably he gave her the same names she'd already heard. She told him that she'd been locked out of using those attorneys.

"What's your attorney's name?"

"Gilbert Stuart. Do you know him?" she asked anxiously.

Know him, Carlson thought, he's so stupid, every time he showed up in court I could hear Avon calling, "Ding-dong." "Yeah, he's no match for Garfield. Albert'll have him rolling over so fast you'll think he's on a rotisserie. What's happened so far?"

Serena went through everything. Carlson closed his eyes and saw Serena Tully on a beach. Albert Garfield and Gilbert Stuart were burying her alive in the sand. A couple of shovelfuls in her mouth and she'd be done for. Lou Carlson felt the same burn that he did every time he'd gone up against Albert Garfield. That burn went back to the first schoolyard bully he'd ever stood up to. Then one day it became a huge fist squeezing his heart, sending white-hot spikes of pain through his chest and down his arm and scaring him more thoroughly than any bully could ever have dreamt.

"Let me call some people I know. They're out of the area. Down in Richmond or Charlottesville. Have them come on board with Stuart. He'll be counsel of record but they'll be the brains and the spine. They'll deal with Garfield. He'll sign the documents. Until then, don't sign anything. Don't agree to anything."

"Should I fire Mr. Stuart?"

"No, that'll alert Albert that something's up. He may pull another stunt before anyone is in place to contest it. Let him think everything is going his way."

"Is there anything else I can do?"

"No. Let Morgan Reece do his thing. That's the best thing you've got going for you. He'll sort things out. It just takes time. Let me give you a couple of books to read. They'll help you think about what you're going through, what the law is trying to do, also some ideas about how to present your case. You may think of things that Stuart hasn't thought of. You'll be in a better position to help your new attorney. I'll try to get someone for you as soon as I can."

"Thank you, thank you." Serena took the books and shook Carlson's hand passionately.

"My pleasure. Please return these books when you're done with them. They're my only copies."

"Absolutely. Again, thank you very much."

Serena glided out of the building. She smiled and pumped her fist with excitement as she walked to the car. She moved effortlessly across the slick surface of her newfound optimism like it was ice on a deep lake.

CHAPTER TWENTY-THREE

Morgan Reece finished scoring the tests the Tullys had taken. Unfortunately they didn't tell him much he didn't already know. Tom Tully's profiles were of questionable validity. He was extremely guarded and defensive. Questions were raised about his impulse control, judgment and level of narcissism. But none of the scores were clinically elevated. He was firmly in the great wasteland called "within normal limits." Serena Tully was less defensive and her profiles were deemed valid. She also looked more disorganized than her husband. She was clearly depressed, anxious and paranoid. So, Reece thought, her reality testing was intact. Her personality style was a mix of histrionic and dependent traits. About as adaptive as hooves on a butterfly.

Reece Xeroxed the consents and mailed or faxed them out. He gave his home fax number for responses.

Serena had gone to Denise's and found her friend sitting, arms crossed, frowning, by the living room phone. The bad news came before she could even say hello.

"Serena, you have to find another place to stay. I'm sorry. Tommy's obviously upped the ante. I can't expose my kids to this. I'm sorry. I really am, but my mind's made up."

Serena felt that lurch, like the room had tipped over on her, that came with every attack Tommy made. She reached out for the arm of the sofa and felt her way around the end to sit down as if she were blind. "What happened?"

"This is what happened." Denise said and pushed the playback button on the answering machine. "Hey girls. This is Bobby at the shipyards. Heard about your offer. Got a bunch of guys here, like to put some miles on your track. Hard ones." He stopped to giggle. "Got a twelve-car train here for you to pull. Now you call me at 410-555-1928, let me know which one of you little locomotives wants to haul all this freight and what it's gonna cost us."

Serena rubbed her head in her palms. "I'm sorry, Denise. I never thought anything like this would happen. I'll get a place to stay, right away. I'm sorry." She covered her face with her hands and silent tears began to drip through her fingers like they were melting icicles.

Denise came to her, put an arm around her and squeezed her shoulders. Braced up by her friend, she stopped being strong and began to scour herself of a lifetime of bad decisions. Sobs and tears rinsed her in regret.

"If it was just me, I'd invite those bastards over and cut their dicks off one at a time. But it's not just me. Brandon went to take that message. I told him it was a wrong number. Thank God, the guy was trying to be funny. What if the next one is more graphic?"

"I understand, Denise. I do. I'll find a place to stay tonight. A motel room. Can I borrow some money just for tonight? I'm going to pawn my watch tomorrow. It's very expensive. Thank God I was wearing it when this happened. I'll live on that until I get some money from Tom. I'm changing lawyers, too. He'll put a stop to this crap. Don't tell anybody, it's a secret."

"I won't. Look, it's late. Don't go anywhere tonight. I'll keep the answering machine off and tell the kids not to answer the phone. You got some other phone calls. One was

117

from your lawyer, the other was from Nordstrom. I gather that you explained your face as a result of dental work. They said to come in for an interview tomorrow about a position in cosmetics. They thought someone with a background as a model could be a real asset."

"The way I feel, I should be selling mace, not mascara."

"You want something to drink?"

"A cup of tea would be nice. Thanks." Serena looked at Denise and saw the sister she never had and never would.

She tried to reach her attorney but only got his answering service. Curled up on the sofa with her tea, she sipped it and closed her eyes as she felt its warmth spread down her throat and into her stomach. She wondered if she'd remember the simplicity and satisfaction of this pleasure in less desperate times.

CHAPTER TWENTY-FOUR

Gilbert Stuart was in court most of the day, so it wasn't until later in the afternoon that Serena Tully was able to speak to him.

Her job interview had not gone well. The store needed someone to start immediately and it was clear from the condition of her face that that wasn't possible. They were sorry but they'd keep her name on file if any future opening came up.

Morgan Reece called Tom Tully's residence and spoke to the nanny, Felicia Hurtado. She would come in to talk to him once she got Mr. Tully's permission and arranged for someone else to watch Tina. Reece suggested that she come in right after he interviewed the children as a way to solve that problem. Heartsick at his ingenuity, she agreed. Felicia only heard one phrase when Reece was talking to her: "Court-appointed." The courts were the police to her and the police here were the police of her homeland, Colombia. You avoided drawing the attention of the police as you would avoid drinking water from a river full of corpses.

Serena got a call from her therapist, Simon Tepper, in the early afternoon.

"Hello, Serena. I have a consent here from Dr. Reece to send him my case file. What's happening?"

"Oh, Simon. Thank God you're back. This has been such a nightmare for me. Tom has taken the kids. He's made up a bunch of lies about me to try to win custody. Dr. Reece is the court-appointed evaluator. Please send him what you've got as soon as possible. He's my only hope of getting the kids back."

"Has Tom asked for a divorce?"

"No. Just the kids. I don't know why he's doing this. I've been reeling from everything!"

"What kind of lies has he been spreading?" Tepper probed gently.

"That I was a danger to him and the kids. That I was suicidal and depressed again. That's not true. You know that." A wave of paranoia swept over Serena. "There's nothing in the file that could hurt me, is there?"

"No. Of course not. I keep only minimal notes. Just enough to satisfy insurance requirements. I told you there's nothing in it that Tom could use to hurt you."

"Please send him that stuff as soon as possible."

"Of course. This must be terrible for you."

"Simon, when can I see you?"

"When would you like to come in?"

"I'll come in whenever you've got time."

Tepper looked at his calendar. "How about this evening? I've got a cancellation at six o'clock. Sounds like we have a lot to talk about."

"It's been awful. I'm so glad you're back. I'll see you tonight at six o'clock."

"See you then."

Tepper went to the file, read through his notes and, satisfied with what was there, he faxed them to Dr. Reece's home, where they would be when he arrived from work.

Serena spent the rest of the afternoon calling other stores about jobs, jewelers to sell her watch and nearby motels to see which ones she could rent by the week and how much they cost. She watched the split between what she was saying and how she felt. Her words should have depressed her and most times they would have. However her meetings with Reece and Carlson and Simon Tepper's return buoyed her and she floated above the words as if she were calling on behalf of a distant relative.

A little after five, Gilbert Stuart returned Serena's call.

"Ms. Tully, Gilbert Stuart here. Sorry I wasn't in when you called. I was in court all day."

Testing her newfound optimism, she asked, "How did you do? What kind of case was it?"

Taken off guard, Stuart stammered while he composed a defensible response. "Uh, it was another domestic case. A visitation matter. My client didn't prevail, but we didn't have a good case. I told him to settle but he wouldn't hear of it. Some people just have to have their day in court. It's their right. You can't make a silk purse out of a sow's ear, though.

"I'm glad you called. Albert Garfield has changed his tack. They aren't just moving for custody, they've filed for divorce. They're seeking it on grounds of adultery."

Serena's stomach tightened as if the floor had fallen from underneath her.

Stuart went on, "They sent over a property settlement and a custody proposal. It's pretty extreme. Garfield said they had some 'devastating proof' of the adultery and that I should tell you he had no compunctions about using it."

The letter and the poem. God she'd been a fool to keep that stuff in the house. When he'd changed the locks, she knew she was in danger. But Tom didn't say anything when he threw all of her stuff out, so she thought she was safe. Hiding it in his space had seemed like such a good idea at the time. She remembered sneaking them out to read. She'd felt so beautiful, so desired. She'd lie back on the bed, close her eyes and be there. The center of the universe. A universe of patient and tender care. Everything Tom was not. Where her every word, look or gesture was bathed, fed and groomed.

Honey on the blade. A taste so sweet, that as you licked it off the razor's edge you couldn't taste the blood filling your mouth. Now the honey was gone, only the blood remained.

"Ms. Tully, are you there?"

"Yes, Mr. Stuart. I'm here." In her mind she reviewed her arithmetic. No, her calculations were correct. The central axiom of her life was still true. All pleasure is paid for in pain. What had she been thinking of? He'd told her it would be different this time. The rules did not apply. They would make their own rules. In the mirror-lined bubble of their folly, they heard only each other's lies, saw only each other's desire, felt only each other's pleasure.

Stuart went on to repeat Garfield's offer. Serena could feel the riptide of guilt and shame that required her to agree, carving the sand away from her feet. She was losing her balance and searched for something to hold onto. It was Lou Carlson's edict, simple and clear: "Don't agree to anything."

"I'm sorry, Mr. Stuart. I can't agree to that."

"Ms. Tully, are you prepared to face whatever Albert Garfield has on you? I guarantee he won't pull his punches."

Serena Tully deafened herself to Stuart's words and her fears. She held on to Carlson's four words with the same strength she'd once used to steady a slippery red razor blade.

CHAPTER TWENTY-FIVE

Serena's leg kicked an invisible enemy as she sat in Simon Tepper's waiting room. She tried to read but the magazines were in Latin. Urging the second hand through its sweep was an agony of effort like stirring cement with a spoon.

Finally Tepper's door clicked open. A young woman emerged, in full Goth regalia. Heavy lace-up boots, torn mesh stockings, ripped vinyl skirt, leather wristbands and chains. A T-shirt with a stencil of two hands gripping prison bars over her heart and enough metal in her face to make you rethink the term "chick magnet." She flipped her thick blue hair back over her ear, and mumbled something back at Tepper.

Tepper said he'd see her next week. She shrugged, and left without seeing the woman with the ashen face and the restless left leg.

"Serena, you look awful. Come right in," Tepper said when he saw her. He hurried towards her, afraid she might collapse right there.

She stood up, smiled weakly at him and took his arm. As he closed the door, she dropped onto the sofa, stretched out and began to cry.

At home, Morgan Reece called Tom Tully. On the third ring, a child picked it up.

"Hello?" Reece could not tell if it was the boy or the girl.

"Is this the Tully residence?"

The child yelled, "Dad." After a second the child said in measured tones, "May I ask who's calling?"

"This is Dr. Reece. Are you Tommy?"

"No."

"Is this Tina?"

"No-o-o. My name is Junior."

"Yes, Junior. Is your father around?"

"He's talking to our nanny."

"Would you ask him to come to the phone?"

Silence. Reece imagined the phone swinging free, as Junior ran off God knows where. If no one picked up in three minutes, he'd hang up and try later.

"Dr. Reece? Tom Tully, here."

"Yes, Mr. Tully. I'm trying to arrange the next step of the evaluation. I'd like to interview the children and their nanny. I'd also like you and the mother to take some more psychological tests."

"Which ones?"

"The Rorschach."

"What's that?"

"You've heard people talk about the inkblots. That's the Rorschach."

"Why didn't we take them at the start?"

"There wasn't time to do them all in that first day. This is routine, Mr. Tully. As we go along, I may ask you to take other tests."

"So you want me and Felicia and the kids there. What time? The club is getting concerned about how much time I'm taking off for this thing."

"First thing tomorrow. Say nine a.m.? I'll try to do as much in a day as I can. After this I'll need three mornings from you for the observation sessions and home visit."

"Okay. Nine a.m. tomorrow. How about you interview Felicia first, then the kids? That way she can take them with her when they're done."

"Fine. I want to discuss with you how I want to be introduced to the children. All I want you to tell them is that I've been asked by you and their mother to help both of you make the best decision you can about how to take care of them. That's it. If they have any questions about me, tell them that I'll answer their questions first thing. If they're afraid that they might forget them, write them down for them and bring them with you. Their mother will meet you here in the office fifteen minutes before the interview begins. So be here at eight forty-five a.m. I'll want you both to bring the kids in when I introduce myself. Then I'll ask you to leave and I'll start with whichever child wants to go first."

"I'm not real happy with this, Dr. Reece."

"What aren't you happy with, Mr. Tully?"

"Lying to the kids like this. You haven't been asked by us to help figure out how best to take care of them. You were ordered by the court to figure out if their mother ever gets to see them again."

"Are you suggesting that I tell the children that?"

"I think you gotta tell the truth. You can paint a smiley face on a dead dog, but it's still a dead dog. These kids are going to have to deal with the kind of woman their mother is. They might as well start now."

Reece was writing as fast as he could, repeating Tully's words in his mind so that the quote was complete and true. "I'm sorry, Mr. Tully, I disagree with you. My charge is to conduct a custody evaluation. That's to determine what's best for your children. What arrangement of time with their parents is best for them. That's what you're telling them. I prefer to keep the court as originator or destination of this work out of it, unless it's absolutely necessary. I think it's better if the children believe that their parents are looking out for them, not a Fairfax County Circuit Court Judge. I'd like you to introduce me exactly as described. If you have a problem with that, advise your attorney and he and I and Mr. Stuart can discuss it."

"All right, we'll be there." Tully was losing patience with this nonsense. He had a season going down the drain and he needed his head on straight. This crap had to stop.

Reece hung up the phone. He scribbled the rest of his notes. As his career had become more and more exclusively forensic, the need to document his activities in detail increased. He was looking for a telephone/tape recorder headset he could wear at all times, making a contemporaneous, true record of all his verbal interactions with anyone.

Morgan Reece called Serena. After exchanging pleasantries, he went on to explain the next day's activities.

"Is it possible for me to be tested first? I'm trying to find a job and I have to move out of the place I'm staying. Tom—well I'm sure it was Tom but I can't prove it—gave the number out along with an obscene message. The family that I'm staying with has children and I don't want them dragged into my mess. So I have to get a room somewhere."

"I'll discuss it with you and Mr. Tully. He says his employers are pressing him about the amount of time he's missing from work."

"Only because they're losing. When you win anything goes. Ask him about the 'Fifth Down Club.' "

"Let me ask you. What is the 'Fifth Down Club'?"

"It's a bunch of guys, players mostly, but there were some coaches, who broke every rule the club had: curfew, drinking, drugs, girls."

"Was your husband a member of the 'Fifth Down Club'?"

"Before we were married, yes. Afterwards, I don't know. I didn't think so, but I also wasn't checking up on Tom either here or on the road. Now, nothing would surprise me."

"Have you considered putting your husband under surveillance to see if he has a girlfriend, as you believe?"

"Dr. Reece, I don't have money for food. I'm going to pawn my watch tomorrow, try to get a motel room to stay in while you do your work and try to get a job with a face that has more lumps than my mother's gravy. No, I haven't even thought of it."

"I brought it up because your husband is moving for a divorce on the grounds of adultery. It sounds like you believe the grounds could go both ways."

"Let me ask you a question, Dr. Reece. Is adultery a factor in custody matters?"

"I don't want to practice law, Ms. Tully. There are cases in Virginia that say that adultery per se is not proof of unfitness to parent. However, it is still a crime on the books. I'd rather you got advice from your lawyer on the legal consequences of adultery."

"But what about you, what does it mean to you?"

"It's a factor, Ms. Tully, like lots of things. I have to see that there's been a direct adverse impact on the children as a result of the adultery for it to be a factor."

"What does that mean?"

"It's a legal concept, Mrs. Tully. Please ask your attorney to explain it to you. He can give you some examples."

"All right. Thank you, Dr. Reece. I'll see you tomorrow."

Morgan Reece spent the rest of the evening working on a sexual abuse evaluation involving the three oldest sons of a prominent Irish Catholic family. While babysitting their eight siblings they took turns sodomizing their twelve-year-old sister. This seemed a reasonable course of action to them considering their fears about her getting pregnant and the prohibitions on the use of condoms.

Around ten o'clock the pizza man arrived with a 'clogger': pepperoni, sausage and extra cheese. When he could not bear to read another page of testimony, he switched to a best-selling thriller he'd recently picked up. So far this one confirmed his belief that inside every fat book is a thin one trying to get out. However as a soporific it was cheap and effective. There was no style to speak of. Just words marching dutifully across the page single file, like pack animals bearing their load of information across the paper desert.

Reece put the book down and thought about Lindsay Brinkman's offer to get an instructor to help him with his fear of heights.

He needed a larger world. He was far too comfortable in his current, cramped one. Bodies at rest tend to stay at rest. Was he ready to defy inertia almighty?

CHAPTER TWENTY-SIX

Felicia Hurtado was in her mid-twenties. She had long black hair braided down her back and her copper skin was free of makeup. She wore a long charcoal grey skirt, a white blouse, black sweater, and sat with her hands folded in her lap. She looked like a parochial school student.

Morgan Reece decided not to beat around the bush. He usually shunned family and friends as witnesses because of the high risk of bias in their reports. That went for employees, too.

"Are you an American citizen, Ms. Hurtado?"

"No."

"Do you have a green card?"

"No. Not yet. Mr. Tully said that he would help me get it."

"How was he going to do that?"

"By sponsoring me."

"What does that mean 'sponsor'?"

"He promised me a job for when I get my card."

"And what kind of job was that?"

"This job. To take care of his children."

"So, you are employed by Mr. Tully alone, not he and his wife?"

"Yes."

"Did Mr. Tully talk to you about our meeting today?"

"Yes."

"What did he say?"

"He said I should tell the truth."

And how much water is in the glass? he thought. "If Mr. Tully loses custody of his children, what kind of job has he offered you?"

She looked down at her nails for the answer, then whispered what she had found.

"None."

"Where are you from?"

"Colombia."

"Is it any different for you here?"

"Sometimes yes, sometimes no."

"Are you a mother?"

"Yes."

"What are your children's names?"

"Guillermo, he is eight and a half. Mayra, she is seven."

"Where are your children?"

"Here with me."

"Who takes care of them when you are at the Tullys?"

"My mother."

"Ms. Hurtado, I do not want to cause you any trouble, but my first and only loyalty is to these children. What is best for them. You can do very little to help Mr. Tully keep his children. If you say that he is a wonderful father and she is a terrible mother, I won't pay much attention to that, I may not even write that down. It could be the truth. It could also be your fear speaking. How can I tell? If the truth is different, that I will listen to. That will help the children. Shall we begin?"

"Yes." She almost said "Commandant," but caught herself. Perhaps he thought he was freeing her from Tully's influence, but what she heard was the police interrogator who came to her village and questioned her about the ambush that killed two of his men.

She was stripped and tied to a chair. He waved the Taser at her like a pet cobra. He, too, knew what answers he would believe. When they put her feet in a bowl of cold water to increase her conductivity, she was finally able to find a truth he would accept.

"How would you describe Mr. Tully as a parent?"

"I have not had much time to see him with the children. When Mrs. Tully lived at home, I would leave when he came home from work. This last week I see him in the morning when I arrive and then for a little bit when I leave. He is affectionate with the children and very generous. He always brings home a toy for the children."

"Does he say why he does that?"

"Because they have lost their mother. So they won't be sad."

"Have you ever seen him discipline the children?"

"No. They are very well-behaved children."

"Have they ever seemed afraid of their father?"

"Not that I have seen."

"Mr. Tully, has he had any woman friends come to the house?"

"No."

"How about Ms. Tully? Any men ever come to the house? Have the children ever mentioned another man being around?"

"No."

"What kind of mother is Ms. Tully?"

"She is a good mother. We did not get along very well when I first came. She only wanted me to clean the house. She would take care of Tina. I understood that. She did not hire me. Mr. Tully did. She relaxed later and let me take care of Tina sometimes."

"When was that?"

131

"The last few months. When she would have to go out to see her doctor. She would leave Tina with me."

"What if she had other appointments, or shopping to do?"

"No. She would take Tina with her. Or do it when she had a nap. But for her doctor appointments, she would leave Tina home. Sometimes he would call her and say he had an opening and she would change her plans and leave Tina with me."

"How often did this happen?"

"She went to her doctor sometimes two or three times a week."

"Every week?"

"Yes."

"You said she had to change her plans when he had an opening. Were the times the same or did they change a lot?"

"Both. She always went on Monday mornings, but sometimes Wednesday afternoons or Friday afternoons. One week I believe she went both days."

"Wednesday and Friday."

"Yes."

"Do you know what kind of doctor she was seeing?"

"No. She said he was very busy, with lots of patients and so he saw her when he had cancellations. It was because she had so much free time she could come in."

"How long was Ms. Tully gone?"

"Usually two hours, sometimes two and a half or three hours. She said she would have to wait outside while he finished with another patient. Sometimes they ran over."

"Did Ms. Tully seem ill to you?"

"No."

"Did you ever see pills in her medicine cabinet?"

"Yes, but I do not know what kind they were."

132

"How was her mood? Did she seem sad or unhappy all the time? Angry, or restless?"

"No. I did not ever see her cry or be unhappy. If she was, she did not talk to me. She spent most of her time playing with the girl or cooking. She would go shopping or to the health club, but she would take the girl with her."

"To the nursery there."

"Yes."

"Did that upset you? That she wouldn't leave the child with you?"

"No. A little bit. It is her child. She can do what she wanted. The house was easy to clean. I had time to study."

"Study what?"

"I take night classes at NOVA. I want to be a teacher. I was a teacher in Colombia."

"How are the children with Ms. Tully?"

"They are very well behaved. Sometimes Tommy is a little difficult. He is just a little boy."

"Like Guillermo?"

"Yes. They need a firm hand sometimes."

"Did Ms. Tully have a firm hand?"

"Sometimes. She would let Tommy test the rules, then she would put him in time-out."

"Did he obey?"

"Oh yes."

"Did Ms. Tully ever have to threaten them with their father? You know, 'wait till your father gets home'?"

"No. She never did that. There was no need."

"Now that Ms. Tully is not at home how are the children doing?"

"They are sad. The little girl, Tina, carries her mother doll with her everywhere. She sucks her thumb and cries out in her sleep. Wherever I go in the house she is just behind me. If

I stop suddenly she will bump into me, fall down and cry for her mother. I cannot get her to stop unless I sit and rock her in her favorite blanket. If there is a loud noise on the TV she will run to find me. If I am cooking in the kitchen she holds onto my legs and tries to hide under my dress."

Felicia Hurtado stopped to tamp out a smoldering memory of her own daughter's nightmares, waking up crying whenever her mother would scream, "NO, NO, NO" into the laughing darkness.

"They need their mother back. They are very scared and sad."

"What about the little boy?"

"He is trying to be grown up. A little man. He will play with his sister when she asks, and if she is frightened, he will go with her."

"Go with her?"

"Sometimes if we are downstairs, she will be afraid to go upstairs alone to get a toy or another doll. Tommy will take her by the hand and go with her. It is cute. He slows down so they can go up each step together."

"Can you tell how he feels? Does he talk to you?"

"No he does not talk. He goes outside to play or he goes to his room to draw. He will do that until his father comes home."

"What does he draw?"

"He draws war. He draws death."

A little man, indeed, Reece thought. "When Mr. and Ms. Tully were together, how did they get along?"

"I did not see them together very much. They did not seem very happy. Mr. Tully would come home and his wife did not go to the door, smile or greet him. He could have been the repairman. He did not go to her either. The children would race to greet him and he would pick them up and hug them and kiss them. I would leave then."

"Mr. Tully says that you saw a fight between them, not too long ago. What did you see?"

"They were in the kitchen. I was in the living room with the children. I had not gone yet because they were painting my portrait. So I was sitting until they were done. I heard Mr. Tully call me by name, to come into the kitchen; when I got there Mrs. Tully had kicked him in the shins and told him that she'd scratch his eyes out."

"What happened next?"

"I said, 'Yes, Mr. Tully, you called me?' He limped away, rubbing his leg and said, 'It's nothing, go home now.' "

"What did Ms. Tully say?"

"Nothing. She looked very angry and pushed past me, out of the kitchen."

"Do you know why she looked angry or threatened him?"

"No."

"Could it be that he had tried to kiss her or more?"

"I don't know."

"But they weren't an affectionate couple."

"No. There was only frost between them."

"Other than that episode, had you ever seen Ms. Tully threaten her husband, or act threateningly in any fashion?"

"No. Never."

"Did she ever strike or threaten either of the children?"

"No."

"Were they ever afraid of her?"

"No. They were very close and loving."

"You said that Ms. Tully was not sad or unhappy while you were there; did she ever do or say anything to make you think that she was suicidal?"

"No. Never. She loved her children."

"Thank you for your help. If anything else comes up, may I call you back?"

"Yes."

Felicia Hurtado left the office wondering what her help had cost her and her children.

CHAPTER TWENTY-SEVEN

The Tullys were facing each other in the waiting room. Tina was draped across her mother's chest like a forty-pound brooch. One arm was around her mother's neck, the other stroked her cheek.

Tommy sat in his father's lap and pointed to the characters in the comic book as his father read.

Serena Tully stood, and holding Tina across the back and buttocks asked, "Can we speak to you before you see the children, Dr. Reece?"

He looked at Tom Tully, who shrugged agreement. He stood and slid Tommy down next to him.

Serena put down Tina, who whimpered and clutched at her neck. "Tina, it's all right. Mommy and Daddy are going into the room across the hall for just a few minutes. You stay here with your blankey and doll baby, honey. It'll be all right. Mommy isn't going anywhere. I'll be right here, honey." She pulled her daughter from her chest, looked straight into her eyes and said, "I promise, Tina. Mommy will be right here. Have I ever broken a promise to you?"

Tina was too frightened to answer that question. She reached out to her mother who pulled back so she only got handfuls of hair. Serena sat down and patiently worked Tina's fingers loose like they were made of gum.

"Junior, you sit with your sister. Play some games with her until we're done," his dad said. Junior walked over to his sister. "C'mon, Eenie," he said, arms outstretched. "Let's play with baby. You be the Mommy. I'll be the Daddy." Tina reluctantly let go of her mother and reached out for her brother. He tried to carry her but staggered and put her down.

"Thank you, Tommy," Serena said.

Her husband growled, "His name is Junior, not Tommy."

Reece followed the Tullys into his office. Serena sat at the far end of the sofa. Tom took the recliner facing her.

"Dr. Reece, I got a call this morning, around eight from your answering service saying that our appointment had been changed to eleven o'clock to accommodate a change in Tom's schedule. Obviously that message was false. I tried to call and got your voice mail, so I used the emergency number. That got me your service. They couldn't get you at home. So I came down here anyway. I'm glad I did. This is another of Tom's stunts. Just like the dinner he planned. If I'd come here at eleven I'd have looked like a complete idiot, too fucked up to make even these appointments on time. Am I right?"

Tully jumped in. "You sound pretty screwed up anyway, Serena. Is this another of your wacko paranoid fantasies? Were you running late again, spending two hours on your face and hair? Need a fallback line? I'm tired of being your alibi, Serena. I want you here. You're the best evidence I've got, Serena. For the record, Doc, I didn't ask you to change the time, did I?"

"No, Mr. Tully. Nor did I ask my service to call you, Ms. Tully. There were no changes in the schedule."

"Oh, I'm sure of that. Tom probably got some friends of his to make the call. I'm wise to you Tom. You sent me to pick up your brother the day of the hearing. Only he never got on that plane. And you lied about me to the judge. You aren't going to trick me again. I know I haven't got any evidence. Maybe I do sound paranoid but I want to be on the record about this. Somebody called me today and tried to sabotage me so I'd miss this meeting. I know it was you, Tom. I just can't prove it." She jabbed a finger in the air at him.

Tully leaned forward and smiled with contempt. "Rag on, Serena. Rag on. You're proving what I've said all along. You're crazy, babe, crazy."

"Why would she make up this story, Mr. Tully? She got here on time. If she was late, sure. Why even bring this up? If it isn't true, she sounds paranoid. Why do that?"

"Because she's desperate. She'll do anything she can to win these kids. If you're gonna lie, lie big, lie often. How do I prove that I didn't do this? I don't have witnesses with me twenty-four hours a day. All she can do is make allegations, throw mud and hope some of it sticks. That's what this is. Trust me. This isn't the last crazy story you'll hear from her. Serena has never taken responsibility for anything in her life. It's always somebody else's fault. She's hoping that if she blows enough smoke you'll be too confused to make a decision. Then she'll trot out 'I'm their mother, children belong with their mother' bullshit and try to steal this one. That's her only hope, doctor. That's what this is. A desperate pathetic attempt to blacken my name. Let me go on record. There's no way that behavior like this is in the children's best interest."

"I don't think there's anything more I can do with this right now. I'm going to bring the children in. I'll introduce myself to them, ask you to give them permission to speak with me and agree not to question them about what is said. Then I'll see who wants to go first and interview that child. When the interviews are done, Ms. Hurtado can take the children home and to school. Each of you will be given the Rorschach by my associate, Dr. Frazier."

Reece stood up and walked to the door. He pulled it open and Tina Tully, who had been sitting against it the entire time, tumbled into his office.

She rolled easily over onto her feet, clambered up the sofa and attached herself to her mother's chest. Tommy had been sitting across the corridor facing Reece's office. He stood up and walked into the room. He surveyed the situation and took up his position on his father's lap, bringing everyone back into balance.

Reece repeated the introduction he'd given Mr. Tully. Then he asked the parents to give the children permission to talk freely with him, since he was a stranger. Then he asked them to promise not to ask any questions about what the children might discuss with him. Last, that they give the children permission to report any violations of the second rule to the doctor. It was Reece's experience that these rules worked best in inhibiting the parents rather than liberating the children, particularly young ones.

There was no dispute over who went first. Tommy yelled, "Me," and Tina turned her face away on her mother's chest.

CHAPTER TWENTY-EIGHT

Tommy Tully looked exactly like his father but with a bowl haircut for his straw blonde hair. He wore a football jersey T-shirt with his father's number on it, blue jeans and sneakers.

"Do you have any questions you want to ask me, Tommy?"

"No."

Reece eased into the interview with low impact questions about school, his classmates and soccer team. A second pass elicited his favorite foods, TV shows, sports team and video games. Tommy had elected to sit in the recliner that his father had occupied. He carefully laid his arms on the rests, stretching his fingers out to see if they would cover the width of the leather. The bottoms of his sneakers faced Reece.

Reece pressed on about Tommy's daily activities and confirmed that his mother used to do all of that, but now Felicia did. His dad liked them to be all ready for bed when he got home. He said it was like being in the army and his dad was the general who did the inspections.

Reece was ready to plunge on. These interviews were like exploratory surgeries without anesthetic. A push here, a probe there. Everything's going okay one second, the next there's a geyser of arterial blood all over the room.

"What's your mom like, Tommy?"

"She's real pretty. She's a good mom. She takes care of me and Tina. She makes what we like for dinner and she takes me to practice. She doesn't know much soccer, but she's learning."

"What is your dad like?"

"He's cool. He's a football player. He was on TV a lot. I have his cards and one of his old helmets. He takes me with him to practices and games. I have autographs of everybody on the team. When I get older I won't play soccer. I'll play football like my dad."

"Do you know why your mom and dad don't live together anymore?"

Tommy's face darkened and he began to play with the adjustment on the recliner. "My mom stopped loving my dad. She took her love and gave it to somebody else. He loves her but she doesn't love him anymore. She broke God's rule and now my dad can't live with her anymore."

"How do you know this, Tommy?"

"My dad told me. He said that my mom loves me and Tina but she can't be with us 'cause she needs to be punished. He told Mr. Gonzo that she had to learn her lesson. I heard him."

"Do you ever have to learn a lesson?"

"In school. I learn them every day."

"How about at home? Do you ever get punished?"

"Sometimes. If I'm bad. I'm not hardly ever bad. My mom puts us in time-out. Me longer than Tina. She cries and gets to get out."

"What does your dad do if you're bad?"

"He talks to me. He tells me to be good. He says he needs me to be good 'cause he has to do everything now that Mommy's in time-out."

"Time-out?"

"Yeah, like when we're bad we have to go off by ourselves and think about what we did. He says that the judge told Mommy she had to go off by herself and think about what she did that was bad. He says she can come back when she says she's sorry and won't do it again. Mommy isn't sorry that she doesn't love Daddy, that's why she can't come back."

"Have you ever been frightened, Tommy?"

"No, I don't get scared. Tina gets scared a lot."

"Have you ever been afraid of your Mommy?"

"No." His face screwed up with the effort of trying to understand the question.

"Your dad?"

"No."

"Has your mother ever hurt you?"

"Yes. She hurt my leg one time. Bad."

Reece looked up. "Can you tell me more about that?"

"I fell on the playground. My leg was bleeding. She put some water on it, but it got all foamy and it hurt like it was burning. She said that was all the germs being killed."

Reece smiled. "I see. How about your dad. Has he ever hurt you?"

"No."

"Your mom came to see you when you were at school. What happened?"

"She did a bad thing. She was trying to steal me from my dad. She came out of time-out but the judge didn't say it was over."

"Did anything else happen?"

"My dad stopped her from stealing me. She tried to bite him and he had to push her down. She hit her head on a rock and fell asleep. It was an accident."

"How did you feel when your mom came to school?"

"I was really happy. I missed her lots. I thought she told Daddy she was sorry and she could come home now. Then she was bad and ran away with me."

"When your Daddy pushed your Mommy down and she

hit her head, what did you do?"

"I wiggled out and . . . I don't remember." Tommy was picking at the buttons on the armrests.

"Were you frightened then?"

"Yes, no, I thought Mommy . . . I didn't know she was sleeping. She did a bad thing."

"I'm a little confused, Tommy. Were you frightened then before you knew she was sleeping?"

"I don't remember." That answer told Reece he needed to back away.

"Tommy, if you had three wishes, what would they be?"

He kept picking at the buttons. Now his feet were drumming the edge of the seat.

"I wish my mom and dad lived together." Then a moment later. "I wish my mom and dad loved each other." Tommy frowned as he searched for a third wish. The first two would have made his life sweet and whole. His last wish cut Reece's heart out. "I wish I wasn't so little."

Reece closed his eyes. The bullet train was picking up speed.

"Doctor Reece, can I ask you a question?"

Reece's eyes popped open. "Of course, Tommy, anything. What do you want to know?"

"Did you talk to my mom?"

"Yes, I did. I talked to her for a long time."

Tommy looked into his lap. "Did she give my love to somebody else?"

CHAPTER TWENTY-NINE

Morgan Reece walked Tommy back to the waiting room. His sister was sitting on her mother's lap. As he approached, she turned her back to him. Reece squatted and tried to make eye contact.

"Tina, it's your turn. Can you come into my office?"

No answer.

Reece motioned to Tommy. "Your brother just finished. Let's ask him how it went, Tina. Tommy, how was it?"

"It's okay, Tina. He just asks you a lot of questions. There's no shots or nothing."

Tina turned her face away from her brother and hung on to her mother's chest as if it was a granite cliff and she had no rope.

"Ms. Tully, why don't you come into my office with Tina and then we'll try to get her to separate from you? You too, Mr. Tully."

Reece ushered them all into his office and left the door open. After assuring Mr. Tully that no questions would be asked in the presence of his wife, he agreed to leave the room. His departure did not alter Tina's cliffhanger position.

"Tina, your Mommy's going to stay right here with us." He looked at Serena. "Isn't that right?"

She said, "I'm staying right here, Tina. Doctor Reece is a nice man. Can you turn around and look at him? I'll hold onto you." She detached Tina's Velcro fingers and turned her around on her lap. With an arm around her belly, she brushed her hair and kissed the top of her head.

"I've got lots of toys and games here, Tina. Let me show you what I've got. If you want to play with any of them, you just slide off your mom's lap and we can play with them."

Tina looked impassively at Reece. She had dark brown hair, pulled back with a bow at the top. Her face was round, her nose upturned and her eyes were large and blue like her mother's. If she would ever smile he would see that the dimples too had made the next generation.

"I've got games: Sorry, Chutes and Ladders."

Nothing.

Reece went over to a cupboard, sat down and slid open a door. "Let's see what I've got here. Hmm." He rummaged around. "How about Legos?" He set them out.

"I have paper and markers. We could draw pictures."

Nothing.

Reece proceeded to show Tina his collection of dolls, Transformers, doctor's kits, art supplies, Fisher-Price house and figures and Duplos. Nothing caused her to leave her mother's lap.

He went back to his chair. "Well, Tina, if anything interests you to play with, feel free to check it out. I'm just going to sit here and talk with your mother."

Serena smiled wanly. "What if she won't climb down? Then what?"

"We wait. We talk about the weather. Once she's sure you aren't leaving, she'll explore and find something that interests her. Once she's done that, I'll see if she'll let me play with her. Then we'll try to . . ." at that point Reece mimed her leaving the room.

"And if she doesn't?"

"We'll give it a decent interval. I don't want being here to

146

be aversive. We'll give it a second try. If that doesn't work, I'll switch the sequence of the evaluation. We'll do the direct observations with you and her and with her and her father. I'll try to interview her after that. She should be more comfortable with me and the place by then. I don't think that'll be necessary. I've never had a child that wouldn't separate from his or her parents, not at her age. Anxious, reluctant, slowly, sure. But absolutely refuse. Never. We'll just take it at her pace."

Reece noticed that she was still holding the child. "Relax. Let her go. She can't overcome your anxiety, too."

Serena colored. "I may be more upset about being separated from her than she is." She let her arm slide away from the child.

Reece, whose daughter had been a select team soccer player for many years, asked some innocuous questions about Tommy's team. He was playing for an under-eight house team in the Vienna Youth Soccer League. The coach planned to take the league all-stars and enter them as a select team when they were nine. He'd already told Serena he thought Tommy would be in that group.

Tina turned over and backed down off her mother's lap. She went to the open cupboard and reached in for the house and figures. They were too big for her to remove. Reece slid off his chair and came up next to her.

"Can I help you get those out?"

She nodded.

Reece set the house up on the carpet. He scooped out all of the figures and laid them in front of the house. He wasn't going to get into her play unless she invited him. Instead he hoped to use her play as an entrance into her world. A way to ask questions that was less formal than an interview. At four she was on the young end of interviewability. Reece preferred interviews to play sessions because the inferential leaps were shorter. As Twain had said, the difference between the right word and the almost-right word is the difference between lightning and lightning bug. So was the difference between "My Daddy hits me" and, dolls in hand, "The daddy doll hits the baby doll." Close, maybe very close, but not the same.

Tina was having trouble opening up the house to expose the rooms. Reece unsnapped the lock.

Tina looked perplexed. "Where's the bed? Baby needs the bed to sleep."

"Let me look." Reece rummaged in the cupboard and pulled out all the loose furniture. "Here." He handed her the bed.

Tina put the bed in an upstairs room. She selected a young girl figure and put her on the bed.

"The baby. Shhh, she's sleeping."

"Reece whispered, "Does she have a name?"

Tina whispered, "Yes."

Reece chuckled. You get what you ask for. "What's the baby's name?"

"I don't know." Tina then selected a boy figure and two adults. She carefully furnished the entire house. The leftovers she looked at disdainfully and pointed to the cupboard. She told Reece, "Put them there." He did.

"Who's that?" Reece asked, pointing to the figures.

"That's the brother, the mom and the dad."

Now was the time to try to get Mrs. Tully out, before her presence could be alleged to have contaminated the child's play or responses. Reece looked up at her. "Tina, your mom has to go to the bathroom. Can she go while we play here?"

Tina looked up at her mother who was sliding across the sofa towards the door. "Okay?"

"Tina, your mom is going to wait for you outside. After

she's done with the bathroom. Like you did when she was talking to me. We'll keep playing here. When you're done playing, we'll go outside and see her. Okay?"

"I'm going back to where I was sitting before we came in here, Tina. That's where I'll be. You can open up the door and you'll be able to see me. Okay?"

Tina said okay and her mother slid past her and out the door. She mastered an impulse to kiss her once before she left.

"That's the brother," Reece reminded her. "And the mother and father. What are their names?"

Tina looked at him incredulously. "Brother, mother and father." She put the mother in the kitchen and the father in the den. The brother and the little girl were sleeping.

Reece attempted to enter her play a number of times but was rebuffed. Tina was intent on playing out a family drama of concern to her but did not want to answer any questions about it. Reece watched and waited.

Tina looked for another figure. A man. She stood him up outside the house. She placed a dog inside the house. She found a police car and put it down the street from the house.

"Who's that?" Reece asked.

"The robber. He wants to steal the children. He's a bad man."

Tina moved the parents together into their bedroom. For the first time she volunteered information. "The Mommy and the Daddy are sleeping too. Like the brother and the girl. The bad man is waiting until they fall asleep. He's going to come in the house."

Tina moved the dog to the top of the stairs and laid him on his side. She put her finger to her lips. "Sleep, Blackie."

She moved "the robber" to the outside of the house.

"He's got a key. He's going to sneak into the house."

She moved the man inside the garage. "Shhh, Blackie. What's that noise?" The dog was up on its legs. So was the girl.

"What is the girl feeling?"

"She's scared. She hears noises at night. Blackie hears them too. He wakes her up."

"What does she do?"

"She has a safe place, where no one can see her. She hides in there."

"Do you have a safe place where no one can see you?"

"Yes."

"Where do you go?"

"In the bathroom. I hide under the sink behind the door. Tommy puts me in there."

"When did Tommy put you there?"

Tina looked away. "I don't know. I forget."

She reached into the house. "The Mommy and the Daddy are up, too. They hear the bad man's noises. Blackie is barking. The Daddy calls the police." She reached down and brought the police car up to the front of the house. She stood the robber up in the back of the police car. "He's going to jail. But the Mommy and the Daddy, the brother and the girl aren't. They all stay in the house. All of them."

Tina looked around and found that the world was not so. She stood up, opened the door and raced to her mother whose absence filled her play, and made it into work.

CHAPTER THIRTY

Dr. Frazier finished with the Bricklin and Roberts tests shortly after Tina's session ended. She scheduled the Rorschachs with the Tullys for the next afternoon.

Reece told them that he needed to discuss the direct observation sequence with their attorneys.

Tom Tully asked, "Why?"

"Because it requires that the children spend equal time with each parent so that it's fair for both parties."

"Wait a minute, let me get this straight." Tully was getting angry.

"No, this is not the place to discuss this. Why don't you both say goodbye to your children, let Ms. Hurtado take them with her and we can discuss this in my office."

Serena moved swiftly, squatted down and hugged her son. She whispered in his ear and stroked his head. He hugged her fiercely and kissed her cheek. She stood up and went to her daughter as Mr. Tully hugged and kissed his son. Felicia Hurtado reached out and touched Tommy's shoulder as they waited for Tina. Serena picked Tina up, kissed her and stroked her, and with great effort separated her daughter from her and handed her to her father. She picked up her purse and fled into Reece's office. Tommy looked past his father at his mother's back.

Tina was starting to cry and Tom Tully looked at Reece. "How about I take her out to the car. I'll be back in a second."

Reece stood in his office and looked out over the top of the curtains. Tully slid Tommy into the car and then disentangled Tina from his neck and put her in the car seat. Without its straps and restraints he might never have gotten loose.

Out of the corner of his eye he saw Serena Tully biting into a gloved knuckle as she watched her children pull out of the parking lot as if they had been snatched by strangers and she would only see them on the side of a milk carton.

Tully strode back into the office. "What's this about her spending time with the kids?"

"Please close the door, Mr. Tully. Just what I said. That's the next stage of the evaluation. It requires equal time with each of the parents. Considering that Ms. Tully has no place to be with the children, that might prove a problem."

"I'm going to get a new place today. I'll get one big enough for me and the children."

"So you're leaving Denise's. She had enough of you, too?"

"No. I've got a job and I'll have a place of my own." Serena hurled back one lie after another.

Reece slipped back into the conversation, "That's only part of the problem. The original order gave *pendente lite* custody to Mr. Tully, but didn't specify visitation for Ms. Tully. Even in emergency situations there's visitation. It may require supervision, but there's visitation. I have to discuss with the attorneys how to address this so I can complete the evaluation."

Serena calmly asked, "So even though Tom has this custody, what did you call it?"

"*Pendente lite,* pending litigation."

"Even with that I'm entitled to visitation?"

"That's correct. Possibly supervised, but visitation, yes."

She almost blurted out, "Then why the hell didn't my attorney get it for me?" but smothered that. She knew for certain that she was changing attorneys and just as certainly that she wanted to surprise the living hell out of Tom Tully and Albert "Mr. Effective" Garfield.

"No way, Dr. Reece. If that's where this is going, I'm out of here. This evaluation is over. She's not getting those kids. That's for fucking certain. I'll fight you on this in court." Tully's jaw was set, his eyes wide. A vein in his scalp throbbed like a snake under sand. He was getting up on his toes, leaning forward, coiled to strike.

Reece stared calmly into Tom Tully's clenched face. "That's exactly where this will be decided. I have an order from the court to conduct this evaluation as I see fit. If you or Al Garfield wants to argue about how it's going to be done, so be it. We'll go before the judge, let him hear both sides and he'll decide, not you or me. Until I'm relieved by the judge, I'm in this matter."

"Not for long, Reece. That's a fact." Tully snarled and left, slamming the door behind him.

Serena Tully looked at Reece. "Aren't you afraid? I'm terrified whenever he gets angry like that."

"That didn't frighten me. I'm sure he could if he really wanted to. I don't know if you've got a new lawyer yet, but you'd better hurry. All hell is about to break loose."

CHAPTER THIRTY-ONE

Between the steak and cheese and the onion rings, Morgan Reece worked on the Tully file. He updated the rolling ledger of his time and expenses. Dr. Frazier had clipped a bill to the Bricklin and Roberts score sheets. Reece separated it, entered it on the ledger and slipped it underneath. He looked at the Bricklin. It favored the mother overall, with her taking the supportiveness scale, the father the consistency and admirable traits scales and a wash on the competence scales. The Roberts showed a little boy who was feeling overwhelmed with problems and unable to fashion successful solutions. His depression and rejection scales were elevated but he had no maladaptives. Not yet.

Reece punched holes in the sheets and slipped them into the file. He slit open the mail from the previous day. The consents were getting very predictable responses. The school had a form letter attached to the questionnaire. It was from the school board's legal department. "Absent an order from the circuit court, the school system will not provide written records in domestic disputes. Subpoena *duces tecum* will be met with a motion to quash. Parental consent is deemed insufficient to release records. Staff has been advised not to respond to verbal requests of any sort. Depositions will be opposed by protective order. If relief is not granted, they will be conducted at the offices of the school board legal department with full representation. All costs to be borne by the moving party." Reece was not surprised. Cancer metastasizes and spreads and the body fights back. These were legal antibodies.

The pediatric records were just that, six years of raw notes, even though his request was for a summary limited to conditions requiring special care by the parents and a note indicating who brought the child in for check-ups and treatment. No, that was too hard to do, he thought. Too hard to spend the time to read the chart, think about the question or compose a reply. Much easier to send a secretary to the Xerox and let the evaluator spend his time translating the hieroglyphics or calling back to ask questions about the runes. Twice as expensive that way. You didn't need health care reform to cut costs; just a little old-fashioned health care would do.

Reece spent the next hour reading and underlining the record to determine that the children were healthy, and he still had no idea who brought them to their appointment although telephone calls were always identified as the mother's.

The therapist who treated Serena Dilworth as an adolescent had no records of her treatment from that long ago. He went on to note that he was now retired and had no recollections of her at all.

The second hospitalization and treatment records hadn't arrived yet. Reece noted the date on the "tickler sheet" and filed the responses. He put his session notes into the chart and looked at the faxed response from Simon Tepper.

Reece stopped, picked up the phone and called his answering service. "This is Dr. Reece, did you receive any calls this morning?"

"No, sir."

"No one identifying himself as me, or with a message from me."

"No, sir. The incoming board is clear."

"How about calls out? Any calls to a Serena Tully?"

"No, sir. Outgoing is clean, too."

"Thank you."

That didn't prove anything. The calls could have come from elsewhere, or there could have been no call at all.

Reece filled his coffee and started to read Simon Tepper's notes. Twice he stopped to think about calling Lindsay Brinkman. Once he even uncradled the phone.

CHAPTER THIRTY-TWO

Serena Tully got only a quarter of what the Baume & Mercier retailed for, but it was two thousand dollars more than she had. She wasn't sure how much Stuart had used up already. She decided to keep half the money as a retainer for a new lawyer and hope she got a job pretty soon. The other half would go to rent a two-bedroom suite in a motel so she'd have a place to stay with the kids. By four o'clock she had a place in an all-suites motel out on Route 7 just before the Dulles Access Road. Two down, one to go. If she was on her own, she'd have thought about a job as a topless dancer. She'd always heard that the money was good and it was cash. Her bruises wouldn't matter. Nobody'd be looking at her face anyway. Not an option if she wanted her kids. Tomorrow she'd go down to the lobby, get a *Post* right off the truck and start her search in earnest. She checked the car clock: four-fifteen. May as well get to Denise's, pack up and leave. Do it before Denise came home from work. That way she could cry if she had to.

Serena slipped the key into the lock and pushed the door open. She went upstairs to the guest room. First stop was the bathroom. She gathered up her stuff, put what she could in the plastic makeup case and filled her arms with the rest. She dropped it all on the bed in the guest room and turned to get her suitcase from the closet.

He was on her like nightfall, silent, black and everywhere. Falling back she tried to scream through his gloved fingers

157

but couldn't even mumble. On the bed she tried to wriggle free. An enormous hand closed on her throat, his thumb pushed on her windpipe like it was a cutoff switch. Her arms flailed weakly. Her legs trembled and shook. This was it, the end. The black ski mask faded out of sight.

"See how easy that was." The voice boomed in her ears. She was coming back. She gasped for air and gulped it down her throat, past the burn. Her eyes watered, but the huge black knitted head stayed right in front of her face. She was afraid to test her limbs, that he might think she was resisting and he'd turn her off again. She felt dead from the neck down. Her mind was filled with the faceless head in front of her.

"You hear me? Nod your head."

Serena nodded.

"Good. Now just listen." His voice was softer now. "See how easy that was. One second you're fine, the next you're dead. Terrible, how close at hand death really is." He shook his head in sympathy. "I can come back and visit you any time I want. You didn't hear me this time; you won't hear me next time. Next time is the last time. You want to see your kids again, sign the papers. You can't hide from me, either. I know where you've moved to. Nice place to visit but I wouldn't want to raise kids there. You understand me?"

Serena tried to speak, but the hand over her mouth muffled it.

"No. Don't talk. Just nod. You understand me?"

Her head bobbed up and down.

"Good. I'm glad we've had this talk. It's late in the day. I expect you to sign those papers first thing tomorrow. If I find out that you haven't, I'll be back. Promise. Now, I'm going to let myself out. You just lie here and think about what you're going to do tomorrow. Count to a thousand. Then get up, take a shower, change your clothes. You'll feel better."

The big man lifted a leg over Serena's body, swiveled on one knee and stood up. He put a finger to his lips, turned and left.

She lay there, rigid with fear, tears running down the sides of her face. Exhausted by her trip to death and back, she couldn't fight any longer.

In his car, the messenger chuckled and whistled a happy tune. Maybe it wasn't too late for a career change.

CHAPTER THIRTY-THREE

Serena Tully hoped that Lou Carlson had a class as she walked down the hall towards his office. If his office was empty she'd just put the books on his desk. If it was locked she'd find the department secretary and leave them there. What to do if he was in was not an option she'd considered.

Outside the door, she leaned forward to listen for voices. A phone call or needy student would be very welcome. The office was silent. She gently gripped the doorknob and turned it, hoping it would catch. When it didn't, she pushed it open slowly and leaned her head around the edge. Empty. She slipped in, went around his desk and put the books in plain sight. She stepped back and surveyed the chaos. No, even in that mess he'd see them. Maybe he wouldn't remember who they were from. She ripped off a piece of paper and scribbled a quick note of thanks. She placed his coffee mug on top of the note and books.

"Hi, there. I've been trying to get a hold of you." Carlson's voice startled her and she flinched. Spooked, her eyes flicked from side to side, looking for a way past him and out the door.

Carlson knew something wasn't right. She looked guilty, like she'd been caught taking something she shouldn't have.

"Sorry, I didn't mean to startle you. I've got the names of some lawyers who . . ."

"That's okay, Mr. Carlson. Really, I appreciate everything you've done, but I won't need those names any more." With each word Serena moved from behind Carlson's desk until she was between him and his bookcases, with the open door only two steps away.

He looked at her closely and revised his opinion. Panic, not guilt, was what she radiated.

"Are you okay, Ms. Tully? You don't look very well."

She put a hand quickly to her throat, felt the turtleneck and smiled weakly. "No, I'm fine, Mr. Carlson."

"Did you and your husband settle?"

"Yes. I signed the papers this morning. The lawyers are down at the courthouse trying to get a judge to sign the order today."

That was odd, Carlson thought. Why not wait until motions day? What was the hurry? Expensive too, running down there with only one order to get signed.

"Things must have changed quite a bit. I guess Stuart did better for you than you thought he would. What kind of settlement did he get?" Carlson was curious at what Al Garfield had to give up. He rejoiced at every setback he experienced, even if he didn't personally administer it.

"I, I, I . . ." she began to sob and pressed her hands to her face, ". . . don't know." She hadn't even read the papers in Stuart's office, her fear compressing each letter, each shape, into a series of black lines on white paper with no more meaning than a seismograph.

She tried to slide past Carlson and out of his office when he reached out and grabbed her by the upper arms.

"Wait a minute, what do you mean you don't know?"

Carlson tried to turn Serena to face him. Her face was contorted trying to suppress her sobs. Her arms were up as if to fend off a blow. "Please, don't hurt me. Let me go."

Carlson looked at his hands gripping her arms as if they were snakes with fangs sunk into her flesh.

"I'm sorry. Please sit down." He steered her into one of the chairs in front of the desk and took the other. The one closer to the door.

"You signed a custody agreement and you don't know what it says: There is something terribly wrong here. A few days ago you came in here and wanted someone to help you stand up to your husband and Al Garfield. Now this. Talk to me. What's happened to you?"

Serena had her face buried in her hands. Gasping for air between the waves of anguish, remorse and self-loathing that broke over her, her words escaped one at a time.

"I can't. He'll kill me. I had to sign it."

"What do you mean, he'll kill you? Who? Did your husband threaten you?"

Serena's head bobbed up and down. Carlson wasn't sure which question she'd answered.

"Okay. One at a time. Someone threatened you?"

Serena nodded.

"Your husband?"

She shrugged her shoulders.

"You don't know for sure?"

More nodding.

"Someone threatened to kill you?"

She shook her head no. Carlson started to relax. Then she nodded yes.

"He didn't threaten to kill you or he did?"

Serena wiped at glistening cheeks. Mascaraed tears zig-zagged down her face. Carlson searched for a box of tissues in his office. Without surrendering his position he reached over to his bookcase, hooked a box with two fingers, pulled it down and handed it to her.

"Your husband?"

"No. Someone else. He had a mask on. I didn't recognize

the voice. He jumped me in Denise's house. I was packing to go to my new apartment. He choked me until I blacked out. When I came to, he told me to sign the papers or he'd come back and kill me. So I did." Sobs exploded out of her. "I gave my kids away."

Carlson sat back and ground his teeth. His gut churned. His chest tightened. He needed Maalox. He needed a nitro. He played mental chess with human pieces. He saw Serena, himself, his wife, Lori, Serena's children, his, Tom Tully and Albert Garfield, Agent Orange. Lou Carlson moved each piece in turn, exhausting their repertoires. They were in the end game and checkmate was everywhere. He rubbed his brow as he contemplated the next move, the only one left on the board.

"Not yet. Look at me. We've run out of time and choices. I'm going to ask you some questions. Think very hard before you answer. There is no going back. What happens to you and your children is going to be decided here and now. This is it. No second chances, no do-overs, no appeals, no excuses, no explanations.

"Do you think your husband would try to kill you?"

"Yes."

"Do you think he should be raising your children?"

"No."

"What do you think is best for the children?"

"To be with me."

"Are you ready to risk your life to do what's best for your children?"

Serena started to answer. Carlson held up his hand.

"Don't answer that. I don't mean here, now, in the light of day in my office. I mean back in that house when you were going under. Are you ready for that?" Carlson tapped a finger on the desk. "Take your time."

Lou Carlson propped his chin on one palm and watched Serena Tully search for the courage that had eluded her for her entire life.

"Mr. Carlson, I'm ready for that. That was just death. Let me tell you it's nothing compared to how I feel when I think about giving my kids away to someone who can't take care of them."

"Take a deep breath and say it again. I want you to be sure."

She'd made the wrong choices so many times. How would she know if this was right? She usually felt much better right after each bad decision. A sure sign of wishing instead of thinking. This time she was still afraid.

"I'm ready to fight for what's best for my kids, Mr. Carlson. No matter what."

"All right. Fasten your seatbelt. This is going to be a bumpy ride."

Carlson went behind his desk, pulled the phone over and called the judge's chambers.

"Johnelle, Lou Carlson, how are you?"

"Fine, fine. God it's nice to hear your voice. Been a long time. How do you like being retired? Piece of cake, uh?"

"Yeah, Johnelle, piece of cake. Could you do me a favor? What judge is hearing a motion to enter a consent order by Al Garfield and Gilbert Stuart?"

"What's the name of the case?"

"Tully v. Tully."

"Hold on a second, I'll look."

A couple of minutes later, Johnelle Murchison, chief clerk to the circuit court judges, returned. "That's Judge Hallowell, they're in with him now."

"Johnelle, would you put me through to the judge, it's an emergency."

"Lou, you know how the judges are. I can't do that."

"I know, Johnelle. I wouldn't ask if it wasn't an emergency. I'm not using the word for effect. This is an emergency. A major miscarriage of justice is about to take place if I can't speak to Judge Hallowell. I will take full responsibility for the intrusion, Johnelle. You know me. Would I say it if it wasn't so?"

"Hold on, Lou. I'll put you through."

"Judge Hallowell speaking."

"Good afternoon, Your Honor. This is Lou Carlson. I apologize for this intrusion; however I have information of the utmost importance about the consent order before you now."

"This is highly unusual, counselor. What is your standing in this matter?"

"I am counsel for the mother, Serena Tully."

Carlson stopped for a second. It had been two years since he'd spoken those words. If he'd been an alcoholic he'd have been staring at his first glass wondering how many more would follow.

"Mr. Stuart is counsel of record, Mr. Carlson. There is no notice of his being replaced or joined on this matter."

"That can be remedied, Your Honor. Would you please put Mr. Stuart on the phone?" This was the turning point. Carlson was in the vast trackless wild of judicial discretion. The judge would do what he damn well pleased and as long as he kept why to himself, answer to no one.

"Hold on, Mr. Carlson. I'll put Mr. Stuart on."

Carlson motioned for Serena to take the phone. He handed her the paper with the words he'd written for her.

"Gilbert Stuart, here."

"Mr. Stuart, this is Serena Tully. I rescind my consent to that settlement. I want you to convey that to the judge. That is your last act on my behalf, Mr. Stuart. After you have done that, you are released as my attorney. Mr. Carlson is now my attorney. Please put the judge back on." She handed back the phone.

"Mr. Carlson, what are the grounds for requesting that I vacate this order? An entered order of this court is no trifling matter. You'd better have a damned good reason to request that I vacate this order."

"Your Honor, my client, Ms. Tully, was assaulted yesterday by a man who told her that unless she signed those papers she would be killed. I would respectfully submit that that renders the consent aspect of that order null and void."

"Let me have a moment to speak with opposing counsel." While the judge spoke to Garfield, Gilbert Stuart snapped his briefcase shut and left the room, mortified by his dismissal.

Carlson looked at Serena and shrugged his shoulders.

"Mr. Carlson, I'm not willing to set aside this court order without a hearing with your client under oath and cross-examined. How soon can you and she be at the courthouse?"

"Thirty minutes, Your Honor."

"Do so. I have other cases to hear. I will be waiting for you in Courtroom E."

CHAPTER THIRTY-FOUR

All the way down to the courthouse, Lou Carlson wondered what he'd tell his wife. While he was easily combustible, she was a smolderer with eloquent eyebrows and pursed lips that whitened from the force of the words withheld. Carlson followed her around, palms up, saying, "What? What is it? Tell me already." When her silence was broken, there was a brief but complete conflagration followed by laborious cleanup and repair.

He looked over at Serena Tully, who was staring out the window, thinking about what she was about to do. The lot around the courthouse was packed, so Carlson drove down the block to a row of townhouses, home to scores of lawyers. He pulled into the patrolled lot and found a spot belonging to a firm he had good relations with, got out and bounded up the front stairs of their office. When he returned, he slipped a visitor's pass under the windshield. He and Serena walked briskly to the courthouse.

Judge Hallowell was in Courtroom E, at the end of the fifth floor. All heads turned when they walked in: bailiff, clerk, reporter, judge and Albert Olen Garfield.

"Mr. Carlson, do you have a motion to place before this court?"

Carlson pulled a chair back for his client to sit, and tried to remember the list he'd made on the trip from his office. Albert Garfield admired Serena Tully. When she caught him staring at her, she tried to meet his eyes but stopped when she saw the smirk on his face. Instinctively she tugged at her skirt.

"Actually, Your Honor, I have a number of motions to place before the court. First, that you vacate the order you signed, because it was entered into by my client under duress. She feared for her life after a brutal assault on her by a person we believe to have been hired by her husband."

"I object, Your Honor."

"Sustained, Mr. Garfield."

"Should Your Honor grant this motion after hearing the testimony of my client, I request that a hearing be set immediately on the spousal violence part of the original *ex parte* order signed by Judge Kenniston. The statute says that such an order is granted for a period of fifteen days."

"Objection, Your Honor."

"Yes, Mr. Garfield?"

"The statute says that a hearing must be granted within fifteen days but that it may be extended. Dr. Reece was ordered to do an evaluation into the spousal abuse question. I think it would not be in the children's best interest to rush such an important piece of work to fit Mr. Carlson's agenda. The proper time for a hearing is when Dr. Reece has concluded his investigation."

"Your Honor, the order was for an evaluation into the best interests of the children, not simply spousal violence, as Mr. Garfield would have you believe. I'm sure the court has a copy of Judge Kenniston's order. You are familiar with Dr. Reece's work. He's very thorough. He may well have an opinion on the spousal violence aspect at this time even if his entire evaluation is not complete. That issue is the one that has forced my client from her home and kept her from seeing her children. Those constraints should be removed as quickly as possible. If Dr. Reece has reached an opinion on that limited question, then we should hear that now in the timeframe of the statute."

"Do you have any other motions, Mr. Carlson?"

"Because of the assault on my client and other forms of harassment, she can no longer stay with the family that took her in. I would request the court grant her temporary spousal support so that she can find a place for herself and her children."

"Objection, Your Honor. There's a *pendente lite* order granting my client custody of the children. I fail to see why he should pay for lodgings for her and the children. That presupposes her receiving custody of the children."

Serena Tully watched Albert Garfield pop up and down like a jack-in-the-box. He wasn't smiling anymore.

"Your Honor, if the *ex parte* order is dismissed then my client will be entitled to visitation at least. If she's to make use of that visitation, she has to obtain housing sufficient to take all three of them. We are all aware of the delays in the court docket; most likely she'll have to take a lease on an apartment or townhouse rather than an efficiency for herself."

Garfield was up again, "Your Honor, this is unnecessary. If Mrs. Tully poses no danger to her husband or children, I'm sure she could return to the marital residence, thereby saving my client the expense of supporting two households."

Now it was Carlson's turn. "That's a gracious offer, Mr. Garfield. As soon as your client vacates the home, she'll be glad to return. She won't return to share the space with him. I contend that it is your client who is dangerous."

"Your Honor . . ."

"Sustained. You are not in a classroom anymore, Mr. Carlson. You remember the rules, I'm sure. Please limit yourself to the substance of your motion."

"Yes, Your Honor. My last motion is to freeze the marital estate. We will show at the next hearing a pattern of asset shifting designed to impoverish my client and force her to settle on adverse terms."

Garfield shook his head as if he had never heard such a pack of lies in his life. "The money has not been shifted to impoverish his client. It was moved to preserve the estate from the hands of an irrational and seriously disturbed woman. Mr. Tully has taken on additional expenses, such as a full-time nanny to take care of his children. He has to know that money exists to continue to care for them and shield them from the tragedy enveloping their parents. We will show no pattern of frivolous spending. The money has always been a phone call away for Mrs. Tully. All she had to do was ask."

"You honor, my motion to freeze the marital estate is bilateral. That protects the children and both of the parents. Those are my motions, Your Honor."

"Thank you. Call your witness, Mr. Carlson."

Serena Tully took the stand, then the oath, and tried to remember Carlson's tips on testifying. He guided her smoothly through the assault, its aftermath, signing the order in Stuart's office and changing her mind.

Carlson sat down and waited to see what tack Garfield would take. He kept his eyes on Serena and the judge. That's where the damage would register. That's where his work would be needed.

"Mrs. Tully, you say you never saw this man before, yet his face was masked. How did you know this?"

"He was very big . . ."

"You saw him standing up?"

"No. Like I said, I turned around and he was on top of me."

"So you don't know how tall he was. You never saw him stand up?"

"No, but . . ."

"Thank you. What race was he?"

"I don't know. It was dark. He wore a mask and gloves."

"Did you recognize his voice?"

"No."

"A complete stranger, then?"

"I believe so."

"What made you think your husband sent him?"

"Because he said if I didn't sign the papers . . ."

"The papers. Not the settlement with your husband, just the papers; is that correct?"

"Yes."

"Did he call you by name?"

"No."

"So he might have thought you were the other woman in the house?"

"No."

Garfield smiled at that answer, nodded his head in understanding and went on. "Have there been harassing phone calls to the house?"

"Yes."

"What sort of calls?"

"Obscene calls."

"To you or to you and Mrs. Fargo?"

"I don't know. No names were mentioned."

"Was the phone call about performing a sex act with some men?"

"Yes." Serena was reddening.

"Are you having an affair, Mrs. Tully? Have you had sex with someone other than your husband?"

"Objection, Your Honor. This isn't relevant to the matter

at hand. We aren't conducting the divorce trial, nor is my client a suspect in a criminal investigation. Mr. Garfield is well aware that adultery is still a misdemeanor in Virginia and my client would be entitled to Fifth Amendment protection. She doesn't have to answer that question, so why ask it?"

Carlson sat, hoping Serena would pick up the shield he had laid at her feet.

"Sustained."

"Well if it isn't you having sex with strangers, perhaps it's Mrs. Fargo. Do you know how they got the number?"

"I'm sure my husband . . ."

"Not what you believe, Mrs. Tully, what you know."

"No, I don't know."

"These men on the phone were strangers too, is that correct?"

"Yes."

"Like the man in the house?"

"Yes."

"This man didn't identify you or the papers. He was a stranger to you. Strange men have called the house asking for sex with the women there. Any woman."

"No. He came for me."

"You don't know that. You can't know that, Mrs. Tully. Did he say, Mrs. Serena Tully, sign the settlement papers?"

"No, he . . ."

"Thank you."

"Did you report this to the police?"

"No, I was too . . ."

"That's sufficient. You told no one about this, correct?"

"Yes, until Mr. Carlson."

"Ah, yes, Mr. Carlson. You went in and signed the documents the next day. Isn't it true you already had an appointment to see Mr. Stuart about the papers?"

"Yes."

"You don't remember reading these papers?"

"No."

"You were so afraid, you were going to sign these papers without reading them, but not so afraid that you'd call the police. Is that right?"

"No, I was too afraid to call the police."

"Too afraid to call the police, the people who are supposed to protect you, I see. Mrs. Tully, have you ever been in therapy?"

"Objection, Your Honor."

Garfield turned to Carlson. "Her mental state is relevant, Your Honor."

"Overruled."

"I believe that . . . no strike that. Are you in therapy now, Mrs. Tully?"

"Yes."

"For how long?"

"About a year."

"How often do you go to therapy?"

"Once a week."

"Do you know what your diagnosis is?"

"No."

"Are these problems similar to ones you had before?"

"Yes."

"Were you in therapy for them then?"

"Yes. I was."

"But they're still with you?"

"I guess so."

"These therapies, were you ever given drugs?"

"Yes."

"Were you ever hospitalized?"

"Yes."

"When you were a model, did you miss jobs?"

Serena was starting to panic. Why wasn't Carlson saying anything? Why didn't he object? She looked like a crazy person. It wasn't true. She wasn't crazy.

"Yes, at the end I was."

"The end. Right before your suicide attempt."

"Yes."

"The first one or the second one?"

"The second one."

Carlson looked at his note pad. He'd drawn a noose. He just needed to put his head into it and finish the job. Just a few facts he'd forgotten to get before leaping onto his white stallion. This would make it easier to deal with Lori. He could come home with a heartfelt *mea culpa,* put his head right on the block, steal all her best lines, beg her to do it. Put him out of his misery. Be over in no time.

"The second time. What did you tell your boss when you missed these jobs?"

"I don't remember."

"Why were you missing jobs?"

"Because I was depressed. I'd sleep through them. I couldn't face going down there, getting made up and trying to look pretty."

"Did you tell them that?"

"No."

"What did you say?"

"I don't know. I don't remember. I made something up."

Carlson grimaced. He looked at Judge Hallowell. If this case was over, he didn't show it.

"So when things got too hard to face, you made things up. Did you accuse your husband of trying to trick you into

174

missing an appointment with Dr. Reece?"

"Yes."

"How did he do that?"

"He had someone call saying that the time had been changed so I'd be late."

"Were you?"

"No, I didn't believe him."

"Did you call Dr. Reece to confirm this?"

"No, there wasn't time."

"Was there a dinner scheduled recently for your family and you sisters?"

"No."

"No? I remind you that you are under oath, Mrs. Tully."

"No." She said defiantly. "My husband says I scheduled one and forgot to cook for it. I never did. He set it up behind my back to make me look crazy, but I didn't do it."

Garfield turned and smiled at Judge Hallowell. "Your Honor, we have a story about a mystery man who threatens her with death if she doesn't sign papers. This from a woman with a lengthy history of mental illness and treatment. When things got too tough for her in the past, she made things up to cover for herself. Those are her own words, under oath. She has a history of claiming that things happened or didn't happen but no one else agrees with her version. This isn't just now but throughout her past. It's always someone else's fault. They told her to do something or not to do it. That's why my client can't live with her any longer. It's never Serena Tully's fault. She can't face that. So she makes things up. This time it's a man who threatened to kill her. Your Honor, the sad truth is that Serena Tully gave up custody of her children and she can't live with that decision. That's what's going on here."

Carlson had waited patiently for the right time to jump in.

It was now. "Your Honor, I think Mr. Garfield has jumped the gun. That sounded a lot like a closing argument to me. I don't mind. He's made his position clear, but I am entitled to redirect, Your Honor. If I may."

When the judge nodded, he added, "Just one point, Your Honor. Mrs. Tully, would you please roll down your collar?"

She pulled the collar down and spread it away from her neck. A purple-black bruise the size of a half dollar was the gemstone of a blue and yellow necklace that ran around her throat.

"That's some imagination you've got, Ms. Tully."

"Objection." Garfield barked.

CHAPTER THIRTY-FIVE

"Gentlemen," Judge Hallowell intoned, "based on the evidence presented today, including the demonstration that Mrs. Tully's hands are too small to have created such an injury, I am moved to vacate the consent order. In addition, I want both of you to contact Dr. Reece as soon as possible and ascertain how soon he can appear to address the spousal abuse part of the original *ex parte* order. Set a hearing before me or Judge Kenniston on that date or fifteen days from the original hearing, whichever shall occur first. I am not inclined to order support today when we will be here in a matter of days to decide whether she can return to the marital residence. The issue of shared residence or temporary support payments can be argued at that time, gentlemen, and a ruling made. However, I do order the marital estate frozen, requiring the signature of both parties before any assets can be moved or divested in any fashion. Get back to my clerk with a date. I'll speak to Judge Kenniston as to which of us will hear this case. Good day."

Lou Carlson gathered up his papers and escorted Serena Tully from the courtroom. In the hall outside he and Albert Garfield exchanged smiles that were a display of canines and nothing more.

"That's the first thing I've won in this whole battle. Thank you so much. I had given up hope of stopping Tom from just running right over me. I don't know how I'm going to pay you. I don't even have a job yet. Once my face is normal, I should be able to get something." She touched her cheek self-consciously.

"We'll work something out. I took this on because it was an emergency. Children should not be hostages delivered to terrorists. This is not going to be an easy one to win. There's a lot about you I found out on cross-examination. That's not a good way to learn things. Your history works against you. I'll need to know all about that stuff Garfield referred to. I presume you've discussed all this with Dr. Reece?"

"Yes, I have."

"Do you have any idea how he took it?"

"No. He's very close-mouthed. I don't know what he thinks of me."

"That's Morgan. You're the kind of target that Al Garfield loves. He's a bully. Like I said, it's going to be a bumpy ride."

"What do we do now?"

"The first thing we do is take you to a police station so you can file a report on the assault. I want the police pursuing this. Make it clear you believe your husband was behind it. I want them asking him questions, too, not just a scene-of-crime investigation that ends up with a smudged print, an unidentified hair and a dead end. After that I want you to move. The police will go to your friend's house. Pack up, and ask an officer to drive you to a new address. Do not go back to the place you rented. We'll try to get your deposit back. I don't think that'll be a problem. Look for a security building. Get it week to week. Call my office, leave a message and a phone number. Do not leave your new address."

"Do you think the police will put somebody there, you know, to keep an eye out?"

"No. I'll ask them to send a patrol car by regularly when you're in your new place. That's all they'll do now. This guy found you because your husband knew where you were staying. You told me that on the ride to the courthouse. You said your husband also knew that you were planning to move. That's probably why he made his move that day. It was the last day that he knew where you were going to be. I think the stuff about knowing where you'd moved to was bullshit. Just something else to scare you with. After the police station, I'm going to get started preparing this case."

"What are you going to do?"

"Get all the papers Gilbert Stuart has for starters. Read them over. He should have sent out interrogatories and requests for documents. If not, that's the first thing I have to do. I want to know a lot more about your husband. Al Garfield has a lot of mud to sling. Right now his client has no reason to tell him not to. I want to see if we can give him a reason. See how he likes it coming back at him. Unless you married a saint, there's something he won't want being part of a public record. It's just a matter of finding it. That'll get you a flat playing field and bring them to the negotiating table. That's what I want.

"After I've read the papers I'll call you and we'll have a meeting. Go over all of it and plan strategy. In the meantime keep working with Dr. Reece. The sooner he's done, the sooner we can get back into court."

"How much importance is the judge going to give Dr. Reece's report?"

"In all likelihood, Dr. Reece's report will be the biggest factor in the judge's decision. That's one of the reasons Al Garfield doesn't like to see him in a case. It takes it out of the lawyers' hands. Al can't beat up on Morgan Reece. Morgan knows all the tricks. He won't give him an opening to question his work."

"Have you ever disagreed with his conclusions?"

"I've had clients who disagreed and we got second opinions of his work. No one ever faults his procedures. He's scrupulously fair, comprehensive to the point of obsessive and he knows his research. They may disagree with his conclusions but they are always credible and defensible. This is not like math or chemistry. It is all human judgment and human error. Morgan's work is important because it defines the reasonable starting point for negotiation and it's not easily ignored by a judge."

Serena Tully reviewed her interview with Morgan Reece. She tried to remember anything she wished she hadn't said, any answer she wanted back. Nothing came to her. She would have to be very careful around him in the future.

Two hours later, Lou Carlson left Serena Tully at the McLean District Police station. She was going back with an investigator and forensics team. Lou had scheduled a meeting at 2941 in Falls Church with private investigator Donovan Blake.

Lou Carlson saw Don Blake at a table in the far corner. Blake waved him over. As he approached a woman came from another direction, looked at him once and sat down next to Blake.

Blake rose as Carlson reached the table and reached out to shake hands. Blake was built like a drum of lead. Five-foot-eight, he weighed two hundred and thirty pounds. His four major food groups were beer, beef, potatoes, and dessert. Exceptional genes and two-hour-a-day workouts were all that kept him out of the ground. A neck wider than his ears rose up to brace a square head topped by thick grey hair swept straight back. Unlike most short men, he cultivated the company of taller women. His current companion was no exception.

"Lou Carlson," he said, pointing with his left hand, "meet

Crystal Cassidy. She's an operative in our Old Town Office."
Carlson pulled out a chair and sat down. "Crys, this is Lou
Carlson. He used to be the best divorce lawyer in Virginia.
Now he's a professor. Isn't that right, Lou?"

"Almost, Don. Sins from a past life have caught up with
me. I've taken a case on an emergency basis. Albert Garfield's
on the other side."

"I sure hope the facts aren't also."

"Too soon to tell. Which tells you how much catch-up I
have to play. Which is why I'm here." Carlson waited a
minute, hoping Blake would offer to have Crystal leave them
alone. When he didn't he said, "I don't mean to be rude, Ms.
Cassidy, but what I have to say to Don is for his ears only.
Could you give us just a moment alone, please?"

She turned and looked at Blake, who placed a broad,
thick-fingered hand on her forearm.

"Anything you want to say to me, you can say to her. We
don't have any secrets. I'm grooming her to take over the
business."

"Don, I'm the only one who knows what I'm going to say.
Let me get it out between us, then you decide. She can come
right back."

"It's okay, Don, really. I'll go powder my nose. I've always
wanted to say that anyway. When I'm done, I'll come back. If
that's too soon, I'll sulk and try to pick up the maitre d'." She
patted Don's hand, stood up, and excused herself.

Blake's eyes traveled up her long, slim body, then the
slender throat to her smiling face. She was as fair as he was
dark, with jet-black hair, tied in a French braid. Both Blake
and Carlson watched her sashay across the room, each step
causing her skirt to twirl around her legs.

"What do you think, Lou? Not bad, eh?"

"Don, she looks just like Margo. I sure hope you aren't

making the same mistake twice."

"I'm not, Lou. She may look like Margo on the outside. But inside there's a big difference."

"And that is?"

"She's got a heart. She doesn't need to rip mine out."

"I hope so, Don. Remember what you said when you came to me that night?"

Blake leaned forward, put both hands on the table, lowered his bull neck and said, "I remember, Lou. I meant it, too. Is this it? Payback time?"

"I think so, Don."

"Don't think so, Lou. I gave you my word. You ever needed anything from me, I was at your disposal. No charge. No questions. All I want to know is that this is it. Whatever I owed you is cancelled with this. We're square. If not, then it's business as usual."

This case was going to cost plenty to prepare adequately. Carlson had no idea what Serena Tully could afford. Do it right or don't do it at all, that's what he always said. If she couldn't pay, Blake would look to him to pay the bill. That's all Lori would need. Her workaholic husband falls off the wagon and winds up five thousand in debt. His salary was only a fifth of what he used to make.

Those reasons didn't cut it. It wasn't fair to blame Lori for this. Clutching his chest in D.C. Superior Court, unable to breathe or cry out for help, he traded every victory he'd ever had for one more minute with her and the kids. They needed him. He needed them. Two years later it was easy to forget that it was his decision as much as her wish. Don Blake would make his job so much easier, would get him home at six, not eleven or one in the morning.

"This is it, Don. I won't come back to you again. Not even for my own kids."

"Done. I'm yours. Whatever you need. I'm at your disposal, without charge."

"I need round-the-clock surveillance on a man, Tom Tully. He's special teams coach for the Squires. I've got to get something on him to force him to negotiate. He thinks he's holding all the cards. I need a joker, bad. Put your best person on it."

"I'm my best person. This one is personal. Me for you. I'll do all the work. What else?"

"An asset search. That's all I know for now. You know how these things change."

"No problem. Get the records over to us and we'll get right on it."

Blake looked up and saw Crystal across the room. She pointed at herself, then at the maitre d'. Blake rolled his eyes and waved her over. Lou Carlson read the menu.

CHAPTER THIRTY-SIX

Don Blake spent the next day reading the background on the Tully case. Lou Carlson sent him the file that Gilbert Stuart had, including the interrogatories, requests for documents and replies. The financial papers were being analyzed by Sid Bowman, a CPA with Trenchcoat Fever, who'd become a private investigator specializing in white-collar crime, corporate fraud, and embezzlement. Blake had finished reading the file by the time he picked up Tom Tully leaving training camp. From six until nine Tully chased skirts at the Fifth Down, a nearby bar. The only common feature Blake could discern was that they all had a pulse. The bartender shook his head every once in a while when Tully made a particularly crude pass. He approached women with all the subtlety of punt coverage.

Blake followed Tully home and called for Crys Cassidy to relieve him. When she arrived he returned to the bar, where he nursed a few beers until closing. The place was just about empty when he motioned to the bartender with his empty glass. He came down and prepared to draw him one for the road.

"No, that's okay. I've had plenty. I want to ask you a question."

The bartender took a step back and sized up the gray-haired man. Not a football player he knew although he was built for it. Too old though, maybe a coach or a scout for another team.

"Yeah, what about?" He kept wiping a glass.

"The guy here earlier, the one chasing all the women. . . ."

"Coach Tully."

"That's right. Tom Tully. I've got some questions need answering and I'm willing to pay for information."

"How much?" He stepped closer.

"Depends on the quality of the information."

"What do you want to know?"

"He pursues sideline to sideline. Does he ever catch anything?"

"And if he does?" He smiled at Blake, like a cat with a tiny tail dangling between its teeth.

"Fifty dollars for the name."

"A hundred."

"A hundred. That's what I meant to say."

"You want a complete list? You better check how deep your pockets are."

"Tell me more."

"Fifty for the game plan, a hundred a name for the players."

Blake opened his wallet. If he spread some money around now, maybe he'd keep the overall cost of this excursion into honor to a minimum. A fifty slid across the bar and into the barkeeper's own deep pockets.

"Tom Tully's an old story. When he played, he was one of the founders of the Fifth Down Club. They'd drink, get rowdy, pick up the groupies, party until we close, then take the party on the road. Same thing every weekend, from the time they got home from training camp until the season ended."

"How many guys are we talking about?"

"Right now? Six, maybe eight. There's McNeil and Broadus, the tackles, a matched pair of idiots. Weems, the linebacker. Fenster, Loomis, the fullback, and Petrillo, the defensive end. Yep, that's it. The Fifth Down Club. Tully was always welcome as a charter member even if he was a coach.

"These guys would come in during the week, too, by themselves. They didn't 'huddle-up,' as they'd call it, until the weekends."

"Tully come in during the week?"

"Sometimes. He'd say he'd been working on things over at the park and come over here late."

"Alone?"

"When he came in? Yes. When he left, sometimes."

"Are we getting ready to name names here?"

"Almost. Tully was different from the others. Plenty of girls here were star-fucking. But Tully wasn't a name to brag about. He had to sweeten the pot. Word was he was a very generous man. He'd chase, some girl would run until he knocked her down with his wallet. Then they'd stay down until they got bored, or the money dried up."

"How many young ladies fit that description?"

The barkeep laughed, "In this place, every one of them. It's worse here than any other bar I've ever worked. In here, the guys really are studs, and the girls are stud-hunters. The competition is brutal. Younger, faster, hotter, that's the motto. People change partners so fast your sweat doesn't dry before someone else is dripping into your tracks. The players here know the score."

Blake pulled his wallet out again, took a hundred out and set it on the bar.

"I'm interested in women who had a substantial history with Tully. Not missed tackles, not one-night stands. If there's a current one, that's the name I want most. If not, I'll take the most recent ones you can recall."

Blake slid the hundred over. The bartender released the names as his fingers walked across the bill.

"Nobody this season. Last year it was Tiffany Ames. Before her it was Brenda Sturgis, but she moved back to West Virginia, if you can believe that. Before that's before my time. Sorry."

"This Ames woman. She still around?"

"Oh, yeah. Tiff's a regular. She'll be here tomorrow night."

"What's she like?"

Paul shook his head. A hundred-dollar bill cured his palsy.

"Dolly Parton look-alike. She doesn't have a chest, it's a mountain range. Petite, everywhere else. Frosted blonde hair. All little ringlets and curls. A helium voice. I guess she can't get a full breath with those things out front. You can't miss her. She's on the all-spandex team."

"Thanks. You've been a lot of help." Blake slid off his stool and headed for the door.

CHAPTER THIRTY-SEVEN

"Dr. Reece? Lou Carlson and Albert Garfield here. We'd like to have a conference call with you. Can we do it now?"

Morgan Reece looked at his schedule. "How long?"

"I don't know. Shouldn't be very long. We want to schedule a hearing and need some information about your availability."

"Okay. Let's do it now."

"Good. I am now the attorney for Serena Tully. I've put a motion before Judge Hallowell to have a review of the *ex parte* order excluding Ms. Tully from the marital residence. That order was granted on an allegation that Ms. Tully was a danger to herself and the children. If she's not, then there's no reason to bar her from the residence. Have you gotten far enough in your evaluation to testify about that question?"

Reece thought about what he had left to do and whether he had formed an opinion on that issue. "Yes, I think so."

"When could you be in court? Either Judge Hallowell or Judge Kenniston will hear this."

"Not today, obviously. Tomorrow I'm in deposition with Joe Anthony and Travis Pruitt. The day after is okay."

"Fine. We'll try to confirm that with one of the judges and leave a message if it's on."

"Doctor Reece, Albert Garfield here. Please bring your entire case file to the hearing."

"Send me a subpoena, please. I'd like that in hand before court."

"I don't know if I can get service on such short notice. I'd rather not have my client pay for a private process server if it isn't necessary. How about if I serve you at the court house?"

"That's fine."

"Dr. Reece, one more thing." It was Lou Carlson, "I'm sending you a transcript of yesterday's hearing. There's information I think you should have before you testify. Mrs. Tully was assaulted by a man who threatened to kill her if she didn't settle with her husband . . ."

"That's an outrageous lie and I won't stand for your contamination of this witness, Carlson," Garfield growled.

"Dr. Reece, Mrs. Tully filed a police report making such a claim. If after you've read the transcript you want to talk with her, please call me for her new phone number. Mr. Garfield's position is obvious from his cross-examination. I'd like you to be able to comment on this incident."

"By all means, Dr. Reece, read the entire transcript, especially the section where I ask Mrs. Tully about her infidelity. I think that behavior is relevant to the children's best interests."

"Dr. Reece, I'm sure you're aware of Brown. Adultery is not synonymous with unfitness," Carlson countered.

"I'm aware of that. There are all kinds of adultery."

"Exactly, Doctor." Garfield was back on. "I'm sure you'll find Mr. Carlson's clumsy effort to advise his client to take the Fifth Amendment very interesting. What does she have to hide? What kind of man has she taken up with? Is it a man? Maybe she's a lesbian. I'm sure you're aware of the Bottoms case. These matters require that you investigate. If she refuses to answer your questions, I think that's very important, Dr. Reece. She's putting that relationship before your pursuit of the children's best interests. That speaks loudly to me, Dr. Reece, and will to a judge and you know it."

Carlson came back again. The conversation was like a dog race. Each animal straining to get its nose ahead, barking once or twice, then falling behind and struggling to catch up.

"To correct Mr. Garfield's hyperbolic distortions, my client has not taken the Fifth Amendment. Nor did I advise her to do so. I mentioned it to the judge as part of an objection to Mr. Garfield's questions. I will reiterate my point here for you, Doctor. Adultery is a crime in Virginia. An individual is entitled to the protection of the Fifth Amendment. In addition you may not draw the adverse inference from the use of the Fifth Amendment. You cannot conclude that she has anything to hide or that she has done anything wrong."

"Like hell, you can't." Garfield shouted. "That's a ruling directed to the judge or a jury, not an evaluator. I don't give a good goddamn who she's sleeping with, but if she is not completely candid with you in this evaluation, I bloody well want to know that. So will the judge. If you don't pursue this matter as vigorously as you do any other in this case, I'll move to have you replaced, Reece. Do you understand me?"

Morgan Reece tried to fix the face of Tommy or Tina Tully in his mind as an antidote to the venom he felt soaked in.

"Is there anything else I can do for you gentlemen? If not, it's been a real pleasure talking with you. I look forward to seeing you soon."

CHAPTER THIRTY-EIGHT

Morgan Reece stared at the phone. What did he want to say? Did he really want to learn to climb rocks? Conquer his fear of heights? Maybe just injure it a little, he thought. He knew that he always felt better after he challenged himself, more alive than before. That was the key. He wanted to feel more alive than he did now.

What could go wrong, anyway? He calls, gets a name. If he changes his mind, he doesn't have to show up. This is foolproof.

This is pathetic, he concluded. She hangs from a cliff by her fingers and you can't pick up a telephone. Maybe that was what was attractive about her. She seemed brave, braver than he was. More alive, less afraid. Sounds like a lite beer commercial, Reece thought, and picked up the phone.

"Rocky Mountain High. Lindsay Brinkman speaking."

"Yes, this is Dr. Reece, uh Morgan Reece."

"Hi, how are you?"

"Um, fine, thanks. I was just thinking that I'd take you up on that idea about learning to climb. You know, get over my fear of heights."

"That's great. What about this Sunday? There are some novice classes out at Great Falls on the Virginia side. Very easy climbs, 5.0's, you can almost walk up them."

"Okay. Where do I go?"

"Just drive to the park, go to the climbers' lot; the instructors meet everyone and take it from there."

"What time?"

"Early. By eight a.m. The rocks get pretty crowded after that."

"How much does this cost?"

"Introductory climb is thirty-five dollars."

"Do I need to bring anything?"

"Bug repellent, sunscreen, sunglasses, lunch. Wear shorts. The instructors will provide the rest. Good shoes make a world of difference. You should stop by the shop and rent some climbing shoes."

"Okay. Maybe I'll stop by tonight."

"Great. It's gonna be fun."

Reece hung up. Like he thought. Foolproof.

CHAPTER THIRTY-NINE

The Fifth Down was packed when the grey haired man came in, pulled off his gloves and surveyed the scene. Against the far left wall, speakers the size of Fijian totems hammered the eardrums of the young and the buffed.

The bar was as crowded as a Metro platform at rush hour. The bartender he had talked to was at one end pouring out some sticky, blended drink for a pinheaded monster he recognized as Leon Broadus, one of the Fifth Down Club. Broadus handed the drink to a brunette he could have used as a swizzle stick.

Two other bartenders were also on duty, moving up and down the length of the polished hardwood surface, keeping everyone's glasses full. Waitresses wedged their way in and out behind the shields of their trays. A huge TV set suspended from the ceiling was showing highlights on ESPN. Stools and small round tables sprang up from the floor like mushrooms. Most of them were occupied by men and women, laughing, talking and eating. Off to the left of the TV screen was a platform set up for arm wrestling matches.

Don Blake found an empty stool at an out-of-the-way table, unzipped his jacket and waved to a waitress. While she swam upstream, he looked at the menu.

"Can I help you?" she chirped.

Blake looked up. The waitress was dressed like a man from the waist up. White shirt, cufflinks, black bow tie. All softened by the stray wisp of hair that escaped being pinned up. From the waist down she was unquestionably female. Short black skirt, patterned stockings and ankle boots.

"Yeah, a mug of whatever's on tap, a plate of buffalo wings and plenty of napkins."

"Sure thing." She spun away and headed for the window to the kitchen.

Blake nursed his beer and wings and watched the crowd for Tiffany Ames. An hour later she came into the bar. The bartender had described her perfectly. Her tiny face was hidden in a mass of frosted curls. About five feet tall, jeans tucked into cowboy boots and a short white fur coat. When she took off the jacket, the whole room watched and breathed, part gasp, part sigh, as she stood there in defiance of gravity and proportion.

Blake watched her flit around the room, looking to see if there was anything new and exciting. He made sure that he appeared bored and that their eyes did not meet. Twenty minutes after she arrived, two other women struck up a conversation that interested her.

"That's him. I'm sure of it," the taller one said to her friend.

"No. Really?" her friend asked before downing half of her alcohol-free drink.

"Yes, it is. I remember seeing photos of him when he played in New York. That's 'Crash' Carmichael. He was their middle linebacker when they won all those championships. Hall of Fame, everything."

The little blonde followed the tall woman's eyes across the room to where Don Blake sat. He looks like on owl, she thought, no, maybe an eagle. The grey hair swept out and back from his widow's peak. Large intense eyes that never seemed to blink. A sharp hooked nose. His eyes scanned the room. His head turned slowly but the barrel chest never moved. She could feel the power inside him. Perched on a limb, ready to strike. Tiffany sought his eyes with hers and followed with a smile.

As he walked over towards her, she heard the tall woman whisper to her friend, "Here he comes; what should I say to him?"

Tiffany positioned herself in front of the other two, pointed her chest at Blake and cooed. "I know you. You're Crash Carmichael, the linebacker. I'm a big fan of yours."

Blake smiled graciously, eyed her with mock delight and said, "And I'm a big fan of yours, little lady. Can I buy you a drink?"

The other women skulked away and left the bar a half hour later. In their car they waited to see if Tom Tully would show up.

The shorter woman, Rachel Pincus, looked at her friend and colleague. "So what do you think? You worried at all?"

"No," Crystal Cassidy said. "He likes his women tall. But I know what perfume she wears. Eve's Secret. I can't stand it. You smell like fruit cocktail. If I ever smell that on him, I'll cut off his 'you know what.' "

Tom Tully did not arrive before "Crash" Carmichael and Tiffany Ames left in separate cars to rendezvous at her apartment.

"What do you think he'll do?" Rachel asked.

"He's a professional. Whatever it takes," Crys answered glumly as she turned the Porsche over and followed them out of the lot.

CHAPTER FORTY

Tiffany lived on the second floor of a garden apartment complex ringing an office park visible from the Dulles Access Road. Blake parked his Z3 next to Tiffany's Audi TT. He opened the door and stepped into an arm lock from Tiffany, who smiled adoringly into his Hall-of-Fame face. His cover story worked better than he'd hoped. He just wanted to attract her attention and create the possibility of a date. The office would do a background check on her while he felt her out for information about Tully. Instead he was walking across the grass in the moonlight with her holding his arm tighter than a cast.

Sometimes investigation was methodical, well planned and carefully executed. Sometimes it was all improvisation, riffs and solos. Jazz detection.

Tiffany let them into the apartment, put her bag down on the sofa table in the hallway, turned and held her finger up to her lips.

"What's the matter?"

She pointed down the hall to a closed door.

"You got a kid?"

"Yeah, he's a real sweetheart. You'd love him. Don't want to wake him though. Then I'd have to explain who you were. We can do that in the morning."

Tiffany leaned up and kissed him lightly and bounced away to shuck her fur jacket.

"Gimme your coat. I'll hang it up."

Blake pulled off his gloves, stuffed them in the chest pocket, and unzipped his jacket. The living room was all high tech and ultra modern. White leather seating faced an electric fireplace. Spindly halogen lamps that looked like Giacometti's men wearing helmets provided the lighting.

"The den's over there. How about I get two drinks? What would you like?"

"Irish Whiskey, if you got it."

"Is that Jameson's or is that a Scotch?"

"Jameson's is fine. Straight up."

"Okay make yourself comfortable. I'll be right in."

Blake watched her disappear into the darkened dining room. She turned right and light poured out from the kitchen. The dining room table was a glacier of frosted glass sitting on a pair of stalactite legs. Blake felt anxiously awkward around furniture like that. How did the kid feel, he wondered.

The den was an electronic temple. The altar was a huge television bracketed by cabinets of stacked tuners, receivers, pre-amps, CD and DVD players, striated like a cross-section of the sediment layers of technology in this century. Huge speakers were the end pieces.

The wall to the right was covered in collages. Selected highlights from Tiffany's life. Blake searched for the child. He found him in the arms of one man as a toddler, then with another, and finally a third. The most recent picture was a school photo with the mandatory faux marble backdrop and cringe-smile.

Blake sank into the loveseat and waited for Tiffany to return. She came in, wearing her blouse and blue jeans but now barefoot. Tiffany handed Blake his drink and as he tipped it back, she climbed astride his lap and began to undo the buttons of his shirt. Blake looked for a place to put his drink as Tiffany enclosed him in a frosted blonde canopy while they kissed. Eager to show off her perfect breasts, Tiffany began to unbutton her blouse.

Blake wondered when to put an end to this and decided to wait until she was partially naked. That would leave her feeling more vulnerable and easier to manipulate. At least that was the reason he gave himself.

Tiffany unhooked her brassiere and presented herself to him. Blake tried to speak, but failed. He raised his gaze and found his voice.

"Tiffany, we've got to talk."

"Later, right now I'm gonna leave you speechless."

She lifted her hips and began to wriggle out of her jeans.

Blake turned to roll out from under her and wound up on his hands and knees with Tiffany, arms and legs locked hanging from him like a tree sloth.

"Now. We gotta talk now. Enough's enough." The edge in his voice cut right through the dreams and the deceit. Tiffany let go and fell back on the sofa.

"The kid. How old is he?"

Tiffany relaxed. That was sweet. He was worried about Alex waking up and seeing them in action. "Don't worry. I'll lock the door."

"No. How old is he?"

"He's eight. Why?" Tiffany tried to scoot away by pulling her legs up.

"Why? Why? You were out in that bar for two hours with me. We come back. There's no sitter here. The kid's by himself. First time we meet, you bring me right into the house. Ten minutes later I got your tits in my face. The door ain't locked. I know I'm not the first. You didn't hesitate for one second once you decided we were gonna spend the night."

"Who are you? Did Roland send you? That son of a

bitch. Well he can't have Alex."

"Lady, your ex is the least of your worries. I'm not gonna call Roland. I'm calling the county. They'll have somebody out here in a heartbeat. With what I tell them, Alex will wake up in foster care."

"You bastard. I'll tell them you followed me home, wouldn't take no for an answer, forced your way in and tried to rape me."

With that, she tried to rip her blouse. Blake reached over, grabbed one hand and began to press her knuckles together. The pain shot up her arm.

"Don't make this any worse. My partners are right outside. They followed us here. They took pictures of us coming in. They've got cameras on us, right now, through that window there. And microphones that'll pick up sound right through the glass. It'll never fly. I'm not interested in taking Alex away from you. I will if that's what it takes to get you to help. I don't care who gets him, Roland or the county. It don't make me no never-mind. You help me and I'm out of your life. You don't, and I smell a shit-storm coming. A big one. What's it gonna be?"

Placating him would be the straight-line answer. And Tiffany was a straight line kind of girl.

"Okay, what do you want?"

"I want Tom Tully. Tell me everything you know about him."

"I tell you what you want to know and you won't report this to anyone?"

"That's the deal."

"Promise."

"Yeah, I promise."

She holstered her breasts, and began to button her blouse. Blake reached into his pants pocket, pulled out a microcassette recorder and set it in front of her.

"Who are you?"

"You've got this all wrong, Tiffany. I ask the questions, you answer them."

"Are you a cop? I want to see some identification."

"No. I'm not a cop. That doesn't help you any, though. Tell me about Tom Tully."

Tom was fun, but this was trouble. Avoid trouble was the prime directive. Tom was replaceable. "What do you want to know?"

"Everything. Start at the beginning."

"I met him at the Fifth Down. I don't know, about a year ago. No longer, cause they hadn't gone to training camp yet. He'd been seeing another girl then, Brenda Sturgis, off and on.

"We hit it off right away." Tiffany stopped. "Your name isn't 'Crash' Carmichael, is it?" Tiffany shook her head in anticipation of the answer.

"No."

"You aren't even a football player, are you?"

"Nope."

"Oh, God." Tiffany looked away, as if sex with a non-player was the worst of perversions.

"So you hit it off. What does that mean?"

"Christ, you're thick. We had a good time together. We liked to party."

"Did you know he was married?"

"So what? If she'd done a better job, he wouldn't have been out with the Fifth Down Club. He said she was such a nag. He used to call her a cling-on. Get it, like Star Trek, Klingon."

"I get it. How long did you two stay together?"

"Most of the season. He decided to cool it in the off-season. Something was up with the wife. He was watching her. I don't know maybe she was finally getting wise to his late hours and 'scouting trips.' She must have had her head in the sand something fierce."

"What about 'scouting trips,' the late hours?"

"Tom'd tell her he was up at the park, watching films. He'd come over here instead and watch them with me. The guys in the Fifth Down always cover for each other. They'll call each other, get their stories straight. Nobody gets wise. Scouting trips, Jesus. The woman didn't even know that they've got scouts for that. Coaches don't do that. He'd tell her he was scouting some college guy. We'd go away together for a few days. Same thing with away games. He'd get me a ticket to the game and airline tickets. Tell the ball club they were for her. I'd fly out, go to the game, stay in the same hotel with the team. Lights out, I'd go up to Tom's room and spend the night. Pre-season I'd go up, Tom'd get me a room in town. After practice and meetings he'd come by. If they had a day off, we'd go out to Atlantic City. Tom loved to play cards, slots, you name it."

"He a winner or a loser?"

"Sometimes he'd win. Sometimes he'd lose. Nothing he couldn't cover. Tom was always a lot of fun. We'd go out to shows when we were out of town. He loved comedy clubs. We'd have dinner out, go dancing, order champagne on room service."

"What about drugs?"

"What about them? Not while that's on."

Blake cut off the tape. "Sure, there were drugs. The Fifth Down Club would get together and do plenty of blow. I don't know who bought it. It wasn't me. I never even did it. I just watched, that's all."

"What about Tom?"

"Yeah, he'd do some. Not as much as some of the others.

Christ, Broadus's girl went after it like a Hoover. That was her nickname, in fact."

Blake turned the recorder back on. "Who paid for all this fun?"

"Tom did. He was generous. That was one of his best features. He bought me that setup over there and the fur coat I was wearing tonight. He even gave me the down payment for my car. Tom was fun. I got to hang out, be a part of the team, get to do things and go places other people would kill for. I'd tell my friends about being at the game, partying with the team, meeting players from other teams. They'd be so jealous. I got autographs for Alex from every player we met and I brought back souvenirs from every place we ever went. See those pictures on the wall? That's Alex with Ox Henderson, down in the corner. And that's T. J. Hoskins with him over there."

"All right, this is how it's gonna go down." Blake turned off the tape. "I'm going to talk to my client about whether he'll need you to sign an affidavit about all this stuff and whether you'll be asked to testify. I don't know."

"But you're not gonna tell Roland or the county are you? You promised."

"No. I'm not going to tell them about tonight. And you're not going to tell Tully either. But I'm going to keep my eyes on you. If you ever leave the kid alone again, you'll wind up being a mother in name only. Do you understand me? No second chances."

Tiffany nodded her head silently.

"Don't get up. I'll let myself out." Blake went out through the living room and retrieved his jacket from the hall closet. Zipping it up, he heard a plaintive voice from behind a closed door. "Mom, Mom, is that you? Can I come out?"

Blake pulled the door behind him, hoping that she'd screw up and do it soon.

CHAPTER FORTY-ONE

Morgan Reece looked at the Rorschach results from Dr. Frazier. Tom Tully's was uninterpretable due to a low number of responses. What a surprise. Tully's defensiveness had rendered the results of all the psychological tests suspect. Dr. Frazier had noted that despite the low number there were two responses that were pathognomic, regardless of what number of responses were made. These were indications of pathological narcissism and were never seen in the "normal" population.

Serena Tully's tests were more amenable to interpretation. She was not "crazy" in that the schizophrenic indicators were not elevated. She was hypervigilant, though not formally paranoid, and clinically depressed. Her short-term suicide risk indicators were close to the cut-off score. Painful self-scrutiny was rampant and her coping skills were taxed to their limit. Emotions were actually fairly well controlled. However, she had not developed a successful problem-solving style, shuttling from trial and error to a feeling-dominated approach.

No news there, Reece thought, rubbing his eyes. The testing confirmed his own observations and gave him reason to trust them. He got up, went to the kitchen, poured himself another cup of coffee and returned to read the old hospital records that had arrived and Tepper's case notes. At ten-thirty he made a last effort to reach Tepper, who hadn't responded to any of his previous calls. This time he got through.

"Dr. Tepper, Dr. Reece here. Sorry to call you so late, but I've got an impending hearing regarding Serena Tully and I wanted to clarify some things that emerged after reading your notes. Could we talk now or schedule another time to do this?"

"If this isn't going to be too long, let's go ahead and do it now."

"Fine. I noticed a change in your notes a few months back. They became very terse, almost cryptic. Not much beyond her attendance. What prompted that?"

"Serena was convinced that her husband was thinking about a divorce. She was afraid that he'd use her mental health against her. As it turns out, he has from what she's told me. I began to keep more skeletal records so that they couldn't be turned into a weapon against her."

"Up to that time things looked pretty stable. Has there been any change in her functioning since then?"

"You mean this recent deterioration?"

"No. I know she's under quite a bit of stress. I mean before that. What of note isn't in the records? Any emergencies, crises?"

"No. Her functioning was really quite stable until her husband declared war on her."

"What was she working on in therapy?"

"She was trying to adjust her expectations of marriage, to get what she could from her husband and find appropriate avenues for getting other needs met. She'd made the decision, at least at this point, to stay together for the children's sake. She felt that a separation would have been very traumatic to both of them. She wanted to ease back into the workplace so that by the time the little girl was in school she could care for them on her own. She felt that money would be the biggest issue with her husband and if she could walk away without child support, alimony or property, he wouldn't contest custody. She turned out to be wrong about that."

"If she's had an affair, that changes the equation quite a bit. Tom Tully's a wounded, angry man. He doesn't want her to have anything. What do you know about this 'alleged' affair?"

"I'm sorry, Dr. Reece. I know we have a consent to exchange information but Mrs. Tully has explicitly directed me not to disclose anything about that, apparently on her attorney's advice."

"I understand. Did you make any changes to your treatment plan in the last few months? Did you consider medication for her?"

"No. I haven't made any changes in her treatment plan. We discussed medication, but she felt that would look bad in court so she's resisted it. I've recommended Prozac, but I haven't pushed it. If she really looks like she can't handle things, I'll be more assertive about that. Right now, it's a day-to-day decision."

"What diagnosis have you used for her?"

"Well, initially I used Mixed Personality Disorder on Axis II and Depression on Axis I. Then I . . ."

"Excuse me, what types did you see on Axis II?"

"There were elements of passive-dependent and histrionic. For a while I thought she might have been a borderline. I'm sure you've seen it, the idealization, the rapid intense attachment, then just as quickly the devaluation and rage. Well, Serena didn't show the latter phase. Her attachments are rapid and intense. She has a terrible fear of abandonment. The histrionic aspect is secondary, a mechanism for creating attachments. The socially approved pathology for many women. Sexy, helpless, accommodating. When needs aren't met and she's disappointed, she has that borderline rage, but she devalues herself and turns it against herself. I guess that's the difference I saw. In our work together we focused on her self-esteem, separating it from the man she was with, developing reasonable expectations from relationships and being more assertive about getting her needs met. I used a diagnosis of Adjustment Disorder with Mixed Features recently. I think she'd be doing much better if this divorce and custody battle hadn't come up."

"What can you recall her saying about the children and her relationship to them?"

"We really didn't focus terribly much on the children. I don't think she felt that they were central to the problems in her life. Mostly we focused on her relationships to men and to herself. I think she felt that she had a good relationship with the children. She was pretty secure in her identity as a mother. The problems were in her identity as a woman and a wife."

"Thank you, Doctor Tepper. I appreciate your help in this matter. It sounds like you've done good work with Mrs. Tully."

"Oh, she's done all the work. I've created the space for it to happen."

"Goodnight, Doctor," Reece said and returned to his preparations. No matter how many evaluations he had done, he approached each one with a good deal of anxiety. He strenuously resisted feeling complacent about his work, sure that it was a beacon for disaster. As a young boy he'd finally stood up to the neighborhood bully and surprised everyone by beating him in a fight. Standing over him he felt the leaden cloud of physical fear fall away. No sooner had he felt free and strong than his foe's older brother clubbed him from behind, drove him to his knees and together the two of them kicked him until a neighbor said she'd call the police.

His brief moment of victory was very hard to recall. But the shame he felt lying face down in his own blood and vomit was never far away.

Life had taught him that if happiness was a butterfly and hard to catch, pain was an anvil and hard to avoid.

He spent the last night before every evaluation lying in bed staring into the dark, sure that it was raining anvils.

CHAPTER FORTY-TWO

Don Blake waved to Crys and Rachel in the parking lot, and then led them back to the office. Rachel drove home. Crys developed her pictures in the darkroom. Don typed out an investigation report to Lou Carlson. When the printer spit out a copy, he went over the conclusions and recommendations.

(1) AVENUES FOR FURTHER INVESTIGATION:

(a) Tully's own adultery to put wife on even footing with the court.

(b) Track flow of money to pay for mistress. Search for hidden assets. Possible perjury for falsehoods under oath in interrogatories.

(c) Fraud in misuse of team benefits, e.g. tickets and hotel room for mistress, not wife.

(d) Drugs? Gambling? More information needed. Tip of the iceberg?

(2) SUGGESTED ACTION PLANS:

(a) Depose the Fifth Down Club. Pop this zit and see what comes oozing out.

(b) Interview bartenders and motel staff in area around club's facilities.

(c) Review last year's schedule. Check for airline tickets and hotel reservations.

(d) Get copy of club's reimbursement guidelines for spouses and others.

(e) Go to training camp. Circulate descriptions of Tully and Ames (very distinctive couple) in motels and bars in town.

(f) Repeat in Atlantic City. Especially comedy clubs.

(g) Cross-reference expenditures with Sid Bowman's reconstruction of income and disbursements.

(h) Pursue Tiffany Ames as information source while she's still vulnerable. If she moves the child out to family, she'll seal over.

Blake signed the report and flipped to the fax number that Lou Carlson had given him. It was the same as the home number. A bad sign. No place to get away from work. That's what Blake's wife said killed their marriage. He'd get out of bed to answer the phone but he wouldn't put the phone down to get into bed. She was right. This time he'd found a girl who'd race him to the phone. Maybe that was an improvement. He fed the report into the tray, dialed the number and waited for a connection. He listened to the paper feed, wondering what he was interrupting on the other end.

Crys came in as the paper began to feed through the fax. She sat on the end of the desk and handed the photos to Don. He flipped them around and scanned them.

"Good. Go ahead and put them in the file." He handed them back to her.

She looked at him, then raised her eyebrows and said, "And? That's it? There's nothing else you want to tell me?"

Blake laughed. "No, Crys, there's nothing else to tell you. Here's my report. I think it covers everything. Read it."

She took it from the paper tray and skimmed it.

"That's polite. Subject was in a state of partial undress. The presence of her child in the next room was no deterrent.

Investigator used this opportunity to break cover and confront subject."

"What do you want to know, Crys?"

"You know what I want to know."

"This is crazy. Nothing happened. You want to know if I would have slept with her, right?"

Crys nodded, grateful that he hadn't forced her to ask. Now if he'd only give her the right answer.

"All right. If I'd had to and there was no way out, yes, I would have. Would I have enjoyed it? To the best of my ability. Would I seek her out on my own? Not on a bet. You do what you have to do to get the job done. I looked for a way out and found one. I owe Lou Carlson a big favor. I'm paying it off. If sleeping with Tiffany Ames would get me out from under sooner, then I'd do it. Okay, can we let this one go?"

Crys had listened to Don's answer without drawing a breath. He had told her that ugly truths were better than pretty lies, and that she could count on him for ugly truths. This time he was as good as his word.

CHAPTER FORTY-THREE

Lou Carlson and Serena Tully met with Don Blake in the courthouse cafeteria. After making introductions, they sipped coffee while Blake expanded on his written report.

"I don't know how to bring this up tactfully, Ms. Tully, but your husband seems to have had a number of extramarital affairs."

Blake stopped and waited to see what her reaction was going to be.

She turned to look at Lou Carlson. When she smiled wistfully, he replied, "That's good news, Don. Get them off the moral high ground. I don't think Ms. Tully is going to be surprised by anything you tell her. You may as well give it to her all at once."

"Okay. Your husband seems to have been part of a group called the Fifth Down Club. In that group, the chief activities were partying with football groupies, drinking and drugs. Seems that when he said he was out at the clubhouse watching films, or in the hotel before and after games, he was really out with these guys. The women he took up with were part of this crowd. I guess he'd pair off with one until the relationship would run its course and she'd be replaced. We've identified the most recent one."

Serena was twisting her wedding ring, which she realized she hadn't taken off yet. "This woman, what does she look like?"

Blake drummed his fingers on the manila envelope of photographs. "Are you sure you want to know? I don't think it's going to do anyone any good to go over the gory details."

Serena snapped at him, "Are those pictures of her in there? May I see them? I presume you both know what she looks like. I'd like to see for myself. May I?"

She held her hand out. Blake pushed the packet over to her. She undid the catch with trembling fingers. Blake noticed and suggested she might want to take them to the bathroom.

"No, Mr. Blake, I'll be fine. May as well see what Tom's been up to with his free time."

She pulled the photos out and stared at the blow-ups of Tiffany Ames. "She's cute in a Barbie doll kind of way." Serena studied the photographs. Abruptly, she slid them back into the envelope. "Too much make-up though," she said and left the photos in front of her.

"Your husband was taking this woman to away games. He was seeing her at training camp. He was buying her expensive gifts."

Serena checked to make sure her hands weren't giving her away. Assured that she looked composed, she smiled at Don Blake, who went on sure that she was anything but.

"I think we have to lean on the Ames woman. Get her to sign an affidavit now. A lot easier and faster than building a paper case, Lou."

"I agree. Do you think she'll pull the kid out of school?"

"Yeah. If she calms down and thinks it through. She'll figure that after some period of time our interest in Tully will pass and so will her usefulness. She'll retrieve the kid and go on like nothing happened. She's scared now."

"Is she afraid of you, Don?"

"Probably. When she isn't pissed."

212

"Why don't you go shake her up again? Let's get her to commit to an affidavit. In the meantime, we should pursue all these avenues in case she stonewalls us or flees. All your ideas are good ones. Go with them."

"Excuse me," Serena cut in. "I've seen that list. This has to be expensive. I don't have any money, Mr. Blake. I don't know how or when I could pay you for all this. Mr. Carlson is hoping to get his fee from my share of the house. I appreciate everything you've done so far, but I'll be left with nothing."

"Don't worry about it. I'm not going to send you a bill for my services. This is an old favor owed by me to Lou Carlson. Now, I'm squaring things."

"Thank you, Mr. Blake. Seems I'm the lucky one, at least on this."

"I want to keep this quiet for now, Don. I don't want Tom Tully or Al Garfield to have the slightest idea we're on to him. Let Sid Bowman prove there's hidden assets first. Then we'll go after him with the adultery, perjury on the interrogatories, maybe even fraud with the club. When we have it all in place, then I want to push this wall over on them. When the time is right."

"Mrs. Tully, did your husband ever buy things for you or the kids, the house, anything, with money you couldn't account for?"

"That's a laugh. Tommy bitched about how little he made as a coach. When he played, he wasn't a big star. And he wasn't into saving money. We got married after he retired and he had to work. He hadn't held on to any of the money he made as a player. No, there wasn't any unaccounted-for money flying around our house. What Tom made, we spent. The only nice gift Tom got me was a very expensive watch, which I just had to sell. But he always made a big deal about what a great price he got on it. How he didn't pay close to what it was worth."

"Well if anything comes . . ."

"Wait a minute. There was something odd. When we first met Dr. Reece and Tom had to pay him for the evaluation, you know the retainer, he handed him an envelope with the whole thing in cash. All eight thousand dollars. I was curious about why he went back into the office to pay him, so when they went into the testing room I pushed the office door open and peeked in. I saw the stack on his desk."

"Really," Carlson said, tapping his finger against his nose as he pondered the meaning of an envelope full of cash.

Don Blake asked, "Did he say where he got the money from?"

"No. He told me it was none of my business. Tom told me that all the time about money. He made it; he could do what he wanted with it."

"Anything else, Lou? If not, I'll be on my way. We'll see what Sid turns up."

"That's fine, Don. Listen, I really appreciate what you've done."

The two men stood and shook hands. As Blake walked away, Carlson looked past him to the entrance.

"One second though, Don. Why don't you stay around for a while?"

Standing in the doorway was Al Garfield, his coattails swept back, thumbs hooked behind his belt. Tom Tully was staring malevolently at them and before him, held in place by his shoulders, was his son, who, seeing his mother, threw his eyes to the floor.

CHAPTER FORTY-FOUR

Morgan Reece woke and spent two hours searching for his blindside in this case. He approached each piece of data from every perspective he could imagine. He battled these spectral foes and his own doubts until he was convinced that his blindside was just that, and no amount of searching was going to make it otherwise.

He heated an artichoke and mushroom focaccia from Cenan's Bakery and ate it with his first cup of coffee. He showered and had a second cup as he put on his uniform. A navy blue suit, plain white shirt and subdued blue tie with red dots. The Commonwealth was conservative and expected its experts to be the same. Over his third cup he reviewed the record one last time. Reece preferred to work without a net, not bringing his files to court unless subpoenaed. That forced the attorney to deal with him, not his jottings and speculations that can take the case off target and into nooks and crannies that fit the attorney's agenda. A photographic memory made this approach possible.

At nine-thirty he walked into the judicial center, checked with the docket clerk for the courtroom assignment, rode the elevator up to the fifth floor and looked for Lou Carlson and Al Garfield. He walked down the hall towards the courtroom, and exchanged greetings with other attorneys he knew until he was outside Courtroom 5A. He peered in and saw Tom Tully and his son in one witness room. Across the corridor, staring sadly at her son, was Serena Tully. The two attorneys were arguing in the courtroom. Reece entered and saw a burly, grey haired man sitting in one corner, his arm stretched across the back of the witness bench.

"Good morning, gentlemen."

"Not for long." Garfield snapped.

"I see."

"I don't think so, Doctor." Garfield said, and cut between Carlson and Reece towards the door and his client.

Reece and Carlson shook hands. "Hello, Lou. Sorry to see you under these circumstances. I thought these days were behind you."

"So did I. So did I. I saw the bruises on that woman's throat and next thing I knew I was in Hallowell's courtroom turning back the clock. It was like coming upon an auto wreck. Somebody's got to do something. You're there, you do it."

"How's Lori taking it?"

"Not too bad. I had good facts to work with. Plus she despises Al Garfield. Always has. He being on the other side clinched it. I do have to turn over my license to practice to her once this is done."

"I remember how you looked in that courtroom, Lou. Your face was the color of your hair there." He pointed at his graying temples. "Your mouth was open, but you couldn't make a sound."

"I was in so much pain, I couldn't scream. I couldn't believe it took so long. I thought your heart just burst and you'd fall over dead. You know, instantaneously."

"Your eyes were completely rolled back in your head. You looked blind and insane until the medics got there."

"You know what the worst part about this is?" Carlson

asked, turning sideways to shield his next comment from invisible ears.

"I can guess."

"I love it. That's what scares me. I could do this all over again. I needed that heart attack to wake me up. Nothing less was going to get me to cut back. Even then I couldn't cut back. I had to quit. This is it for me. One and out. Then back to law school. Do what I can to keep the Albert Garfields out of this line of work." Carlson turned back.

"I'm going to ask you to go beyond the judge's question about dangerousness. I want to get her equal access to the children. Do you have an opinion on that?"

"Yes, but I'm the court's witness. You want to hear it, go get Garfield over here. I'll be glad to tell you both."

"What about letting the little boy testify? I don't know why Tully's got him here but I have to figure the worst."

"Lou, you know my position on that. If you want to hear it about this case, go get . . ."

"Albert. No thank you."

The big man in the corner got up to leave. He glanced briefly at the other two and pushed through the door.

"Who was that?" Reece asked.

"No idea." Carlson said. No need to give Reece information he couldn't protect.

"I thought he might be their expert, here to listen to my testimony."

"No. If they want to second opinion you, they'll go to Henry Pecorino. Why shop, when Henry always has the opinion you need."

"I'll wait outside until the bailiff calls me. Good seeing you again, Lou."

"Likewise, Morgan."

Reece went out into the hall and paced back and forth, his

mind empty, waiting for the questions to bring all of his experience to bear on the data he'd collected. It was too late to prepare any more. He knew what he knew. What he didn't would become abundantly clear in the next few hours. One last time he reminded himself that expertise was not omniscience.

The bailiff brought the parents into the courtroom. Tom Tully took his son with him. Not a good sign. Reece went back to pacing. The man from the courtroom was seated at the far end of the hall, intently reading a newspaper.

A few minutes later, little Tommy came back out. Reece went over to him.

"Good morning, Tommy."

"Hi."

"Can I sit here with you?"

"Uh-huh."

Reece sat and looked down at the boy. He was sitting on his hands and kicking his legs vigorously. "Day off from school, huh?"

"Yeah. Dad said he'd take me out to McDonald's after this is over." Tommy looked up, smiling at the thought.

"Do you know what this is?"

"Yeah, this is the court. The man on the high chair is the judge. He's the one who decides things."

"What's he going to decide today? Do you know?"

"Yeah, my dad said he's going to decide if my mom can come back to the house."

"That's right. Do you know why your dad wanted you to be here today?"

"So I could talk to the judge."

"I see."

Reece sat back and stared out the window across the top of the Fairfax skyline. Nearest were the colonies of law offices that surround the judicial center, then the original county courthouse, in use for almost two hundred years, and beyond that the commercial crossroads of the city that sprung up around the courthouse and the government center. In the distance, he could see the campus of George Mason University.

"Doctor Reece," Tommy asked, tugging at Reece's sleeve.

"Yes, Tommy."

"Do I have to talk to the judge?"

"Do you want to?"

"No. Not with my Mommy there."

"What if she wasn't there? Would you talk to the judge alone?"

"I won't be alone. That man said he'd be there to ask me questions."

"The man who is sitting with your dad?"

"Yeah. He said it was important for me to answer his questions."

"Do you know what his questions are?" Reece was skating perilously close to violating the rule forbidding witnesses to discuss their testimony.

"Yes. We talked in his office, before we came over here. He told me what to . . ."

"That's okay, Tommy. Suppose you were alone, all alone with the judge, would you talk to him then?"

"I don't want to," Tommy said, kicking out a foot. He tried to steady a trembling upper lip with his lower one, but couldn't.

"Dr. Reece, Judge Kenniston is ready for you."

Reece started and looked up at the bailiff in the doorway.

"I'll be right there."

He looked back at the little boy struggling to control his face and everything behind it.

"I don't know, Tommy. I'll see what I can do."

CHAPTER FORTY-FIVE

Morgan Reece settled into the witness box, adjusted the microphone and nodded towards Judge Kenniston.

"Good morning, Doctor. Do you understand the purpose of today's hearing?"

"Good morning, Your Honor. The purpose is to determine whether Serena Tully constitutes a danger to her husband or her children such as would warrant exclusion from the marital residence. This is a portion of the scope of the entire custody evaluation I am conducting."

"Are you prepared to address that question today? Have you proceeded far enough in your evaluation to reach a conclusion on this question?"

"Yes, I have, Your Honor."

"Dr. Reece is the court's own witness. As such he will present his testimony in response to questions from the bench. The parties' attorneys, Mr. Carlson and Mr. Garfield, will each have an opportunity to cross-examine the witness. Are there any questions before we begin?"

"Yes, Your Honor, I have some questions." Albert Garfield stood. "Though Dr. Reece is the court's expert witness, we are entitled to cross-examine him as to his qualifications, or to accept the proffer of his expertise and stipulate to his qualifications. I would like to know what types of opinions he's going to offer today and his qualification to render each of them."

Lou Carlson's antennae were quivering. Something was wrong here. Very wrong. Nobody challenges the qualifications of the court's chosen expert. Why would Garfield have let him be appointed if he had grounds to challenge? Had he learned something new in the course of evaluation? Why do this now? Why not wait for Reece's opinion, attack him on cross-examination? Al must know his client's story was a scam from the start. There was only one certainty. Al Garfield didn't posture, he didn't grandstand. He never pulled a trick he didn't think he had a decent chance of winning. And he did his homework. He was on to something; something he thought would carry the day.

Morgan Reece told himself to relax. You have no idea what Garfield's up to. You know his client hasn't got a case. Attacking the expert is the weakest form of cross. He's got to do something. This case isn't all that unusual. Relax, you always expect the worst, he reminded himself. Most of the time it didn't happen. When it did . . .

"Dr. Reece will be asked to reach a conclusion about Mrs. Tully's dangerousness. The foundation for that opinion being the data he's collected in his evaluation, interpreted through a combination of his experience and knowledge of his field. What part of this do you wish to challenge, Mr. Garfield? To explore these matters in any depth will require allowing Dr. Reece to testify at some length. Do you wish to make your objections to Dr. Reece through questions prior to a presentation of his foundation? How else are we to know the areas that he has ventured into and to assess his expertise in these areas?"

"I withdraw my objection, Your Honor. I believe they will be best saved for cross-examination."

Interesting move, Carlson thought. How much will it distract Reece, wondering what he's got up his sleeve? Will it

force him to hedge his bets, qualify his opinion until it's as en-
lightening as a sampler?

"You may begin, Dr. Reece. Please tell the court what
your data base is."

Reece recounted his interviews, the collateral records he
reviewed, the tests he administered or had done by his con-
sultants. Garfield and Carlson scribbled furiously. Reece
scanned the courtroom. The bailiff was obviously bored,
Tom Tully scowled at him and Serena was biting her lip and
had started to blink with anxiety. The court reporter's stac-
cato clicking was the only other sound in the room. Reece
caught Judge Kenniston's eyes for a second and went on to
finish laying his foundation.

"Dr. Reece, these information sources, are they typically
relied upon in the practice of custody evaluations?"

"Yes, Your Honor. Custody evaluations should always
use multiple methods of data collection. These are the funda-
mental methods used by evaluators. I have not yet done my
direct observations of the children with the parents, but everything else is completed."

"Is an assessment of violence or dangerousness a routine
part of a custody evaluation?"

"Not routinely, Your Honor. If the particular facts of the
case include allegations of spousal violence or child abuse,
then it is essential to evaluate those issues in a custody evaluation. It doesn't show up in every case, but where it does it
must be attended to."

"How long have you been doing custody evaluations, Dr.
Reece?"

"About fifteen years, Your Honor."

"The number of evaluations you've conducted?"

"Approximately two hundred custody evaluations. An
equal number of evaluations of abuse in the context of a cus-

tody or visitation dispute, and probably half that many case reviews of other evaluators' work."

"How many of these cases included the issue of spousal or domestic violence?"

"Allegations of such violence occur in the majority of these cases, probably sixty to seventy percent. Demonstrated or proven histories of spousal violence are actually rare. They are generally dispositive of the question of custody and as such aren't referred for evaluations."

"Have you formed an opinion in regards to the allegations that Serena Tully posed a danger to either her children or her husband, Thomas Tully, and if so, what is the foundation for your opinion?"

"I have formed an opinion, Your Honor." Reece began. Everyone in the courtroom leaned forward. All eyes were on Reece; the court reporter's fingers were poised over her transcriber. Carlson and Garfield both knew that the court's expert's opinion was the single biggest factor in predicting the court's ruling. This was the unveiling, the presentation of Morgan Reece's sculpture, his construction of the truth of this family. Who would be going for the jackhammer?

"My opinion is that Serena Tully is not a danger to either her children or her husband. Starting with the children, my opinion is based on the following: my direct observation of her interactions with them in my office. Granted her sudden absence is probably a factor in the degree of attachment I saw, they did not act at all like children afraid of their mother. In addition the report of Felicia Hurtado was consistent with this. Her observation over a number of months of the children with their mother did not include any reports of harsh discipline or fear. This woman is an employee of Mr. Tully's. If there is any likelihood of bias in her reporting it would be to favor Mr. Tully, her employer. Her green card application is contingent upon his sponsorship of her. The fact that her report goes against this pull is noteworthy. The children's psychological testing is also consistent with these reports. The mother figure is perceived as quite nurturing and supportive on both tests. The boy, Tommy or Junior, did not express any fear of his mother. In fact, the question itself struck him as very odd. The little girl, Tina, seems to be suffering a good deal from her mother's absence. She was not interviewed, but her play indicated a wish for her family to be intact, with the mother back in the house.

"The question with her husband is a little more complicated. Ms. Tully has no history of violent behavior directed at anyone but herself. In the course of the recent stresses two allegations have been made and one act of violence appears to have occurred. The allegation that led to the original exclusion order was that she 'threatened to do a Manassas,' or sever Mr. Tully's penis. This threat is alleged to have occurred in the context of an argument in the home. A fight was observed, or rather the end of an argument was observed by the housekeeper, Felicia Hurtado. She confirmed that Ms. Tully kicked her husband in the shins and threatened to scratch his eyes out. Later an altercation broke out at Tommy or Junior's elementary school. The report of both parties is consistent. Ms. Tully fled with the child. Mr. Tully pursued. He caught up with her, grabbed her by the hair, took the child from her and flung her to the ground. She got up and pursued Mr. Tully, now fleeing with the child. She attempted to regain the child. As part of her efforts she bit her husband. He retaliated, striking her with sufficient force to render her unconscious and produce a large contusion on the side of her face.

"Mr. Tully in fact was the first to resort to violence in this matter. Ms. Tully reciprocated and so did he. This points up the difficulty in assigning 'danger' to one of the parties in some of these domestic situations. What is occurring is a cycle of mutual provocation escalating until one or both cross over into violent behavior. Who crossed the threshold first may vary from situation to situation in these volatile pairings.

"The 'fight' that Felicia Hurtado witnessed was by Ms. Tully's report the end of a cycle in which Mr. Tully had restrained her against her will and provoked her by making offensive remarks about sex acts he wished to perform on her.

"My opinion is that an exclusion of Ms. Tully from the marital residence is unfair to her. She poses no more of a risk to Mr. Tully than he does to her.

"This is a very volatile pair. Subsequent to her exclusion, Ms. Tully was apparently assaulted by someone who said she would be killed if she didn't sign a settlement. Her belief is that this person was employed by her husband to intimidate her into relinquishing any claim to property or the children. I understand this matter is being investigated by the police.

"I believe Ms. Tully poses no threat to her children. Her ban from seeing the children has had an adverse impact on the children and should be lifted immediately. The exclusion from the marital residence is a more complicated matter.

"I think that if Ms. Tully's rights as a parent were abridged because of a concern over dangerousness to the children, they should be fully restored as I find no grounds for that concern. However, I think that putting Mr. and Ms. Tully together under one roof is unwise. To exclude Ms. Tully on the grounds that she is the dangerous or violent one is not accurate. This is a volatile pair. In fact, should her allegation about Mr. Tully prove true, then the evidence would tilt towards him as the more dangerous. Witnessing conflict and especially violent conflict between parents is indisputably harmful to children. Putting these two together is an invitation for that to happen. They should be kept apart, at least until I can finish my evaluation and the court can rule on the custody issue. That determination will have substantial financial consequences and may clarify the options for living arrangements for this family."

"How much more do you have to do in your evaluation?"

"The direct observation and home visit sequences. One of the requirements for this aspect of the evaluation is that the children spend an equal amount of time with each parent before I observe them so that what I see is not a function of stranger or reunion behavior or a transition effect."

"How do you accomplish that, Doctor?"

"Either equal time spent in two different houses or, when the parents haven't separated, equal time under one roof."

"But you think these parents should be separated."

"Yes, Your Honor."

"Do you have any other conclusions or recommendations for the court at this time, Doctor?"

"No, Your Honor."

"Thank you. You may cross-examine now, gentlemen. Mr. Garfield."

"Thank you, Your Honor." Garfield leaned forward at the lectern, adjusted the microphone and began. "Dr. Reece, are you a trained psychotherapist?"

"Yes."

"Do you recognize the concepts of transference and counter-transference?"

"Yes."

"Please tell the court what they mean."

"They refer to the 'transfer' of important elements of one relationship to another."

"Why do psychotherapists care about that?"

"Some schools of psychotherapy believe that it's these

transfers that are at the heart of dysfunctional relationships."

"I see. So if I had a rotten relationship with my father, I'll be prone to transfer that to my relationships with other older males, like the judge here, and have a rotten relationship."

"That's only one determinant of the actual relationship; the other person's transferences are also a part."

"That's counter-transference, right?"

"Counter-transference refers to the therapist bringing aspects of old relationships into a current one with a patient."

"I see. Now, is this restricted to psychotherapy relationships?"

"No. It can happen in any relationship."

"I see. Are therapists supposed to do anything about their transferences?"

"They're supposed to be aware of them and make efforts to ensure that they don't distort their relationship with the patient."

Carlson sat and listened as the questions began to collect like vultures circling lazily over a corpse. "Objection, Your Honor. I fail to see the relevance of this line of questioning about psychotherapeutic esoterica."

"Where are you going with this, Mr. Garfield?"

"This isn't esoterica. Dr. Reece has already said that it can come up in all kinds of relationships and that psychologists have to be on guard that it doesn't affect their work. That's the relevance."

"Objection overruled. Proceed."

"You've written extensively on the subject of custody evaluations, haven't you, Doctor."

"Yes."

"One of your positions is that the evaluator has to be objective, neutral and impartial. Isn't that correct?"

"Yes."

"So that your opinions don't reflect bias on your part, or are colored by your feelings."

"Correct."

"You said you've been doing these evaluations for fifteen years. Now, Doctor, I don't remember seeing you in court until the last few years. Where did you previously practice?"

"California."

"California. What brought you out here, Doctor?"

"I wanted a change of scenery."

"A change of scenery. Don't be coy, Doctor. You moved all the way across the country. What were you running from, Doctor?"

"Objection, Your Honor, this is argumentative and irrelevant."

"Sustained. Do not badger the witness, Mr. Garfield. Ask your questions, do not answer them also."

Garfield nodded to the judge. Carlson's heart was going like a boxer's in the late rounds. He poured himself a glass of water and took out a pill and downed it. What had Garfield discovered? Reece was a charlatan, an imposter? He'd lost his license? He was a sex offender, a pedophile?

Carlson waited for his pulse to leave his ears and thought some more. Nothing that glaring. There'd be no need for this roundabout foundation. It was more subtle. It might be repaired.

Garfield stepped around from the lectern and faced Reece. He swept his coat tails back and dug his fingers into his waistband, his trademark stance in court.

"Are you married, Dr. Reece?"

"No."

"Objection, Your Honor. We do not require defense attorneys to be felons also," Carlson snapped.

"Your Honor, I'm trying to make the issue of transference

relevant to this particular case. By exploring Dr. Reece's previous relationships."

"Overruled."

"Do you have any children, Dr. Reece?"

So it had come to this, Reece thought. His oath robbed him of any hiding place. His private scourgings were one thing. This was another. He knew when to stop, when he'd had enough. He was adrift. It was so warm here.

"Did you hear me, Dr. Reece? Do you have any children?"

"No."

"No? Didn't you have a child, Dr. Reece? A daughter. What was her name?"

It had been years since he had spoken her name. Tears clouded his eyes and the microphone seemed to be swaying in its stand.

"Danielle."

"Danielle. How old was she when she died?"

"Sixteen."

"Sixteen. And how did she die, Doctor? Remember, you are under oath."

"She committed suicide." Reece had never been able to say that she killed herself.

"Why was that, Doctor? You're a trained professional. I'm sure you must have some thoughts on her motivation."

Reece shielded his face from Garfield and answered the question. Judge Kenniston leaned over and said gently, "Doctor, you're going to have to speak up. We can't hear you."

Reece nodded and winced. "She had been arrested for shoplifting. The police wanted to teach her and her friends a lesson, so they locked them up in the adult detention cell. She was so ashamed that we'd find her there that way." Reece stopped. He'd lost his train of thought. The words wouldn't lie in a straight line so he could just repeat them until he got to the end. They kept flying away in all directions. "She asked to go to the bathroom. They didn't watch her very well. She found some bleach in a custodian's closet and drank it. She died two days later."

"Pretty extreme reaction, don't you think? But she was a troubled child wasn't she, Dr. Reece?"

Reece was lost in the ever-present past. He was at his daughter's bedside holding her hand, stroking it over and over. They couldn't talk. Her ruined throat wouldn't permit that. Nor could she eat. The bleach had burned holes in her esophagus and trachea. She was on a respirator that entered through the new mouth she had between her collarbones. Her skin was now grey. Even her famous red hair seemed dimmer. Reece put Vaseline on her blistered, raw lips and watched her die without ever regaining consciousness. Her death was their last conversation.

"Doctor, I asked you a question."

"Yes, I'm sorry. Could you repeat the question?"

"Your daughter was in therapy before her suicide, isn't that true?"

"Yes."

"What for, Doctor?"

"Objection, Your Honor. Dr. Reece's mental status is pretty far afield. His daughter's is entirely irrelevant to the matter before the court."

"I don't think so at all, Your Honor," Garfield interrupted. "We've entrusted the fate of this family to a man whose judgment I think is profoundly flawed. His own child was in treatment for depression. She killed herself rather than face her parents. What does that say about him as a father? Should we be letting him sit in judgment of other families? His wife left him . . ."

Kenniston slammed his gavel. "Enough Mr. Garfield. This is cross-examination, not summation. Dr. Reece does not sit in judgment of anyone. If you will notice, he's a witness. I am presiding over this matter. His job is to collect information and evaluate it according to his profession's tenets. If you cannot show a connection between this material and his judgment, and I mean promptly, I will disregard this entire line of questions as a fishing expedition and a barren one at that."

Garfield approached even closer to Reece. "Your daughter was in treatment for depression, correct?"

"Yes."

"After your daughter's suicide, your wife left you, isn't that also correct?"

"Yes."

"Why did your wife leave you, Doctor Reece?"

"She blamed me for Danielle's death. We never got over it . . ."

"It was more than that, wasn't it? The records of your divorce in California indicate that she believed you were depressed and suicidal yourself, Doctor. That she attempted to have you involuntarily committed to a psychiatric hospital for treatment. That you never received treatment for your depression. That your depression is what drove her away. Your inability to relate to her."

"Objection. There's no foundation, Your Honor."

Garfield reached into his briefcase and pulled out a file. "This is a copy of the entire case file of Reece v. Reece in San Diego County. I ask that it be entered as evidence in this matter pertaining to the emotional fitness of Dr. Reece to conduct an evaluation of anyone."

Garfield presented the case file to the judge.

Carlson stood up to object. "Your Honor, we have not had

any time to review these documents, to check that they are complete, unaltered."

"May I respond to Mr. Garfield's depiction of my divorce?"

"Mr. Carlson, do you have any objection?"

Lou Carlson had to protect his client. Reece had a haunted look that did not inspire confidence. Could he take a chance and let him try to rebut Garfield's indictment or was he going to decompensate right there on the stand and prove all of Garfield's points? Worst case, they'd be back to square one with a new evaluator. Maybe Reece could pull it together. He didn't have a bad feeling when he thought about saying no, and so he did.

"All right, Doctor."

"After our daughter died, we were devastated. Neither one of us could reach out to console the other one. We did things that drove each other away. Mr. Garfield is right about one thing. As a trained professional it's easy to believe that you have the tools to make you immune to the mistakes that other people make. And so, you're even harder on yourself than other people are when you turn out to be just like everyone else. Danielle paid a terrible price, one that her perfectionism demanded of her. I've come to accept that it wasn't all my fault. What exact part is my fault is a piece of knowledge that I'll never have. That I have any part of the responsibility is a stake in my heart every day.

"I get up every day and live with it, around it and in spite of it. I do my work with it, around it and in spite of it. My wife tried to have me committed. She was unsuccessful. I was not a danger to myself or anyone else. I was grieving for my daughter. Later, for myself. I was not able to grieve for my wife and her loss until it was too late. We both lost, twice.

"That was four years ago. Mr. Garfield thinks I may have a

transference relationship with Serena Tully. That her suicidal history reminds me of my own daughter. That I'll try to protect her like I couldn't protect my own child. Very perceptive of Mr. Garfield. I'm aware of that. I have been every step of the way. That's why I had the psychological testing done, interviewed her current therapist, the housekeeper, read the old therapy records. To get other perspectives. To make sure that no 'bias' was running uncorrected through my work.

"My work is transparent. My files are open for discovery, the foundation and reasoning for my judgments are clear in my reports. I am subject to deposition, cross-examination and rebuttal testimony. If my reasoning is flawed, for whatever reason, it will be obvious to the court. If Mr. Garfield disagrees with my judgment, he should demonstrate its weaknesses. You can allege the operation of bias in any case. I will be like each parent in some ways and different in others. How many different biases might be at work? Do they all point in one direction or do they cancel each other out? If bias is the explanation, you should see that I didn't pursue the parents' concerns equally, didn't weigh the same data equally. If you can't show that, then you're crying wolf in the courthouse."

CHAPTER FORTY-SIX

"Does either of you gentlemen intend to call any other witnesses?"

Carlson said no. Garfield stood and announced, "We would like to call Thomas Tully, Jr. as witness."

Kenniston looked up from his writing. "Approach the bench, gentlemen."

Looking down at them, Kenniston turned towards Garfield, "To what end would you put a six-year-old on the stand, Mr. Garfield?"

"To dispute Dr. Reece's testimony. He told his father that he didn't feel comfortable with Dr. Reece and so he didn't tell him how he really felt. He is afraid of his mother and has been showing symptoms of stress as the court date approached."

"He has? Really? How is it that he knew that a court date was approaching, Albert? How would he know that increased time with his mother was the issue?" Carlson snapped.

"Perhaps his father was discussing it with me on the phone and he overheard him."

"Your Honor, if you recall Doctor Reece's testimony, he had another psychologist administer and score those tests to the children, the results of which were consistent with the notion that they were not afraid of their mother. Mr. Tully's nanny, who has seen the children daily for three months, says they aren't afraid. Mr. Garfield did not dispute the evidence. He attacked Reece's personal life. Maybe he thinks we should put all those people on the stand to see if their lives have been free of any incident that might 'transfer' to the case at hand. Perhaps we should subpoena the people who made the tests, see what their life histories are? This transference stuff seems to cut two ways, Your Honor. Going through experiences like your patients do can deepen your understanding, your empathy for others, like nothing else. I don't think that Dr. Reece has given Serena Tully a whitewash here, nor did he rely on his perceptions alone."

"As for putting the child on the stand," Kenniston enunciated his next words clearly and slowly, "not while I'm on the bench. That was the point in having Dr. Reece do an evaluation. Barring extraordinary circumstances, six-year-olds will not be asked to testify in front of and about their parents. Are we clear on this matter, Mr. Garfield?"

Garfield nodded. Time to get Pecorino started on that shadow evaluation.

"Good, gentlemen. If you'll return to your clients. I'm ready to rule."

Kenniston folded his hands on the desktop in front of him and looked out at the couple and their attorneys. He wondered if there was anything worse than a ground-zero custody case. The preponderance standard made so much depend on so little.

"The court rules the temporary custody award to Mr. Tully be vacated. Mrs. Tully is restored to full rights as a custodial parent for the minor children, Thomas Drew Tully, Jr. and Tina Nicole Tully.

"The decision to freeze the couple's assets will remain in place. Mr. Tully shall pay spousal support to his wife according to the guidelines. I will rely on you gentlemen to do the calculations and have them filed with the clerk promptly.

"As for the exclusionary order, I will vacate that also. I am troubled by Dr. Reece's testimony as to the volatility of this couple. Having them both under the same roof does not seem to be in the best interests of the children. Considering Doctor Reece's comment on the need for equality of time for the evaluation and stability for the children, I rule as follows. The children shall remain in the marital residence. Mrs. Tully shall return to the residence and spend whatever percentage of time with the children Dr. Reece shall deem necessary to allow the evaluation to proceed to its conclusion. Mr. Tully shall not be in or near the premises while Mrs. Tully is there until the direct observation and home visit sequence with his wife has been completed. Then the situation will be reversed, with Mrs. Tully vacating the house until Mr. Tully's portion is completed. From that point until this matter is heard by the court, only one parent shall reside in the residence with the children at any time. The cost of the lodgings for the non-resident parent shall be factored into the spousal support award."

The attorneys sat waiting for Kenniston to continue. When he didn't, Carlson rose.

"Excuse me, Your Honor, do I understand your ruling to be joint legal and physical custody with the time share to be determined by Dr. Reece until his evaluation is complete?"

"You understand me correctly, Mr. Carlson."

"And that for the duration between the end of the evaluation and settlement or trial date, we are to work out a time-sharing arrangement and lodgings for our clients, provided only that they shall not both reside with the children at any time nor shall the children leave the marital home?"

"Retirement has not dulled you, Mr. Carlson."

Kenniston had put the burden on the two attorneys to try to settle the case as soon as Reece's work was done. Either both parents would shuttle back and forth from an apartment to stay with the children on an alternating basis, an expensive proposition, or custody and visitation would be negotiated and possession of the marital residence would flow from that. Considering that the first available trial date was a year away, his ruling created substantial motivation to settle the case.

Outside in the hall, the two attorneys spoke to their clients. Tom Tully scooped his son up in his arms, stormed past Serena Tully's outstretched arms and headed for the elevator. She turned and looked helplessly at Lou Carlson.

"Albert, what is your client doing with the child?" Carlson gave no sign that he saw the hawk-nosed man enter the elevator with Tully.

"The order said, and I quote, 'Mrs. Tully shall spend whatever percentage of time with the children as Doctor Reece shall deem necessary.' Dr. Reece hasn't deemed anything. Your client may be joint legal custodian but that doesn't give her exclusive use of the children. Mr. Tully was taking the boy back to school. I'm sure we can agree that's in the child's best interests. Away from this volatile couple, who shouldn't be under the same roof. That's what your expert said, isn't it?"

"Bailing out already, Albert? He isn't my expert. He is the court's choice. Let's go see Dr. Reece, right now. Get his recommendations on the time split. Kenniston wants us to settle this. That's what his ruling was all about. The sooner you and I get to the negotiating table, the sooner this family can get on with their lives, or what's left of them."

Reece, seeing them talking, walked over, forcing the issue. Garfield would have to actively avoid him. Not something Judge Kenniston would want to hear about.

"This seems like a good time to hear my recommendation about time-sharing," he began. "I would like Serena Tully back in the house immediately. I want her to be the primary caretaker of the children. If Mr. Tully wants to keep Ms. Hurtado during this time, that's fine; however, her involvement in child care will be determined by Ms. Tully. Ideally, Mr. Tully would vacate the premises for the next week or so and Ms. Tully could reside in the home."

"I don't see any reason for my client to vacate his home. She's already got an apartment to stay in. Let her go back there at night. In a week, that's where she'll be anyway."

Reece started to reply when Carlson cut him off. "I think that's okay. This is a very short-term situation. Once you're done, we have to find interim housing until we settle this or it goes to court. May as well keep the number of moves to a minimum."

"Okay, but I want Ms. Tully there at eight a.m. to get Tommy off to school and she stays until bedtime for the kids, say eight p.m. Then Mr. Tully can enter the house."

"How do we handle the switches? You can't leave the kids alone," Carlson asked.

"Maybe Ms. Hurtado will come first and leave last. That way the kids aren't alone but the parents won't meet in passing," Garfield offered.

"That's fine with me, if she's willing to."

"I'll have my client ask her today."

"I'll do my home visit in a week. Then the direct observation in my office. After the direct observations are complete, Ms. Tully will return directly to the residence and prepare to turn the children over to Mr. Tully. The access will reverse at that point, until I'm done with Mr. Tully. My report will be ready one week after I've completed the direct observations with Mr. Tully. Any questions? No. Fine. You'll hear from me when my work is done."

Reece nodded to Serena Tully as he passed and walked down the hall to the elevator.

Watching him walk away, Lou Carlson turned to Albert Garfield. "That was a new low today, even for you. You pulled that stunt just to try to see if you could rip his stitches. You knew it wasn't going to work. There was no point in doing it."

"You should go back to teaching, Lou. You've lost your taste for combat. This is no place for the squeamish. Your girl hasn't even begun to feel my heat."

"What's that supposed to mean? Another of your 'Mongol replies'?"

"Who knows?" Garfield said.

Carlson watched him saunter to the elevator, enter, turn crisply and shake his head ruefully, as if things were beyond his control, as the doors closed.

"But where are the Mongols now, Albert?" he said to himself. "It's still the thirteenth century in the land of the yak and the yurt."

CHAPTER FORTY-SEVEN

Don Blake followed Tully's Jeep Cherokee out of the court lot, left onto Route 123 and across Fairfax City to I-66. Tully sped up the eastbound ramp and took the interstate towards Washington. At the beltway he got off and headed north around the city. Blake followed Tully across the American Legion Bridge into Maryland, past the I-270 cutoff and up I-95 towards Baltimore.

Forty-five minutes later, he watched Tully's car roll slowly down an alley parallel to ' The Block.' Blake parked his car illegally, grabbed a video camera with a telephoto lens and sprinted to an observation point between two buildings. He ducked behind a fence as Tully got out of the car, then turned back to shout something angrily at the little boy.

Blake adjusted the focus and followed Tully to the back entrance of a building. Tully pushed a buzzer by the door. A metal slide moved back. Blake framed Tully at the door with the address number stenciled across it. The door opened and a huge man held it open for Tully. Blake shot them shaking hands, then Tully going into the building. As the door closed, he swung back to the car and the little boy's head.

Blake panned to the back of the Cadillac parked next to the door and made sure he got the license plates.

He pulled off his watch, set it in front of the camera and kept watching the door, the little boy and the minutes roll by.

★ ★ ★ ★ ★

Tully slid past Carmine and walked down the hall to Vinnie's office. He knocked on the door and was told to come in.

Vinnie was finishing off some Osso Bucco. He was hunting for the marrow with a tiny fork. When he found it, he pulled it out and then spread it on a slice of bread.

"The fuck's so important you gotta see me right away, huh?"

Tully looked at the chair and motioned to it.

"Yeah, sit down."

Carmine stood by the door and quietly closed it.

"I need some more money, Vinnie. For this court case I got. The bitch is gonna get support while this evaluation is going on."

"You ain't paid off what I already loaned you. We been holding back your money, but you ain't touched the vig."

"Hey, Vinnie, I'm good for it. How long have I been working for you? You haven't had any complaints. Haven't my tips been good? I've made plenty of money for you."

"That's true, Tom. That's why we're even having this talk. How much you need this time?"

"I don't know. Figure a couple of thou for the bitch, another five for the lawyer if we have to go back to court, five for the new evaluator."

"What new evaluator? I thought we were already paying for one?"

"That bastard. She's probably sucking his dick, too. He fucked me over in court today. My lawyer says we've got to get another evaluation done. A shadow evaluation that they don't know about, so that when this fucker's done, if he comes out for her we can neutralize him."

"Sounds like a good racket, this evaluation stuff. Five

grand a pop. If you don't like the first one, buy a second. Maybe we should get into this stuff. What do you think, Carmine?"

"Whatever you say, Vinnie." The big man swayed from foot to foot, arms crossed in front of his enormous chest.

Vinnie went looking for more marrow. There was never enough for him, so he had the cook put three shanks on his plate.

"This evaluator, the one who fucked you over, what's his name?"

"Reece. Morgan Reece."

"What do we have here? Twelve grand. That's your biggest loan, Tommy. The vig on that's twenty-five hundred dollars a week. That's more than you make from us. You'll keep falling behind, Tommy. That isn't good business. Tell you what I'm gonna do. I'll give you the first two, for the bitch."

As he spoke, Vinnie reached into his desk and counted out twenty one-hundred-dollar bills.

"The vig's the same as before. Maybe you won't need a new evaluation, or more legal fees. Shit happens. Sometimes you just gotta wait till it does."

There was a knock at the office door. Vinnie yelled, "What is it?"

"It's me, Jerry. I got a kid here."

"What the fuck? Carmine, open the door."

Carmine pulled the door back and a young man wearing an apron pushed Tommy into the room.

"What the fuck is this?" Vinnie yelled, "You want to get us busted? Who brought his kid in here?"

"Nobody, Mr. Colabucci. I went out back to put some trash out from the kitchen. The kid he was standing by the door. Before I knew it, boom, he's past me going down the hall, yelling for his father."

"Tommy, come here," Tully said and reached out for his son, who ran to him and buried his head in his father's chest.

"You came up here with your kid? Are you out of your fucking mind, Tom?" Vinnie was on his feet, waving his fork, spraying marrow all over the room.

"I told him to stay in the car. How was I to know he'd do this?"

"You fucking moron. It's bad enough you and me gotta meet. You tell me it's a fucking emergency. But you bring your kid, too. Who else you got in the car, Tom? Fuckin' *Sixty Minutes*?"

Vinnie was bug-eyed with rage. He caught himself and sat down. Taking a deep breath, he pulled his napkin loose and wiped his mouth. He set it down next to his plate, then put his knife and fork on the plate.

"What's your son's name, Tom?"

"Junior."

"Junior. Well I think I should have a little talk with Junior. Man to man. About things. Why don't you step outside for a minute, give us a little privacy."

"Hey, Mr. Colabucci, I don't think that's . . ."

Colabucci's face was white. "That's right, you don't think. Now put your son down and go outside with Carmine. I ain't gonna tell you again."

Tom put the boy down. "Its okay, Junior. Daddy'll be right outside. Mr.—uh, the nice man just wants to talk with you. About things."

Tom stroked his hair and slowly turned the boy around. Vinnie smiled at him.

"Put him in the chair. Pull it closer, so we can have a private little talk. Everybody else, outta here."

Carmine put his arm on Tully's back and pushed him out of the room.

"Hey, Jerry, come here, take this food away."

When Jerry came back in, Vinnie pulled him close and whispered in his ear.

"Go get me one of those rabbits you got in the kitchen."

"One of the live ones?"

"Yeah, and a tablecloth, and a sharp knife."

CHAPTER FORTY-EIGHT

Blake turned the camera off when the boy entered the bar. Twenty minutes later the door opened. Blake aimed and began to shoot. Tom Tully came out first, his son in his arms. The boy look dazed. He'd gotten into something. There was a large dark stain all over his T-shirt. Godzilla followed him out, then another man appeared in the doorway. He jabbed a finger at Tully and his son and pulled the door closed. The muscle watched them get into their car and pull out of the alley. When they turned at the end of the block, he put a key into the lock and let himself back in.

Blake ran to his car, tossed in the camera and went west on Baltimore Street, hoping he was parallel to Tully's Jeep. On Greene, he saw the Cherokee heading south and fell in behind him heading back to I-95.

Inside, Vinnie settled behind his desk and told Carmine to bring Wanda Perkins back. Two minutes later, Carmine pushed the door open and Wanda stepped in. Vinnie looked up and smiled at her. She was nice to look at, especially those soft tits with the nipples on them firm as erasers. She had beautiful hair, too. He loved stroking it while she went down on him.

"Sit down, Wanda. Got something I want you to do."

Oh, no, she thought. She'd sucked this weasel off plenty when she needed a job. She had plenty of fans now. She'd just go to another club. Did Vinnie have enough juice to keep her off the block? There had to be other club owners who'd hire her just to cut into his share of the market. She smiled nervously and waited for the worst.

"I want you to go down to Virginia for a week, maybe two. Here's the address. Make yourself comfortable. It's a place I keep for business. I want you to call this guy."

Vinnie pushed a piece of paper over to her. "He's a shrink. Get an appointment to see him. Make it as soon as possible. Soon as you do, call me back. Here's five hundred bucks for the first week. You stay longer, I'll see you get more money."

Wanda reached for the money, counted the bills and stuck them in her garter. She frowned, waiting for the slimy part. Dealing with Vinnie was like finding an oyster sleeping in your beer.

"Don't look at me like that, Wanda. I'll give this to one of the others girls in a fuckin' heartbeat. This is a piece of cake. You just stay in the apartment, eat what you want, drink what you want, sleep in, watch the tube, use your vibrator. You see no one and you talk to no one except me. All you gotta do is see this shrink for an hour and call me. Pretty cushy for five hundred. You want your regular nut? Stay here, dance ten hours a day, six days a week. I'll send down that Brazilian cunt you hate so much."

"No, no, it's okay, Mr. Colabucci. It's just fine. You're right, it's easy money." She succeeded at looking grateful. Maybe there was a chance here. If she didn't fuck this up, she could get other jobs from Mr. Colabucci. Get off the stage. Make more easy money. She had to keep her head. Pay attention to things, do a good job. "What should I tell this guy?" She looked at the note. "Morgan Reece. Why do I want to see him?"

"I don't care Wanda. Make something up. Just get an appointment fast. Don't worry about anything else. Call me. I'll give you more instructions. When you're in there with him, keep your eyes open. Pay attention to the set-up, how he does things, what kind of guy he is. You understand?"

"Yeah, Mr. Colabucci. Thanks for the job. When should I go down there?"

"Right away. Go get dressed. When you get in, call his office and set it up. I'll expect to hear from you by tonight. Call Carmine here at the club. He'll get in touch with me and I'll call you back."

Vinnie watched Wanda rise and had a sudden urge to throw her across the desk and fuck her. What great legs. The urge passed. Hell, Vinnie thought, he felt that way about all the girls. God, the pussy business was sweet. If only everything else was as easy. Tully was still an investment worth protecting. But how long?

CHAPTER FORTY-NINE

Don Blake followed Tom Tully home, where he changed his son's shirt, and then to his son's elementary school. Tully left there and went to the club's training facility. Outside, Blake called his office and had Crystal come out to pick up the surveillance on Tully.

Back at his office he called a friend in the Maryland State Police and asked him to run the Caddy's tags. The answer came back Frutti di Mare Shellfish Company, based in Baltimore, Maryland. Then he called Sid Bowman.

"Sid, how's that paper chase coming?"

"Not bad, Don. Should have it done in a few days. End of the week for sure."

"Can I add something to the search?"

"Sure. What?"

"Company out of Baltimore. Frutti di Mare Shellfish Company. I want to know who the officers of the company are, also if they're connected to other companies. A complete family tree."

"How soon, Don? That's at least a day in corporate records in Baltimore."

"As soon as you can after you've finished with Tully's finances."

"I'll call you when I'm done."

Blake called his Maryland connection back and arranged a late-night showing of "The Alley" with a recently retired

Baltimore police detective. His last call was to Rachel Pincus, who was following Tiffany Ames. The little boy had gone to school today and Tiffany was working at a unisex hair salon.

Blake told Rachel to stay with her and that he'd be over for the tag around four-thirty.

None of the other operatives had filed reports yet, so he had no idea whether they had been successful in placing Tom Tully and Tiffany Ames in any local motels or at training camp. By four o'clock nothing had changed and he left the office.

Blake pulled up behind Rachel's car, walked over and let himself in.

"Who's inside?"

"Just the Ames woman. Last customer left a few minutes ago. Shop closes at five. I don't think anybody else would be scheduled this late in the day. There were only two stylists in the shop. Ames and an Oriental woman. She left about an hour ago."

"So, what do you think? Take a little off the top?" Blake asked as he slid out. "Turn your motor on. She may come out in a real hurry."

Blake strolled across the street, pushed open the door and listened to the bell affixed to the frame announce him. Tiffany Ames was kneeling between two chairs sweeping up the last of the day's hair.

"Just a second. Be right with you," she said without looking up.

Blake walked towards her, deeper into the shop. Away from the sidewalk and the windows. Tiffany felt him before she saw his shadow.

She spun around, lost her balance and fell backwards between the chairs, up against a chest of drawers.

"What do you want?" she asked, sure that there was no answer she'd like.

"A haircut, of course. Why else would I be here?" Blake said, and reached out to help her up. "Don't worry. I won't hurt you."

Tiffany Ames slowly extended her hand and placed it inside Blake's. Gently, he closed his fingers and smoothly pulled her to her feet, backing away so she could escape from her prison.

"You're shitting me. You want a haircut?"

"Yeah, it's getting a little long on top and the sides. Just a trim."

Tiffany kept turning his request over in her mind, looking for the booby trap. She was sure it was a trick but refusing it might make him angry. She didn't want him angry. That was for certain.

"You want a shampoo?"

"No, that's okay. I just washed it last night. Trim is all."

"Why don't you take this chair up here?" she suggested, pointing to the one nearest the front door.

Blake walked over and settled himself in the chair. Tiffany snapped the loose hair from the smock and draped it over Blake's chest. He watched her fasten it behind and counted the scissors and razors on the shelf.

"This is how you usually wear it?" she asked.

"Yeah, straight back. Me and Mike Ditka."

"Right," she said sullenly and began to comb the hair to check the length.

"Got a proposition for you, Tiffany."

She stopped, comb and scissors in hand, and looked at Blake's face in the mirror. He returned her gaze.

"Don't get fancy in your thinking, Tiffany. I've got people right outside watching the salon. You can't run from here.

Why don't you just cut my hair and listen to what I've got to say?"

Tiffany worked slowly, trying to keep her hands steady. She didn't want to cut him, at least not accidentally.

"We're not interested in causing you trouble, Tiffany. I think we've found a way that you can help us and not hurt yourself. Tom Tully's in a heap of shit. You want to be as far away from this guy as you can get. You come down and make a statement, under oath, about your relationship with Tom Tully and we'll do everything to keep it out of the papers. Nobody has to know, least of all your ex. We want to leverage Tully into settling this matter out of court. No public records. No media. Just quiet and dignified. Your statement will let us do that. If you don't, we'll subpoena you. Then we'll call the *Post* and the TV stations. I'm not talking leak, I'm talking a flood. There won't be ten people in this city that don't know everything about you. Last night included. We're already checking out motels at training camp, here in town, away games for the last two years. We'll put you and Tom together whether you help us or not. Your only hope of keeping this quiet and going on with your life is to co-operate. You help us and we've got no reason to hurt you or your child. What'll it be?"

Tiffany, whose life had become a maze with moving walls, desperately wanted to see an exit, even if it turned out to be painted on the bricks.

"All right, all right. Let's do it. I just want out of this."

"Excellent." Blake stood up and reached back to undo the smock. Tossing it over the chair's arm, he checked himself in the mirror. "Nice job," he said and followed Tiffany Ames to the front door. He waved Rachel off while Tiffany locked up.

CHAPTER FIFTY

Morgan Reece waited for his new patient. In the evening, after his secretary left, he utilized a light system to tell him that patients had arrived. A switch in the waiting room turned on a light in his office. He'd had to give the woman the access code to the front door three times. She was clearly distressed and disorganized, but wouldn't say why. She said she was at work and didn't have any privacy. He offered her his last appointment of the day: seven p.m.

The light on his desk lit up and Reece went to the waiting room. His office suite had two consulting rooms in the back. One for therapy and interviews. The other room was for testing. The therapy office had two leather recliners, a love seat, a wall of cabinets with books, tests, and hidden from view, toys for his child patients. A desk and file cabinet stood against the far wall. The hall from these two offices ran past his records room, the secretary's space to the foyer and the front door. The waiting room was off to the left of the secretary's space.

Reece walked around the corner towards the waiting room, his fingers drumming lightly along the top of the half wall that enclosed his secretary. He poked his head in and saw his new seven o'clock: Thelma Bouchard.

"Ms. Bouchard, I'm Dr. Reece."

Thelma stood up and smiled. She walked over on extreme heels and held out a boneless hand for Reece to shake.

"Won't you come this way, please." Reece said and pointed around the half wall to the doorway on the left. He let Ms. Bouchard pass and was enveloped in her perfume.

She was wearing a black beret, a black cape that hung like the folded wings of a raven and black tights. Depressive haute couture.

"Where should I sit?"

"Wherever you like," Reece replied.

She took the loveseat and kept her hat and coat on. Reece sat in his chair, leaned back until he was comfortable, put his feet up and waited. Thelma slipped her bag off her shoulder and looked around the office. She nervously fingered one of her large dangling earrings.

"What brings you here, Ms. Bouchard?"

She looked at her hands. "This is kind of hard to talk about, really. I have this problem. It's a sexual problem." She looked at Reece to see how he was reacting.

Reece had spent years developing his poker face and it was working fine as he watched and waited for her to continue. Thelma waited to see if he'd ask what kind. When he didn't, she went on.

"I have this compulsion to have sex with strangers. I'm starting to get scared. You know AIDS and all. I don't want to die, but I can't seem to stop myself."

"You say 'compulsion'?"

Oh shit, Wanda thought. Why is this jerk asking me questions? I don't fucking know. Why doesn't he hit on me? What kind of an invitation does he need?

"It's a little warm in here. Can I take my jacket off?"

"Of course. Make yourself comfortable."

Thelma took her beret off and ran her hands through her hair, pulling it up from her head and letting it fall slowly back down. She stood up and looked down on the doctor. Maybe she should just go over and climb into his lap? No. A little tease first. Make him come over the line to her. She undid the buttons to her cape and slowly slid it off her shoulders. The see-through blouse did the trick. Poor doctor. His eyes looked like they were gonna come out of his skull. Nothing to it, Wanda thought. Vinnie told her to get his attention, keep him occupied. That she knew how to do.

Johnny Lentini hit the numbers Wanda had given him and slowly turned the doorknob. The door opened and closed quietly. He walked casually down the hall. First rule of theft. Look like you belong there. Secretary? He peered over the top of the wall. Desk was clean. He walked around the corner. No purse under the desk. Johnny walked back to the waiting room. Empty. The door on the right said "Bathroom." Johnny pushed it open. Dark. Wanda was in with the putz. Johnny moved back around the corner and saw the three doors at the end of the short hallway. Doctors? Only one nameplate by the entrance. Maybe he rented the other offices. Fuck. He hated no-look jobs. Why couldn't Vinnie wait? He'd go in as a fireman. Unannounced inspections were the perfect cover. You got to look anywhere you wanted, ask all the questions you needed, write notes to yourself. Just leave a receipt for the inspection. Tell them to post it in an accessible place. See you next year.

Johnny tried one door handle. Locked. He pressed an ear to the door. Nothing. Then the other. With his ear to the door he could hear a woman's voice. Wanda was still talking. He'd have felt better if he'd heard wet, slurping noises.

Lentini went to the records room and pulled on the handle. Unlocked. Beautiful. The guy had no idea he was a target. Slipping inside, he scanned the records files. He pulled out a shelf. It squealed. Lentini stopped, squatted down and peered at the folders. What was the system? Names, not numbers. Thank God. Alphabetical. Lentini thumbed back the names on the second shelf looking for Tully. These were the first letters A to H. He squatted down looking for the T's. Terwilliger, Titus, Tjader, Tolan, Truman, Twayne. Shit. Where was the fucking file? Coming back here to B & E, the joint was such a hassle. Why couldn't it be easy?

Lentini looked at the top shelf. More files. Fifteen or so. Alphabetical, too. Open cases? Maybe the others were closed. He quickly flipped the tabs. TULLY. Thomas Jr. and Tina. Bingo. He pulled out his mini-camera. Vinnie said shoot the whole file. He opened it up and began. Click and flip. Click and flip. Christ, the damn file had to be two inches thick.

Suddenly he heard Wanda's voice as clear as if she was next to him. What the fuck? Shrinks were supposed to give you, what, fifty minutes, an hour? Johnny closed the file until it squealed again and slid himself into the space next to the file cabinet. He slid the folding razor out of its sheath in his waistband, snapped it open and held it up next to his ear. Don't come in here, Doc.

Morgan Reece thought he'd heard something in the office. "Excuse me for a second. I think someone has come in, and I have no other appointments."

He closed the door behind himself and went to check the waiting room. Empty. He walked around the secretary's desk, turned immediately and pushed open the bathroom door. Also empty. Once inside, he flipped on the light and ran water in the sink.

Reece filled his hands with warm water and then put his face in them. Then he reached out to get a paper towel and dry off.

He remembered one of his first custody cases. He went out to do a home visit. The mother was an exotic dancer. She came to her hearing dressed for work. High heels, mesh stockings, a neon green sheath held together by a pin next to her left breast and slit all the way up the side. She crossed one leg over the other and gave old "Sleepy" Duncan a good look-see from her ankle to her armpit. When she commented on how the nice doctor came out to pay a call on her at her home, "Sleepy" came to real fast. Reece was so glad for the female social work student he'd brought along for that home visit.

Stay in your area of competence, he reminded himself. Primary sexual disorders was not his. She needed to be referred on. A female therapist for sure. She hadn't said anything about sex with female strangers. Not yet at least. She eroticized everything. She had stroked the shaft of the table lamp next to her, running her thumb around the rim just below the bulb the whole time she had talked. He needed to close things up, explain to her that this was outside his area of competence and make a referral. Once that was clear, he finished drying off, turned off the light and stepped into the hall.

The records room was open. That was odd. Had he left it open? No, he never did. Unlocked, yeah. Open, no. He had been distracted by the Tully case before she arrived. He clearly remembered putting the case file back. Had he closed the door? Reece stepped towards the records room.

Johnny Lentini peeked around the edge of the file cabinet and saw the shadow on the floor. Too bad, Doc. One swift slash, a sheet of blood as thick as paint, you're dead before you land. Lentini tightened his grip on the razor.

"Doctor Reece, are you okay?" Wanda called out.

"Uh, yeah. Be right there." Reece pulled the door closed and walked back into his office.

Lentini relaxed, counted to thirty and slid the razor back

into its sheath. He went back to copying the Tully file.

Thirty minutes later, Morgan Reece escorted Thelma Bouchard out of his office, the referral to Dr. Maxine Crosby tight in her fist. He wrote up his notes on the intake, turned off the lights, locked his desk and went to the records room. Everything looked normal. Nothing was out of place. He filed Bouchard in Closed, turned off the waiting room music, the inside light and locked the records room. He darkened the waiting room, then stepped outside to lock the front door, more than ready to put this day behind him.

CHAPTER FIFTY-ONE

Morgan Reece almost forgot that he'd told Lindsay Brinkman that he would come by to pick up some climbing shoes. When he remembered, he was halfway between the store and his home. By the time he got home, it would be too late to call. What the hell, he'd swing by the store, get the shoes and go home. Still didn't mean he had to go climbing.

Reece walked into the store and scanned the merchandise. Books and maps to the left. Harnesses, ropes, anchors, carabineers and crampons all over the wall. Chalk bags, chalk, sunglasses, bug repellant, helmets on shelves and in bins. Tables of clothing for summer climbs, spandex and other synthetics, shorts, socks, shirts. Down jackets and parkas for winter or ice climbing. He saw shoes on the back wall and headed towards them. He stared at the models and admired the prices. Serious climbing meant serious money.

"I thought you weren't coming," she said as she came up from behind.

Reece spun around. "Oh, hi. Yeah, well I almost didn't."

"Why?"

"A lot of reasons. I had a rough day at work today. I just wanted to go home, go to sleep and forget it. I'm ambivalent as hell about climbing. It scares me, I think it might be exciting and . . ."

"What are you afraid of?" she asked.

"Falling. Getting killed. How's that for starters?"

"Not going to happen. We'll be top-roping. You'll be well anchored. I'll belay the ropes myself. It's the safest thing you'll do all day. Climbers are obsessive about safety. Good ones anyway. And I'm a good climber. A good teacher. What else are you afraid of?"

Reece frowned. "Isn't that enough?"

"No. I want to know what to expect. You remember what you said about climbing being simple. Well that's partly right. The rock is the rock. It doesn't change very much. But people do. When you climb by yourself, you can't have a bad day. It can kill you. You need to know yourself as well as you can every time you go up. Especially when you push your limits. I won't flash a climb unless I'm sure I can do it. When you climb with other people, especially strangers, you need to know what to expect. So you can help them and not get hurt either."

"Okay. What else am I afraid of? I'm afraid of looking like I'm afraid. Of going out, trying it and chickening out, in front of other people. This is all about me licking my fear, not getting beaten by it."

"I understand. We'll take it real easy. You'll do fine. It'll be good." She reached out and squeezed Reece's hand.

Neither one looked down, but each counted the seconds until she took her hand back.

Reece looked at her. She didn't look anything like any woman he'd ever been attracted to. Totally uncharted territory. Physically and emotionally. He didn't know what he wanted or how to get it.

"Lindsay, we're closing up," boomed a ruddy blond with an abundance of muscles.

"What size do you wear?" she asked.

"Eleven, D-width."

"I'll be right back." She ducked behind a curtain. Lindsay

returned and handed a pair of shoes to Reece. He shed his loafers, jammed a foot in, hauled the heel up and repeated the process with the other foot. He laced them up; Lindsay knelt down and felt to check the fit. Reece quickly scanned from her shoulders down her flanks to the swell of her hips and back to her face.

"Can we continue talking, after we finish with the shoes?" Reece asked.

Lindsay looked up. "Okay. We can get some coffee downstairs. The food court is still open."

"These are strange shoes. They've got soles right up to the laces," Reece said.

"That's because when you climb you use all the surfaces of your foot. You brace yourself with the sides, the top. You need traction everywhere. This is more shoe than you're going to need, but it's what we had in your size."

Reece stood up and checked them out in the mirror. He sat down, unlaced them and slipped his feet back into his loafers.

"How much is the rental?"

"Twenty bucks. Don't worry about it. You can pay for them at the climb."

She handed him the shoes; Reece took them and smiled. "Okay."

Lindsay stood up, went behind the curtain and came back fastening a waist pack. She said goodnight to the other employees and bounded down the stairs to the restaurant.

Inside, they sat at a table along the wall facing the bar. The waiter brought their coffees and they declined dessert.

"What did you want to talk about?" she asked.

"I don't know. I had questions when we were talking. Now they seem, I don't know . . ."

"Go ahead. Ask me."

"I was wondering why you offered to help me with this."

"You have nice eyes. They're kind. And I liked what you wrote about abused children and what you said when we met. You seemed to be a . . . I don't know. I didn't think about all this. I just thought it might be nice if you weren't afraid of heights, I mean, you know, nice for you, and that was all I thought."

"And that was something you could do for me. Help me with that."

"Yeah."

"Thank you. I'm kind of excited about shedding some of that fear. I think you're very brave. Braver than I am."

"I'm not. There's plenty of things that scare me. Heights just isn't one of them."

Reece started to speak, but Lindsay held up her hand. "But don't ask me what they are. I'll see you on the rocks Sunday. Okay?"

"Yeah. I'll be there," Reece said.

Lindsay stood up, dropped a couple of bills for her coffee and said, "I've got to go. Bye."

"Bye."

CHAPTER FIFTY-TWO

Wanda stretched out in Vinnie's hot tub. Too bad she couldn't think of someone to share this with. She felt the jets of water massaging her. Best time she'd had being naked in quite a while. She poured herself another glass of champagne and sipped it slowly, savoring the chill in her throat and the warmth everywhere else. Why couldn't every day be like this? What had gone wrong for her? Vinnie didn't seem all that smart, and he sure didn't work any harder than she did. Was it just 'cause he was connected? How come they didn't teach that in school? A course on "How the Real World Works." It ain't what you know, it's who you know. With a special class on how to identify who you should know. Maybe this was her chance. She knew Vinnie, Vinnie knew God, or so it seemed. She set down her glass, picked up the cordless phone and called the club.

"Hi, Carmine, it's Wanda. Is Mr. Colabucci there?"

"So Wanda, how'd it go?" Vinnie asked as soon as he got on.

"Fine. I had a session with the doctor. That guy you sent down, he said he got in, copied everything and got out. The doctor won't even know he's been hit."

"Good. Is he on his way back here with the film?"

"Uh huh. He said he'd develop it first and bring it to you later tonight. He said you should call him and tell him where to deliver it."

"Okay. Good. What's this doctor like?"

Wanda thought about telling him the truth. If she couldn't get back to see Reece, what use was she to Vinnie?

"He's nice." Actually she thought he might be gay. The guy seemed terrified to be in the same room with her.

"He's nice. That's it? You get him to play with your toys?"

"No. I didn't want to make it too easy. I got him all worked up and then I cooled him off. That way he'd be sure to want to see me again. I thought that was what you wanted. So I could get back into his office if you wanted me to."

"Yeah. That's good, Wanda. After I read the file and figure out what this putz knows, where he's been stickin' his nose, I'll call you back, tell you what to do next. You think you can get this geek to put his hands on you?"

"Oh, yeah, Mr. Colabucci. He was hot for me. Wouldn't be hard at all."

"Good. If we want to get him off this case, that's the easiest way. Some eight-by-tens of him showing you his stiffy and he's history. You figure out a way to get him alone with you. Out of the office, someplace he's got no reason to be. We'll plant a camera, long lens maybe. Catch him being a bad boy, boom, we got him."

"Okay, Mr. Colabucci. I'll come up with something."

Wanda put down the phone and then slowly lowered herself entirely under the water. Doctor Reece actually seemed like a nice guy, real skittish, though. Maybe a suicide attempt? Bet that would get him. Late at night. I can't talk to anyone but you. Get him to come up to the apartment. Hide the cameraman in the closet, or maybe use a hidden security video camera, like behind the bar at the club. Wear something hot, like that black lace teddy she just got for work. If he was gay, she could always jump him. Once they got all tangled up and her boobs were in his face, it'd be pretty hard to figure out who started what.

Happy with that plan, Wanda came up for air, sipped some more champagne and admired her toes, breaching so far away.

Two hours before Johnny Lentini showed up with the developed film of the Tully file, Vincent Colabucci got another phone call at the club.

"Hey, Mr. Colabucci, this is Danny Gillespie. I got something you might want to hear."

Gillespie was a bartender at the Fifth Down Club, hired by Vinnie long ago to keep tabs on the possibilities of expanding his influence with "The Squires."

"What is it?"

"The police were here today. Asking about Tom Tully. His wife filed a complaint against him. Said she was assaulted by some guy that Tom hired so she'd settle with him. They were asking about his whereabouts, who he hangs out with. They figure it was a player, because she said he was huge. They wanted to know if anybody has showed up with sudden money or running mouth. Whether I heard Tom threaten the bitch."

"What'd you say?"

"Nothing. Nothing to say. If Tom did it, I don't know anything about it. Just thought you'd want to know, Mr. Colabucci."

"Thanks Danny. There'll be something in this for you. Keep your ears open. You hear anything else, call right away."

"Sure thing, Mr. Colabucci."

Vinnie hung up the phone. The cops. That fucking moron tried to muscle her into settling. Trust me, Mr. Colabucci. She'll roll right over, no problem, Mr. Colabucci. It's a mortal lock. He mimicked Tommy as a falsetto, a castrati. He backhanded the phone off the desk. His grimace forced his eyes closed.

"You fuckin' imbecile. I'm gonna fuckin' kill you," he bellowed. "Carmine, get the fuck in here."

The door bowed, before it snapped back. Carmine filled it, his hands flexing in anticipation of tearing someone's head off, and blinked with disappointment when he found only his boss in the room.

Vinnie ground his teeth. His head throbbed. He knew the blood vessel over his left eye would be up and pulsing. He was so mad, he wanted it to explode, to spray blood all over the room, like champagne, to celebrate his rage.

"What do you want, Boss?"

"I want that mother fuckin' moron Tully. Find him. We're gonna have a talk."

CHAPTER FIFTY-THREE

Four days later, Morgan Reece got a call on his emergency line.

"Dr. Reece, this is your answering service. We have an emergency call for you. It's a Mrs. Nash. She says she's Tommy Tully's teacher. She wants you to call her right away. She'll arrange to get out of her classroom."

"What's the number?" He wrote down her number, and then dialed it.

"Wintergreen Elementary School. How may I help you?"

"Mrs. Nash, please."

"She's in class. Can I take a message?"

"This is Dr. Reece. I'm returning a call of hers. She said she'd arrange to get out of class."

"Yes. Please hold, Dr. Reece. I'll page her."

Moments later, he heard faint voices in the background.

"Dr. Reece, this is Monica Nash. I'm Tommy Tully's teacher."

"Yes. What can I do for you?"

"Well, I'm calling since I didn't hear from you."

"I'm sorry. Were you expecting me to call you?"

"Yes. I told Mrs. Tully I was worried about Tommy. That was on Monday. I knew the family was being evaluated. Mr. Tully told me about you. I don't know if you're aware of the big scare we had here not too long ago."

"Yes, I am. You told Ms. Tully you wanted me to call you on Monday, is that right?"

"Yes. I'm very worried about Tommy. Has anything new happened? Any major changes?"

"Did you explain to Ms. Tully what you were worried about?"

"Absolutely. I didn't have to. She could see it with her own two eyes. I told her I thought it was important to have you talk to Tommy right away. She said she'd call you, Doctor. I've been waiting. Things aren't any better, so I thought I'd call you directly."

"Ms. Tully hasn't been in touch with me. I'm glad you called. What's going on with Tommy?"

"What isn't? It started on Monday. We have a rabbit in our class. He's in a cage in the back of the classroom. We use him to teach the kids responsibility and caring. He's also a reward. They get to take him out of the cage and sit and hold him. Tommy never showed a particular interest in the rabbit. He didn't dislike the animal, but nothing especially positive either. Anyway, he was going to wash his hands at the sink in the back. He'd been painting. Tommy saw that rabbit and just freaked out. He wet himself and then he started screaming. He went to the rabbit cage and tried to open it. I'm the only one with a key to the lock. He couldn't get it open. He was sobbing hysterically. I was afraid he'd pull the cage over on himself, and hurt himself and the rabbit. So I ran back to stop him. I tried to put my arms around him and support him there, then let him let go of the cage when he was ready. He was in a frenzy. I've never seen him like that before. He was trying to bite me, then he slammed his head back; I thought he'd broken my nose. We both fell over. It was a mess. There was rabbit stuff all over the floor: water, food, wood chips, rabbit pellets. The rabbit was terrified, sitting in the corner of the cage shaking. I had blood running down my face from my nose. Tommy saw that and it just set him off again. It was dripping from my chin to my dress. He started screaming, 'I'm sorry. I'm sorry. I'm sorry.' Over and over again. I tried to tell him it was okay. I'd be okay. The rabbit was okay. He'd be okay. He didn't hear a word. He just kept saying he didn't want the rabbit's foot. He was sorry. Then he broke down and started saying 'red luck' over and over again. I had one of the other children get the principal. We called his mother and had her come in to get him. He was still crying a bit when she got here. I told her what happened. I asked her if she'd noticed anything different at home. If he might have seen something bad that happened to a rabbit or another animal. She said no. She did say he'd had problems sleeping at night. Nightmares and he wet the bed. She wasn't sure what to make of it. Maybe just a reaction to her being back in the house with them and his father being out until they're in bed. She thought he'd be angry and sad and confused. She was going to watch and see if it got better after a while."

"What happened next?"

"She got him calmed down and then she took him home. He came back the next day, but things still weren't right."

"How so?"

"He stayed away from the rabbit. In fact he wouldn't even look at it. I tried to take him over to see it with me. Convince him it was okay. He wouldn't have any part of it. He just said the rabbit wasn't okay and wasn't ever going to be okay and it was his fault. I didn't push it. He's been completely out of it this week. He can't concentrate. He doesn't follow any directions. When you ask him where he is, what he's thinking about, you get nothing. That's new for Tommy. He's never been a particularly open or expressive child, but he's also not been spaced out like that.

"It's been getting worse each day this week. He doesn't eat his lunch. He won't even unpack it. I tried to help him. When was it, Wednesday, I think, I tried to open it for him, see if he'd eat a little. He got very angry and knocked the bag out of my hand. Technically, we have to report any assaultive behavior to the district office. They'd send out a school psychologist who'd make recommendations about whether he can be contained in a regular classroom. I didn't do that. I figured it was so recent and you were already involved, but when you hadn't called back, I was getting concerned.

"Today, he started pulling his hair. He'll sit quietly in the back. He doesn't get angry or out of control unless someone approaches him and tries to make him do something he doesn't want to. Otherwise, he's lost in space. I was walking around the class, quizzing the kids on some work we'd done yesterday. Tommy won't answer any questions at all, even about schoolwork. He can't use school the way he is now. Anyway, I saw him twirling his hair and then tugging at it. When I looked down, there was a pile of it on the floor. That's when I called you. I wanted you to know that I'm going to have to report the situation to the principal."

"Absolutely. I'm glad you called me. I had no idea that any of this was going on. I'm going to call Ms. Tully right away, ask her to bring Tommy right in."

Reece put the phone down. What the fuck was going on? The kids had been with their mother less than a full week, and Tommy was a supernova of symptoms. And why hadn't she called me? She'd had all week to follow through.

Reece dialed the Tully house. Felicia Hurtado answered.

"Is Ms. Tully there?"

"No. She is out. Can I take a message?"

"Yes, this is Dr. Reece. Is this Ms. Hurtado?"

"Yes."

"Have you been there all week?"

"Yes. I have."

"How is Tommy doing?"

"Not good, doctor. I don't know what is the matter with him."

"Is he acting like before?"

"No. It is different. He does not sleep at night. His father said one night, he had a nightmare he could not wake him from until he slapped his face."

"Did he say what his nightmare was?"

"He said his Daddy had no skin and no feet. That he gave him 'red luck.' Do you know what that is, Doctor?"

"I haven't a clue. What else is happening?"

"He does not eat very well. He had a hot dog for dinner one night, and he threw it up. Every night he waits by the phone for his father's call. When he's late, Tommy is very upset. He will tear up his drawings or throw his toys. He has even hit his sister. That is not Tommy, he loves her. Even when the mother was not here he did not do that."

"Is Mr. Tully late with his calls?"

Felicia skipped a beat before answering, "Yes."

"How often?"

"He is always late. Sometimes he does not call until after Tommy is in bed. It makes a big problem. The mother wants him to call on time so that he is rested for school. She tells him that he does not sleep until he hears from his father. He will lie there and wait. He says he is afraid that bad men will come into the house and he cannot sleep until his father calls. Then they will be okay."

"Has he told his father this when they talk?"

"I don't know about that."

"Are these all things you've seen yourself or just heard from Mrs. Tully?"

"I have seen them myself."

"Have you been taking care of the kids?"

"Yes. Mrs. Tully, she has not been feeling well. She asked me if I would stay to help out."

"Is she sick?"

"I don't know, Doctor. She is always tired and says she wants to sleep. She does not look very good. I have heard her on the phone calling her doctor for an appointment. That is where she is now."

"When do you expect her back?"

"I don't know. Not for an hour, I would say."

"Tell her I called. Ask her to call me as soon as she walks in. If she can't get through to me, ask her to use my emergency number. My service will find me and I'll call her immediately."

"Yes, Doctor."

Working with the Tullys left Reece feeling like he did about his own family. The longer he looked, the less he understood.

CHAPTER FIFTY-FOUR

An hour and forty minutes later, Reece's direct line rang. His service said that Mrs. Tully was returning his call. He took her number and rang back.

"Ms. Tully, this is Dr. Reece. I was called earlier today by Tommy's teacher." Pause. This is your chance to jump in with an explanation, apology, anything. Nothing.

"Ms. Tully, she says that Tommy's been behaving very strangely at school. She said that she shared this with you. That she asked you to call me back at the first of the week."

"I just thought that he was having trouble adjusting to all the changes. Me back, his dad out. I figured I'd wait a little bit longer before I called."

Adjusting to changes? The kid sounds like he ate the DSM and was regurgitating it one page at a time. "I'd like to talk to Tommy. Today." Reece flipped his daybook to the evening. "I have an opening at six. Please bring him in then."

"Can I have Felicia do it? I'm not feeling too good."

"No. I'd really like you to do it. If Tommy's having problems, I think you'd make him more comfortable than she would."

No reply. Reece sealed the deal. "See you at six."

He hung up and wondered at all the things he wasn't hearing in her voice.

Six o'clock came and went. His compass on this case was spinning.

The light on his desk was on. Reece went out to the waiting room. Serena Tully was sitting there with Tommy. Her face was unmade, her eyes dull and empty. She looked every second of her age. Tommy sat in the chair next to her, staring at the floor.

"Hello, Tommy," Reece said, kneeling down trying to make eye contact. "Can you come into my office? I'd like to talk to you."

Tommy kept his head down. Reece put out his hand. Nothing. "Ms. Tully, would you come into my office? I'd like to talk to you."

Serena Tully reached for her son's hand and preceded Reece into his office. He motioned her to the loveseat, which she took. Tommy climbed up next to her and put his head in her lap.

"Tommy, I wonder if you could help me today. I have a real problem."

Tommy shook his head.

"Well, let me tell your mother about it. She might be able to help." Reece fixed on Serena's face. She was quite pale and her left eye had a tic.

"There's this little boy I'm seeing in therapy. He's just about your age. Well, this little boy, he has something on his mind all the time. He can't stop thinking about it. I'm not a little boy anymore so I'm having trouble guessing what it might be. What do you think it could be, Tommy?"

"A secret," he said, his head still down.

"A secret. That makes sense. Well there are good secrets and bad secrets. Can you tell me what a good secret might be?"

"A good secret is all pluses on your report card."

"That's right. I'd want to tell someone about that. I'd keep it a secret until the time was right. Then I'd tell when it was a big surprise. I don't think this little boy has a good secret, but I'm not sure. How can I tell if it's not a good secret, Tommy?"

"I don't know."

"Bad secrets make you feel bad inside. You worry all the time that bad things will happen to you. That makes it hard to sleep. I've asked the little boy what makes him feel so bad, but he won't say. Do you know what he does instead?"

"He hits you."

"That's right. Why would he do that, Tommy?"

" 'Cause he's angry."

"Who's he angry at, Tommy?"

"He's angry at everybody."

"Is he angry at himself, too?"

"Yes."

"Why is he angry at himself?"

"I don't know."

"Is it something he did?"

"I don't know."

"Is it something someone else did to him?"

"No."

"Geez, you sound angry. Just like that other boy. Are you angry at me?"

"Yes."

"What did I do to make you angry, Tommy?"

"You're bothering me. I don't want to talk about it."

"I'm sorry, Tommy. I don't want to make you angry. I have a problem, though. This little boy is so unhappy. I just don't know what to do. What should I do?"

"I don't know."

"You know, when I don't know what to do, that's when I need help. I need a hero to help me. Do you know any heroes?"

"My dad."

"Your dad. That's right. Do you think your dad can help us with this?"

Tommy shook his head. He looked terrible.

"Why not Tommy? Heroes help people."

"My dad can't do it. He's not big enough. The bad man is bigger."

"Really." Reece flicked his eyes at Serena. Her lifted brows said that she had no idea what Tommy was talking about.

"You know one good thing. No matter how big the bad guys are, there's always a bigger hero. You just have to know which one to get. Who is the biggest hero you know?"

" 'Credible Hulk."

"Yeah, he's pretty big. Is he big enough?"

"I don't know."

"Tell you what. I know lots of heroes. To get the right one, we need to know how big the bad guy is. Can you draw him?"

Tommy shook his head.

"Okay, how about if I draw him? Can you help me?"

Silence is not a no, Reece reminded himself as he went to get his sketchpad and pencils.

"Okay. First, let's draw me." Reece sketched himself, with his thinning hair and beard. "Okay, now your dad. Is your dad bigger than me?"

"Yes."

"Okay. Let's see, he's got no hair on top and his beard is different from mine. Is that right?" Reece sketched Tom Tully as a slightly larger, more muscular figure, trying to get the proportions right.

"Now, how about the bad guy? How tall is he?" Reece put his pencil to the paper and moved it as Tommy nodded his head until it was right. He drew an egg for a head. If Tommy was a good judge and not relying entirely on "the feel" of the man, he was a giant, easily six-foot-eight or more. "How big? How wide, Tommy?"

Again Tommy nodded and Reece adjusted. The man was huge, fully half again as wide as his father. Reece started to draw him with the same wedge-shaped muscularity.

"No. He's fat. He's got a big tummy."

Reece doodled another larger egg for the torso.

"Does he wear a uniform? Or just regular clothes?"

"Regular clothes. They're all black. He has sneakers. I saw them."

"Black ones?"

"Yeah."

Reece covered the shape in black.

"How about his head? Does he have hair?"

"Yes."

"Light like your mom's or darker like mine?"

"Darker than yours."

Reece scribbled hair, but Tommy said it was shorter so he re-did it.

"Does he have a beard?"

"No. He had black on his face."

"Black on his face? Is he a black man? Is he black all over?"

"No. He has black dots on his face."

Reece drew generic lips, nose and eyes, then peppered the face with black dots for heavy stubble.

"Anything else? Is that him?"

"Yes."

"Okay, does he have a name?"

"No."

"All right. I think I know a hero who's bigger than that. I'll call him and tell him we have to stop this bad guy. All I have to know is what the bad man did, so we can stop him."

"He didn't do anything."

"He didn't? Why is he a bad guy then?"

"The other man did it. His friend."

"Oh, his friend. What did his friend do?"

Tommy buried his head in his mom's lap.

"You know, moms can be heroes, too. Can you tell your mom what he did?"

More head shaking.

"Are you afraid, Tommy?"

The head bobbed up and down.

"What are you afraid of, Tommy?"

Nothing.

"Did the bad man say he'd do something to you if you told?"

Nothing.

Reece went over everything the teacher had reported.

"Did the bad man hurt an animal?"

Tommy was burrowing into his mother's lap.

"Did he hurt the rabbit?"

Tommy burst into tears. Reece leaned back in his chair, counting the questions answered against the ones raised. Serena stroked her son's head and told him the oldest lie of all, that things would be all right.

CHAPTER FIFTY-FIVE

When Reece gave Tommy some toys to play with, he was willing to stay by himself in the waiting room. Reece returned to the office and closed the door. He sat down and picked up his notepad.

Reece wished he'd been able to interview Tommy alone, see if he'd confirm what Hurtado said about Serena. Not this time. Maybe after the home visit he'd try interviewing him again.

"When you were out, I had an opportunity to speak with Ms. Hurtado. How do you feel about having her in the house?"

"She's a lot of help. I'm glad to have it."

Reece studied her face. Her eyes were deeply shadowed. Problems sleeping?

"What does she do to help out?"

"A little bit of everything. She's really quite good with the kids."

"You weren't comfortable with her taking care of the kids before. What changed?"

"That was before. This is now." She pulled her jacket tight around her and jammed her hands in her pockets.

"That's right. This is now. Let me tell you how now looks to me, Mrs. Tully. Maybe you can help me with it. I see a woman who looks pretty bad right now. Your looks have been very important to you. Even after you were thrown out of your house, you came in here made up, accessorized. Not now. You've got your kids with you. You're in your home. Things should be looking up and you look worse. I'm confused."

"Maybe it's just a delayed reaction," she said, her chin quivering with the effort of that evasion.

"I don't think so. Ms. Hurtado says you're always tired. You have no energy. She's been helping with the kids. You aren't taking care of yourself. Sounds like depression to me."

"So maybe I'm depressed. I've got a right to be depressed, after what I've been through."

"True enough. However your depression seems to be affecting the children."

"That's not true. You heard what Tommy said. Some bad man hurt a rabbit. Probably one of Tom's macho asshole friends. If he's having problems it's not my fault. I didn't do anything to scare him."

"Perhaps you're right. What do you think you should do?"

"About what?"

"Indeed." Reece smiled sadly. "Mrs. Tully, have you discussed what's going on with Dr. Tepper?"

"What do you mean?"

"I mean your recent depression. Are you discussing this with Dr. Tepper?"

"I'm not seeing him anymore. We've terminated things."

"And whose decision was that?"

"It was mutual. I thought it made me look bad, like I was the crazy person Tom said I was."

"And Dr. Tepper agreed with this?"

"It was my decision. He didn't have any right to keep me there. It's not like I was committed."

"Mrs. Tully, why didn't you call me on Monday? After you saw Tommy, after the teacher suggested it to you?"

"I told you. I thought it was just a reaction to all the changes. I was waiting to see if it passed."

Reece rubbed his beard, struggling to stay calm. "I can see not wanting to rush out and put him in therapy, but why not call me? Just let me know what was going on, see what I thought?"

"I don't know. Okay? Is there anything else, or can I go now?"

"Mrs. Tully, I don't often do this, but I'm going to make an exception here. I strongly recommend that you get Tommy to a therapist right away. He's been traumatized and apparently very recently. The sooner efforts are begun to help him deal with it, the easier it'll be to help him recover. I'll be glad to give you some names or you can get a referral from Dr. Tepper. I'll let both attorneys know that this is coming from me and why."

"Fine. I'll call for those names tomorrow. It's late and Tommy needs his dinner."

Serena stood up and left, pulling back the door so hard she barely kept it from hitting the wall. Reece rose and followed her out. In the waiting room, she told Tommy it was time to go home. He left the Legos he was playing with and dutifully took the hand she gave him. Reece watched them from his doorway. When they left the building, he went into the waiting room, knelt down and began to clean up after them. A very angry woman, Serena Tully. Morgan Reece wondered why.

He went into his office, flipped through his Rolodex and wrote down the names of three child therapists. He'd follow up and make sure the Tullys executed consents for him to talk to the therapist. What was the secret Tommy held? Had someone hurt a rabbit to ensure his silence? He'd run it by Child Protective Services in the morning.

Reece knew that this was a borderline case. No real disclosure. They'd send out an investigator, probably get no farther than he did. Hopefully a therapist over time would get all of it from Tommy. He didn't mention his father doing anything to him or anyone doing anything to him at all. Maybe he saw some slasher film and it scared him, or someone kill a rabbit for food.

What had he said? Reece flipped the chart open and went over his notes from the teacher. "I'm sorry. I didn't want the rabbit's foot, and 'red luck.' " Red luck? Good luck? Bad luck? Reece kept looking. Hurtado said he'd had a bad dream about his father losing his foot and having "red luck." Reece hated dreams. Royal road to the unconscious. Fat lot of use that was to him. That was the easy half of the trip. If he couldn't connect it back to reality it was a dead end.

This case had gone out the window. Reece had been leaning towards primary physical custody with Serena Tully. Right now, foster care was starting to look pretty good. Why had she gone south now? She'd hung in through tougher times.

Tommy's acting out all over the place and she's sleeping in and handing off to the nanny. Reece wondered if this was the craziness her sister described in the transcript or what Tom said she'd been like.

Why screw this up now? Maybe she didn't really want the kids? Maybe it was Lou Carlson storming into court for the kids and she just bobbed along in his wake. She seemed pretty vulnerable to the influence of powerful men. That's what attracted her to Tom. Lou Carlson could be very persuasive. Maybe he needed a cause to go back into court, to "unretire," without choosing it.

Reece felt like he'd just run over something in the road. Nothing big. Just a little bump. No swerve, no screech of tires. He began to back up slowly.

An hour later he hadn't found a thing. He called out for pizza and started a new pot of coffee. Thirty minutes later, the pizza arrived as promised. Reece sat at his desk, took the entire file apart, got a new notepad and began to examine every page. He went over all the collateral records, the transcripts, the questionnaires, the test results, his interview notes. He ate pizza. He drank coffee.

Every once in a while he scribbled a note. When he was done, he reassembled the file and closed it. He stacked the pizza box on the file and poured out the rest of the coffee.

Reece scanned his notes, tore the pages off and began to copy them, rearranging and numbering them as he went along. Reece looked at what he had. The dark, wet shape of what he'd run over earlier in the evening. Late at night, in this light, who could tell? Was it a dog, or just a pile of rags? Only one way to find out. Walk over, squat down, put your hand on it and turn it over.

CHAPTER FIFTY-SIX

Don Blake pulled to a halt on Toone Street. He was in Highlandtown, home of the marble steps in East Baltimore. Each block looked like a medieval castle, unbroken stone from end to end, anchored at one corner with a church and by a bakery at the other. One block German, then Slovak, the next Russian, then Ukrainian.

Retired Detective Emil Radechenko opened the door to Don Blake's knock. Radechenko was a tall wiry man with a prominent Adam's apple and a flat top that looked as stiff as quills.

"Lieutenant Radechenko?"

"Retired. You Blake?"

"Yeah."

"Come on in." Radechenko stepped back and let Blake enter the foyer. Blake, seeing the immaculate interior, took an extra second to wipe his shoes on the mat.

Radechenko pointed to the living room. "You said you had a tape you wanted me to see, that right?"

"Yeah. Here it is."

Radechenko held out his hand and took the tape.

"TV's in here. Go ahead, sit down. You want a beer?"

"Thanks."

Radechenko disappeared into the back of the house and returned with two bottles of beer and frosted mugs.

Blake poured his carefully, watching the head rise like a

pompadour. It crested before he had to take a pull and Blake set it on a coaster.

Radechenko inserted the tape and hit Play.

"Where'd you shoot this?"

"In an alley behind 'The Block.' It's the back entrance of a strip club called the Passion Pit. I need to ID two of the guys in the tape. My friends say you knew all the bad guys and never forgot a face."

"Well, let's give it a look-see here. Then we'll know if I'm as good as your friends say."

Radechenko leaned forward, his elbows propped on his knees, his chin tucked behind his closed fists. Blake sipped at his beer and scanned the room as Radechenko watched the tape. The walls next to the TV were covered with commendations and a mirror. In the mirror, Blake saw a picture of suffering Jesus hung over the velvet sofa.

Radechenko spoke, "Those the two guys, right there?"

"Yeah, that's them. You know 'em?"

Radechenko went over to the VCR, hit Stop and Rewind.

"Yeah, I know 'em," he said. He returned to his seat and took a long draw on his beer.

"And?" asked Blake, who had not retired, and wanted to get back to D.C. before he did.

"Let's start with the big one. That's Carmine. Carmine used to be even bigger. Had this disease, Pickwickian Syndrome. He used to fall asleep standing up, sitting down. So much weight pressing on his heart and lungs, it cut off the oxygen to his brain. Not that he needed a whole lot. Out like a light. Pretty fucking funny. Sometimes Vinnie 'The Bat,' he'd scream and yell, threatening to kill somebody, and he'd point to Carmine, and there's Carmine snoring away, sounds like he's fartin' out his mouth.

"They did this thing, they staple your stomach, so you

can't eat so much and you lose weight. Worked for a while. Looks like he's putting it back on, though."

"This guy trouble, or just big?"

"Oh, he's trouble. A regular juggernaut. He's inhumanly strong. I've seen street bulls break nightsticks on him, three or four at a time. He didn't even know they were there. We tried to tag him for three killings when I was on the force. All three were hits ordered by 'The Bat.' Know how they died? Their heads were twisted around one hundred eighty degrees. Medical examiner said a human being couldn't do that. Rumor was that there were witnesses, that a lesson was being taught. Guess what? Nobody saw a thing. Lesson learned.

"Only good thing about Carmine is he's too stupid to play with himself. Unless Vinnie tells him what to do, he eats, he sleeps, he watches the girls and he shits. That's it, start to finish."

"What about Vinnie? Why's he called 'The Bat'?"

"Vinnie 'The Bat' Colabucci. Story is one of his girls was gonna go down on him, so she unzips him, pulls out his lumber, takes one look at it and says no way. She says it's as big as a Louisville Slugger. So he became 'The Bat.' Personally, I think he paid her to say that. I used to call him 'The Pencil.' Boy did he hate that." Radechenko chuckled. "Vinnie's a pretty big player here in town. He's connected to one of the New York Families."

"What's his action down here?"

"You name it, Vinnie's got a piece. Gambling, loan sharking, whores, money laundering, drugs."

"He ever do time?"

"When he was a kid. He went down a couple of times. Nothing major. Since then, he's been arrested half a dozen times. Never spent a day in jail. Vinnie's a scumbag but I couldn't ever prove it. Not to convince twelve of his peers beyond a reasonable doubt."

"They got a file on him downtown?"

"Big as this room."

"Thanks, Lieutenant. You've been a big help. I'd like to pay you for your time."

"Hell no. You gonna stick something on Vinnie?"

"I'm trying."

"Good luck. Being retired doesn't mean I quit hating Vinnie or Carmine or the rest of them. Just let me know what happens, okay?"

"Absolutely."

CHAPTER FIFTY-SEVEN

The next morning Don Blake rolled out of Crys Cassidy's embrace, quietly closed the bathroom door and took a shower. She'd been out all night watching Tiffany Ames. He dressed, put some cream cheese and smoked black drum on a bagel, brought the paper in for her and fixed himself a road mug of coffee.

Blake went back into the room and looked down at her. He reached out and traced a line with his finger along her elegant swan's neck. Blake remembered the story about Carmine's handiwork, shuddered and pulled back. He'd felt so vital and young with her; now he felt old and vulnerable again.

Crys stirred and curled up into a tuck with one hand under her cheek. Blake kissed her cheek and left for work.

Sid Bowman was deeply tanned, tall and pot-bellied. He rose when Don came in and gave him a big hug.

"Nice to see you, Don. How you been?"

"Fine, Sid. And you?"

"Good. Good. You ready?"

"Let's do it. Where do you want to work?"

"How about the conference room? Let me spread my stuff out."

"Fine. Want a cup of coffee?"

"No. Had my one for the day."

Don and Sid walked past the receptionist's area into the

conference room and closed the door.

"What do you have, Sid?"

"It's what I don't have that's interesting. I recreated Tom Tully's income and expense pattern and compared it to his tax returns. Nothing. A perfect fit. Money in. Money out. The guy spent every penny he made, but no more.

"Then you send me all that stuff from the Ames woman. I start looking for credit cards entries or checks to cover airfare, hotels, the fur, the loan, the jewelry, the dinners, everything, gambling in Atlantic City.

"It ain't there. He hasn't got it. I went back five years. I looked at all unaccounted-for cash. You know, cash taken out of deposits, cash advances on credit lines, checks to cash. Still doesn't make it. There's only one answer. He has another income. A hidden one, with hidden accounts, credit cards and investments. If so, he lied on his interrogatories, and he filed fraudulent tax returns. That puts him in a heap of shit.

"How about this, Sid? A hidden income, all cash. No investments, no bank account, nothing. Say twenty thousand in a coffee can in the garage. I knew a guy once carried fifty thousand dollars sewn in his jacket."

"Works for me. What do you know, Don?"

"Let me play Karnak with you. You went to corporate records in Baltimore, right?"

"Yes."

"Frutti di Mare Seafood Company is a . . ."

"Subsidiary of The Blessed Virgin Olive Oil Company."

"Which is . . ."

"Part of the Consolidated Food Importers Conglomerate."

"A . . ."

"Division of the FCF Holding Company."

"Okay, let's see. Which one is based in Baltimore?"

"Blessed Virgin Olive Oil."

"The others are in New York."

"Right."

"The CEO of Blessed Virgin is, wait a minute, it's coming to me." Blake slapped a hand to his forehead. "Vincente or Vincenzo Colabucci, yes?" Blake smiled.

"Not bad, Karnak. Close. He's the treasurer. The CEO is . . ."

"Of course, Carmine Rivera."

"Bingo, Karnak. How'd you know?"

"I got an ID on the owners of the car. They're the source of Mr. Tully's secret income. It's all cash, it's small bills in a brown paper bag in a dark alley. It's drugs or gambling or whores or all three. Not only is it hidden, it's dirty money. I'm going to call Lou Carlson with this. See what we do next."

Blake dialed Carlson at the Law School. "Lou, Don Blake. Got some good news for you. You ready for it?"

"Let me clear my desk so I can take notes."

Carlson lifted piles, intact, and set them on a chair or on other piles. He pulled a pad into the clearing and said, "What have you got?"

Blake brought Carlson up to date on the investigation.

"I think he went to 'The Bat' because he needed more money. You'd just stuck him with spousal support. He's not just going to lose his kids; he's out of a job. The league won't tolerate coaches hanging out with known gamblers. He could even be looking at a criminal investigation. This guy is breaking out in trouble like an Israeli marketplace."

"Beautiful, Don. Put it all together. The books, Ames' affidavit, the tape, everything you've got and get it over to me as soon as you can."

"What are you going to do to him, Lou?"

"I don't know. It's what I don't do that gives me leverage to get this settled. It won't do his kids any good to have all the assets vaporize into my wallet or Al Garfield's. This whole family could go down the shitter in a hurry. If he loses his job, there goes the money. I don't know what Serena can earn, but it isn't going to be near what her husband makes. Not for a while at least. Goodbye house and everything else."

Carlson thought about his options for a minute, and then asked, "How do you think Colabucci got his hooks into him?"

"Tully's no Boy Scout. He likes to gamble. He chases anything in a skirt. Maybe he lost more money than he could cover. A guy like Vinnie would love to have a hook into a pro ball club. My source says he runs the typical one-stop vice shop: sex, drugs and gambling. Tully could be providing these services to players. In exchange he's now getting a salary. Maybe he's leaking information on injuries, or other performance-related things, like who's drinking more, whose wife left him, to affect the betting line."

"How would Colabucci go about doing that?"

"If Tully exploits the time lag, and leaks information to Vinnie before the team files its report with the league, Vinnie could be putting down significant money before a game gets called or taken off the board. He could be creating middle, so he can get bets in on both sides of the final line.

"That's if Vinnie's gambling with the information. Suppose he's passing it on to the Vegas line. That's the mother of all lines. It's like an earthquake. You get a tremor on the Vegas line, you've got aftershocks all over the country. It affects gamblers everywhere. Vinnie could be using it that way. In exchange for a piece of the take on the games affected.

"Maybe he's running a renegade line with this information. People laying off bets against the prevailing line with him. He shouldn't do that too often or he'll get an all-expenses ride out to BWI in the trunk of his Cadillac, where he'll stay until he smells. There's lots of ways he could be using information from Tully. A coach is perfectly placed to leak that stuff. The more I think about it, the more I like it. This could be worth millions to Vinnie. I'm sure Tully paid his debt off long ago, but once you're in, you can't back out. Maybe he'll roll over on Vinnie. He'll lose his job, but he'll be out from under," Blake mused.

"Don't even think that, Don. If he rolls over on Vinnie, he'll have to go into a witness protection program. So will Serena and the kids. They'll spend the rest of their days looking over their shoulders. That's a hell of a price for custody. I want to get it for her without risking that. If I can. As soon as Tully and Garfield know that we know about the connection, it's out of our hands. I don't trust those bastards to look out for anyone but themselves. This information is a doomsday weapon. Once it's unleashed there won't be any winners, just survivors . . ."

"What are you going to do then?"

"The perfect outcome is for Reece to find in favor of Serena. Then I can sit down with Albert and show him some of the cards we've got. The ones we control completely, and use them to dictate a settlement. It's up to us to press the perjury issue on the interrogatories. Tully won't fight it because he knows that's the doorway to his cash income and his ties to Colabucci."

"But that still leaves Tully in with the mob. Someone else might discover the connection and your client has the same problems."

"Maybe after the custody is settled and they're disconnected we leak some low impact stuff to the club. Enough to get him fired and out of football but nothing more. That makes him useless to the mob without exposing the connection. They can both go their own ways. There's no reason for either side to bring it up. Serena and the kids can get on with their lives. It'll cost her money but she'll have to get a job anyway."

"Suppose Reece goes the other way, then what?"

"Then I'll really wish I was retired. I'll have to tell her. It's her decision, not mine."

"And if she decides to blow the whistle, what then?"

"Let's not go there. Not until we have to."

"Any way to get a read on which way Reece is leaning?"

"Not without putting Albert Garfield on the phone. Reece won't talk to either of us alone."

"You want to send any of this over to Reece?"

"No, not yet. The fewer people know about this the better. Anybody other than Bowman know what you found?"

"No."

"Let's keep it that way. Put the originals of your notes and the tape in your vault."

Carlson hung up and thought about how to negotiate with Agent Orange. The key was misdirection. Garfield would only give away what you didn't appear to want.

CHAPTER FIFTY-EIGHT

Vinnie calmed down after some serious head from one of the dancers. With a criminal investigation underway, it was clear he and Tully shouldn't meet. Not even Carmine should see him. That putz. Running right up here for money, straight from the courthouse. He was lucky nobody followed him. Vinnie's contacts in the police told him that the investigation still hadn't come up with anything. Forensics was negative. Mrs. Tully's statement hadn't provided any suspects. The private opinion of at least one officer was that one of the Squires was doing Coach Tully a favor. Tom Tully claimed he knew nothing and had a wonderful alibi for the assault. He was at a meeting with the other coaches to review game films, a meeting that included a shrieking tirade directed at him by the head coach after a particularly poorly-covered punt.

The investigation had turned up a couple of reports of a very large black man in the neighborhood before the assault. One resident saw him sitting in a sleek dark green car watching the house. They didn't get a tag number, and the car disappeared around the time the neighbor had become suspicious. Another neighbor had reported the same man and car parked behind the house and watching it through the yard. No one had actually seen a man enter the house or leave it.

Another neighbor reported seeing a black or maybe dark green car speed through a stop sign a couple of blocks from the house. The investigation was ongoing.

Vinnie had read the psychologist's entire file. There was nothing in there that linked them together. Her first lawyer was a real chump. He could see how Tully thought this would be a walkover. The new guy was no dummy. He'd be looking into his assets. Nothing there, since they only dealt in cash. But Tully was not reliable. He was impulsive. He could have done something stupid that Vinnie didn't know anything about. It was time to call a halt to this. There was way too much money at stake here. Tully's three tips last season had moved the line enough to bring in over two million dollars. Not a bad investment on his hundred-thousand-dollar salary. Of course, Tully didn't know what he was worth. He'd have asked for more money. He'd paid off the hundred K he'd lost a long time ago. But, you can't be a virgin twice. Tully was theirs and it was time for this shit to end.

Vinnie dialed Tully's home.

"Hey, Tommy. It's Vinnie."

"Yeah, what's up?" Tully was wary. Vinnie had already stiffed him on the money. Albert Garfield was making noises that without more money he couldn't go on in this case. Whatever he'd said to Junior had scared the shit out of him. When he came back into the office, there was blood all over the desk and Junior's shirt and something moving in the wastebasket. Junior was unhurt but he wouldn't say anything at all on the way to school and he hadn't seen him all week.

It probably wasn't smart to take Junior with him. He should have dropped him at school first. But he told him to stay in the car. Kid wouldn't follow orders. If he'd only followed orders, nothing would have happened.

"This is what's up, Tom. I been thinking about your situation. There's a lot more at stake here than your kids. I was gonna change my mind, send you the money for this, but I got a call from somebody told me about this criminal investigation. Somebody beat up your wife. Tried to get her to settle. That was pretty fuckin' stupid, Tom. No subtlety. Why didn't you come to me for this? You were getting desperate? There were other ways we could have fixed this. Put a cunt into that shrink's office. Get him to dip his wick in her. Then we got him, the evaluation and the kids. But no, a two-by-four you gotta use.

"I can't have this shit going on, Tom. We got an arrangement, you and me. There's a lot of money at stake here, Tom. A lot. I ain't gonna have you fuck this up. Not over your kids."

"Vinnie, You ain't got kids, so you . . ."

"Shut up, Tom. You don't give a fuck about your kids. Up until you caught somebody laying pipe to your wife, I never heard one word out of you about your kids. This is about your bitch fucking you over and you having to take it. If you'd a come to me with that problem when this first started, we could have taken care of that. But no, you had to get fancy and punish her. I read the fuckin' file, Tom."

"What? How'd you get that? What does it say?"

"That ain't the fuckin' point. You ain't fuckin' listening to me. This is over. I'm telling you this is over. Not just I ain't giving you any money, but you're going to your attorney and tell him to settle this thing now. You take whatever they give you, you say 'thank you' and sign the fuckin' papers. I don't want anybody messing into our business. No shrinks, no lawyers, definitely no cops. I don't know why I listened to you in the first place. I should'a put a halt to this as soon as you told me."

"You listened to me because you need me. I heard what you said. There's lots of money at stake here. You're making that money 'cause of what I give you. You don't want to piss me off, Vinnie, because then I won't make you rich any more. You're right. This is about that whoring bitch cunt, my wife. She's gonna pay. I am not gonna take this lying down. I ain't gonna take nothing lying down."

As Tom's voice grew shriller, more out of control, Vinnie calmed down. The conversation was over but only he knew it.

"I ain't gonna take nothing. She's gonna pay. Just like I said. She ain't gonna walk away with anything. No money, no kids, no house, nothing. You ain't telling me what to do, Vinnie. Nobody tells me what to do. She's gonna pay. You're gonna give me the money to do it with. You don't and I got nothing to say to you. The golden goose ain't laying no more eggs."

Vinnie was completely calm when he replied. "Let me make sure I understand you, Tom. I asked you to put this aside and not jeopardize our mutually beneficial business and you tell me that if I don't give you the money, our business is over. Did I get that right?"

"You got it, Vinnie. Dead right."

"Okay, Tom, if that's your decision. I guess I'll just have to take it. Our business is over. You do what you gotta do."

Hanging up, Vinnie said to no one in particular, "And I'll do what I gotta do."

CHAPTER FIFTY-NINE

"Lou Carlson for Albert Garfield."

"Hold please."

"Albert Garfield, here."

"Al, let's talk about this Tully case."

"So, talk."

"We've got proof of adultery on his part. His girlfriend was an expensive hobby. We've been going over your client's answers to interrogatories and his financial records. Your client lied under oath, Al. The money doesn't add up. Now I want to talk settlement. Mrs. Tully has no assets. I haven't collected penny one on this. I'd like to wrap it up and go back to teaching law without taking a bath on this. If we slug it out in court, I'll win, Al, but I'll lose my shirt on this. I don't need the aggravation."

Garfield doodled, arrows and boxes, all looping back on themselves. Tully's retainer was gone and he said he couldn't come up with any more for the case. He wanted Garfield to take it out of the proceeds of the house. Even in this market, he'd be fifty thousand in the hole before they sold it. This was fortuitous timing. He wouldn't have to drop Tully as a client, just get him a good deal. Tully was a dangerous client. Adoration in the front door, a malpractice action out the back, if he didn't get what he wanted. He'd have to sell him on the idea of how hard he fought for him, how bad the situation turned out to be, emphasize his fault for lying.

"Okay. What's your offer?"

"Let's turn it over to Reece. He's the court's expert. We can't take him out of the equation. Kenniston will want to know what Reece thinks. If we agree to his recommendations, we look like heroes to Kenniston. Sparing the children the bloodshed of a custody battle. Who'd expect it of us? I've got nothing to prove, Al. I'm retired. I like it that way."

"If you want to hear what Reece has to say, I'll go along for the ride."

"Let's get him on the phone now, while we're both here. That's the only way he'll talk to us."

Carlson relaxed for a moment. He hadn't lost his touch, not entirely. Custody cases with Al Garfield were a poker game with a pot full of children. He was dealt the cards, he upped the ante, made the raises, called the bluffs; but it was Serena Tully who would read 'em and weep.

"Morgan Reece."

"Dr. Reece, this is Lou Carlson and Albert Garfield. We're exploring a settlement in the Tully matter. Do you think you could spare us a few minutes of your time? We want to know if you've reached any conclusions about the custody of the children."

Reece was stunned by the question. He never spoke to the attorneys until he was done with his work. Why were they asking?

"Uh, I'm not done, gentlemen. When I'm done, I'll call you and the clients and give you my conclusions and recommendations in a formal report."

"We understand that's your normal procedure." This time it was Garfield. "But we're trying to settle this matter in as timely a manner as possible. Some insight into your position would be enormously beneficial."

"I'm not sure I understand. You want an interim report?"

"Yes, that's a good way to put it," they chorused.

"I don't know. I've never done this before. I'm very reluctant to release information before I've collected all my data. My impressions at this point are just that, impressions. Nothing more."

"We could depose you, Dr. Reece."

Good old Albert Garfield. Two minutes trying to co-operate was all he could endure. What did Carlson have that brought him to the negotiating table?

"And I'd get a protective order. We could waste a lot of money they don't have."

"Dr. Reece, perhaps we can get your input without pinning you down to an opinion. First, how close are you to completion?"

"I'm going out to the house for a home visit on Saturday. Then the direct observations in my office on Monday and Tuesday. Same thing with Mr. Tully next week. If you put a gun to my head, I could have everything else pulled together and be ready Wednesday a week."

"Okay. Thank you. Ten days or so. We can do the rest of our negotiating in the meantime."

"Dr. Reece, let me ask you this," Garfield said. "Are you leaning in either direction? Are you leaning strongly? Without telling us who. Let us both assume the worst for our clients. Is this a done deal or not? Are you going through the motions for protection on the stand or do you really need more data?"

Reece mulled this one over. "Let me be very candid. I have grave concerns about both of your clients. This is not a good parent-bad parent case. Secondly, I really do need all of the data I can assemble. I don't know which way this is going to go. As for assuming the worst for both of your clients, I think that's a very prudent course of action. I'm not going to say any more about this."

"Thank you, Doctor."

The phones were cradled, leaving the three to wonder what was going on and what to do next. Playing poker for children was bad enough, Carlson thought, but it was insane to do it in the fog, when you couldn't see the other players' faces and, until the bets were laid, you didn't even know how many were at the table.

CHAPTER SIXTY

Albert Garfield called Tom Tully at the team's headquarters.

"Tom, Albert Garfield. We need to talk."

"I can't now. I've got to get to a meeting."

"Be late. You're in a lot of trouble. I want to know what kind. I can't do anything for you, unless I know the truth."

Tully did not recognize the instant chill that Garfield's words evoked as anything but the ignition for his rage.

"What the fuck did I give you all that money for? You're supposed to be the best, a fucking killer attorney. Why am I listening to this?"

"You're listening because if you don't, I'll fire you. What have you done? Lou Carlson thinks he has you by the short hairs. I don't think he's bluffing."

"I haven't done anything. I don't know what he's talking about."

"Okay for starters, he says he's got proof of adultery on your part. What's that about?"

Tully wondered who they'd found. Tiffany probably. She was the only one still in town. He could deal with her. Love her up a little, she'd tell the right story. What if it was someone else? Had they been investigating him?

"Hey, even if I was unfaithful, I had plenty of reason. Serena wouldn't have sex with me. What was I supposed to do? Play spank the monkey? No thank you. I've got needs. She was supposed to take care of them. When she didn't, I

301

went elsewhere. That ain't adultery.' "

Garfield pressed on, wondering how much rehabilitation Tully would require. Send him to Pecorino for some pre-trial work, clean up his image, at least get him to say the right things. "Help me with this, Mr. Tully. How is that different from your wife having a lover, whom by the way, we still haven't found?"

"What do you mean how is that different? I was always ready to give it to Serena, whenever she wanted. There was no reason for her to go elsewhere. That's the difference. I can't believe you're even asking me this."

"I'm asking you because you didn't tell me you'd had sex with other women."

"What for? I didn't do anything wrong."

Garfield didn't know whether to be more worried if Tully believed what he said, or if he didn't. "They also say you lied on your interrogatories. That you have money that you didn't declare. How would they know that? What are they talking about?"

"I don't know."

"Let's try a different question. Is that the truth? Did you lie on your interrogatories?"

Tully felt like he was watching a motion offense. Lineman up and down, backs shifting, receivers in motion, then back. He'd never solved those deceptions and was burned in coverage. That was why he'd never made it beyond special teams. All the recklessness, the savage hitting, wasn't enough. He still didn't understand why.

"No. I don't have anything else."

Garfield scratched his head. Carlson or his client? Who was lying? Was Carlson bluffing to force him to negotiate because he had nothing or was he loaded? Was Tully lying? No, how much was Tully lying?

"Tom, the money you used to pay my retainer, where did that come from?"

"What's that supposed to mean?"

"Seems pretty simple, Tom. Where did the money come from?" Garfield had copies of all his bank records. Any withdrawal would be there.

"It was a loan."

"A loan? From whom? I don't remember seeing it on your list of debts."

"Not a *loan* loan. It was a gift. If I couldn't pay it back, that wasn't a problem."

"Wonderful to have the trust of others. Who gave you the money?"

"That's none of your business. You got paid."

"That I did. But if there's no problem, why won't you tell me who gave it to you?"

"A friend."

"Tom, this is pathetic. Do you have any idea how this will sound in court? The judge can compel you to answer. Who gave you the money?"

When Tully didn't answer, Garfield went on. "I don't think I want to know who gave you the money. I think Carlson has you. I don't know how; maybe you bought some chippy a gift that he can't find. That's not important. You lied under oath. That's a crime. Perjury. If you've hidden income, you could be looking at tax fraud. You can't take this to trial.

"Your only hope of coming out with anything is for Reece to grant you custody because Carlson won't use this if it'll hurt the kids. You can ride that for child support, maybe keep your share of the house. If he goes the other way, you're shit out of luck. She'll get the kids, support, alimony, the house, everything. You'll get whatever Carlson and your wife want to give you.

"I recommend you fold your cards and walk away from this. I can't negotiate without them being afraid of litigation. I don't have enough to hurt them with. You're gonna have to take what they give you."

"What the fuck is going on? I don't get this. I had her. I did everything you said. She was out on the street. She had no money. She had nothing. I had her. What do you mean I have to take what they give me? The fuck I do. I don't have to take anything."

"I'm afraid you will. You lied to me. You've done things that were illegal. You've undone all the leverage we created for you. That's what's going on. You did this to yourself, Mr. Tully, and now it's too late to help you."

"Fuck you, Garfield, you sorry son of a bitch. Don't tell me I did this to myself. I did it your way and it went to shit. As soon as that bastard Carlson got in there, you were about as useful as a one-legged man at an ass-kicking."

"Mr. Tully, I wasn't the one who assaulted your wife. That tactical masterpiece is what got Carlson in this case and we both know whose idea that was. You wouldn't wait. You had to rush things. You better hope they don't tag you with that. Goodbye football, hello prison.

"When we had that moron Stuart, we were doing fine. I told you at the start this would work if we had the right lawyer on the other side. We did. Once that changed, the flaws were exposed. You provided Carlson the information to turn this around, not me. If you'd told me this up front we'd have played it differently, or I'd have had a chance to put the proper spin on it. It's too late now. Your only hope of walking away with anything is for your wife to fuck up the home visit this Saturday. What do you want me to tell Carlson when he calls?"

"Tell him and my wife to go fuck themselves. You can join

'em. Fuck you all. Fuck you to death."

Garfield was never so glad to be fired. He dictated a letter of termination, attached a final bill and informed his malpractice carrier that he had ceased to represent a disgruntled and uncooperative client.

CHAPTER SIXTY-ONE

"Please come in, Ms. Tully," Morgan Reece said as he stood back from his office door.

Serena Tully walked in. She wore a leather jacket and boots that disappeared into a long shirtdress. She hesitated to remove her sunglasses, then did so and sat down.

Morgan Reece sat and stroked his beard with indecision. Where to start? He knew where he wanted to end up but could not force the result. Back to basics, he thought. Start with what is foremost in your mind and work from there.

"Ms. Tully, I have a serious problem. I called and asked you to come in because I need your help with this. I'm leaning strongly towards giving custody of the children to their father and unless you help me see things differently, that's probably what I'm going to do."

Serena sat silently and still. Her stomach churned and rolled like a washing machine and the elevator bringing air to her was stuck in her throat.

"Why?"

"You tell me, Ms. Tully. Can you think of any reason that I might feel that way?"

"No. I don't know. You seemed upset about Tommy."

"Anything else?"

"Well you were angry with me because I didn't call you."

"That's part of it. I was concerned that you didn't seem to understand how troubled Tommy was."

"I told you I thought it was just an adjustment thing."

"I don't believe you, Ms. Tully."

"How can you say that?"

"I think you knew your son was in trouble."

"That's crazy. If I thought Tommy was in trouble, I'd do anything for him."

"And you did. You kept Felicia Hurtado around because you knew he was in trouble. And because you were in trouble."

"I don't know what you're talking about. What trouble? I haven't done anything."

"How do you feel, Ms. Tully?"

"I'm okay."

"I don't think so. I told you last time you looked and sounded depressed. You still do. Your eyes are red; your face is puffy and blotchy. Takes a fair bit of crying to do that."

Serena touched her hand to her face. She'd thought of putting on makeup, but couldn't get her hands to stop shaking. Two tries and she looked like Tina had done it with crayons.

"Why are you depressed, Serena?"

"I'm not. I'm just stressed out about everything. It's all just caught up with me."

"I don't think so. You looked a lot better when your life was a complete shambles than you do now. This isn't idle curiosity. Depressed parents have a hard time being available for their kids and that's bad for the kids. You're depressed and you've stuck Felicia in there to pinch hit for you. You know that you and Tommy are in trouble, but you won't get help for him or yourself. That's my problem, Ms. Tully. Right now you can't take care of yourself or your children. I don't know why. When I know why, I'll know what to make of this."

Serena hugged herself. Her pounding heart was the truth knocking louder and faster, demanding to be let out. First, it had to be let in and she couldn't bear that.

Morgan Reece leaned forward. Surprised, he felt the old thrill of standing with someone on a narrow ledge as she readied for her leap of faith in herself and life. It was for the privilege of those few moments that you slogged through the countless hours of returning to square one in therapy.

"Why aren't you in therapy, Ms. Tully? Now when you need it more than ever?"

Serena gasped for air. A lie surfaced and rode its way to shore. "I thought it wouldn't look good with the court date coming up." Serena wondered how long the lies would find their way to her tongue.

"And you told this to Simon Tepper. What did he say?"

"He agreed that it would be best for us to stop for awhile."

"I see, and then what?"

"We would begin again when the hearing was over."

"I see. Does this feel like it's best for you? How does this feel, Serena? Have you thought about going back to see him? Have you called and said maybe this isn't such a good idea?"

Serena clasped her hand to her mouth. The churning in her gut was climbing up her throat. She felt like vomiting the poisonous truth, but holding it in was all that held her together.

"We're at a crossroads, Serena. You and me, Tommy and Tina. Hard choices. Irrevocable ones."

Serena was paralyzed, drawn and quartered by love and its counterfeits. Reece had no idea if she'd go off the ledge like a bird or a rock. He pushed her closer.

"Where's your anger, Serena? You've been left to do this all alone. Does that sound like love? Is that how you love Tommy and Tina?"

Serena leaned forward, groping for the trashcan by the sofa. She fell to her knees, retching. Reece came out of his chair, knelt next to her and pressed a hand to her forehead, something he had not done since Danielle had been a child.

Serena pushed him in the chest. "Don't touch me."

Reece let go and sat back listening to the last wracking spasms.

Serena reached out blindly for a tissue. Reece pushed the box over to her. She wiped her mouth with one then blotted her eyes and blew her nose. She sank back against the sofa.

"Let me get that out of here," Reece said, and carried the can from the office. He returned and sat facing her on the floor.

Serena covered her eyes with her hand and turned her head away. "He told me we had to stop seeing each other, until the hearing was over. That it made me look bad being in therapy. I said, couldn't we meet anyway, not as therapy but as lovers? He said no. We had to keep it a secret."

"So he asked you to protect him. That's why you wouldn't answer any questions about who you were seeing. Does Lou Carlson know any of this?"

Serena sniffed and shook her head.

"Did you ask Simon to see you after you got depressed?"

Serena nodded.

"What did he say?"

"He said it was too dangerous. He was afraid we'd be found out."

"Did he refer you to anyone else?"

"No."

"So he left you all alone. He abandoned you, Serena. I knew all about your history. We went over that. It didn't mean anything unless it impaired your parenting. I didn't get

309

concerned until you checked out while Tommy was falling apart."

"I didn't know that. You're so cold, so flat. I had no idea what you thought of me. You don't give anything away, Dr. Reece."

Reece pursed his lips. His renowned inscrutability. So well practiced. The professional mandate that masked the personal need. A shell, impermeable: nothing in, nothing out. He wondered if it could be dismantled.

"He wasn't looking out for you. He was looking out for himself. He's in enormous trouble ethically, legally, professionally, personally. You name it. How did it start?"

"I was lonely and depressed. My marriage was dead. I felt like a failure at everything. He was so patient and understanding. Different from any other man I'd ever known. I felt so safe with him, so good. It was like he knew my feelings before I did."

Sure he did, Reece thought, grinding his teeth. The stunningly accurate insights, the relentless focus on the other person as infinitely worthwhile. Finally, the uncontested center of attention, just for being yourself. Wasn't this the love we all sought? Simon Tepper was a homely middle-aged man with a homely middle-aged wife. He'd never been within hailing distance of a woman that looked like Serena Tully.

"When did you become lovers?"

"I don't know. I mean I felt like I was in love before we ever did anything. I thought he loved me. One session, I was crying about my father, how I always disappointed him, no matter how hard I tried. I felt very little and alone and ugly. Simon came over and put his arm around me. I remember holding onto him and crying on his chest. The next thing he lifted my chin up and we were kissing. I knew what I was doing. I wanted to kiss him. He told me we shouldn't be doing this, but he couldn't help himself. He loved me too much."

"I guess that's a special kind of love when a man would risk everything for it. And from a special man."

"I thought so." Serena said and grimaced, trying to hold back her tears.

"So you began to see him more often."

"Whenever we could. He'd call from his office and I'd go to see him. One time Tom and his wife were both out of town. Simon and I spent the weekend at a local hotel. Tom came back unexpectedly early. I wondered if that was when Tom found out. Simon dropped me back at the house and Tom came in right after he left."

"What did he say when he told you that you had better stop meeting?"

"He said we had to stop. That we shouldn't have done it. That it was a mistake. That he'd looked deep inside himself and realized that he only meant to comfort me, to make me feel better about myself."

Looked deep inside himself, now there's a contradiction in terms, Reece thought. He marveled at the "we" Tepper used. Given enough time he'd convince her that it was all her fault or a hallucination or both.

"I pleaded with him not to. Tommy was acting strangely. I was frightened. When he said no, I felt like the bottom of my world had given way."

"What kept you from revealing the secret?"

"The last time I went to see him, I was desperate. I didn't call. I just showed up. I made him see me. I told him I was suicidal. I was. I meant it. It was just like before. Like nothing had changed."

"What did he say?"

"He said he couldn't stand to see me like this. That I had

to be patient. That once the custody was decided we could start seeing each other again. I asked him what as, patient or lover? He said he didn't know. That I still had things to work on. That we had to look at our relationship as part of the therapy. That there were important things to learn from this. That we learn the most from our mistakes."

Reece massaged his forehead. He was dizzy from the mad self-serving logic of Simon Tepper. More than Tepper's abuse, Reece detested his cowardice, his refusal to accept responsibility for what he had done. He'd tried to tie her hands with knots of her own complicity. Where he had no guilt, she had enough for two. Reece was sure Serena Tully had not been the first.

"And you'd have held onto that hope unless I threatened you with an even greater loss?"

"Yes," she whispered, head down. "Why did you do that?"

"I had to know. Would your kids come first, or protecting your relationship with Tepper?"

"So you knew. How?"

"Like I said. You kept it together while your husband was blitzing you, then all of a sudden you fell apart when you got the kids and the house back. That told me you'd lost something really vital to you. Essential. What? What made you depressed in the past? What made you suicidal? You'd been betrayed by men you loved. You don't love your husband. His betrayal of you by his sneak attack scared you and angered you, but you weren't devastated. That said to me you had a lover, someone else who was more important to you. Your husband showing me the letter confirmed it. You fought back because you had the support of someone you loved and you thought loved you. When you got depressed and stopped attending to yourself or the kids, I was pretty sure you'd been abandoned again. The question was who, and why weren't you getting help.

"I knew you were seeing Simon more than once a week. Felicia told me when I interviewed her. In your testimony you said you saw him for therapy once a week. His clinical notes matched that. I figured you were telling Felicia you were going to therapy as a cover for seeing your lover. It's a great cover story. You're gone a couple of hours. You're legitimately incommunicado. It wasn't until you told me that Simon had agreed not to see you that I began to wonder. No therapist would cut you loose at a time like this, not the way you looked.

"So I went over everything I had in the file. Way back when I first saw your husband, he said that the private investigator following you said that you didn't go anywhere except to the doctor. I took out the copy of the poem that your husband gave me and compared the handwriting with his session notes. They're a match. What I had to know was how far you would go to protect him and your relationship with him. Now I do."

"What are you going to do to me?"

"To you? Nothing. Simon Tepper exploited and abused your trust and vulnerability. He betrayed your love and abandoned you when you needed him most. On top of that he's tried to make you feel like it's your fault, or just a mistake in technique."

"It is my fault. He didn't force himself on me. I wanted to have a relationship with him. I was in love with him."

"Ms. Tully, you'd have more of a relationship with an ATM machine. Regardless of what you were willing to do, it was Dr. Tepper's duty not to use his relationship with you for his own needs. Period. If Tommy would let you touch his penis or wanted you to, would that make it okay? No. You're not responsible for what he did."

Serena faced the fact that once again she had been played for a fool and sold herself cheap. The bitter tide of self-loathing rose again and she raced to the bathroom.

Morgan Reece sat alone, adrift in a sea of easy wisdom that he would not drink from.

CHAPTER SIXTY-TWO

When Serena returned, she sat on the sofa, took a tissue and held it at the ready. Morgan Reece climbed back into his chair.

"Mrs. Tully I have to put this in my report. I can't keep it out. Your relationship did affect your parenting. The problem was with Dr. Tepper, not you. Ultimately, your kids did come first, even at the expense of any hope of a relationship with Dr. Tepper. His behavior is a clear violation of ethical standards. There are a number of avenues available to you if you wish to take any action. You can report him to the American Psychiatric Association or the state health care board. You can sue him. Whatever you decide to do, I will be available to provide information on your behalf. Right now the most important thing is for you to get a new therapist for yourself and one for Tommy. If you want, I'll make a recommendation to you."

"Please."

"There's a pair of therapists that work over in Bethesda. Bryce Kaplan is an excellent child therapist. Sandi Myers is also very good. I'd recommend you see her."

Reece turned to his desk, found their addresses and phone number on his Rolodex, wrote them down and handed them to her.

"What about Tom? Do you have to tell him?"

"No. I'd strongly recommend that you tell Lou Carlson, though. Once my report is released, it won't be a secret to anyone. Lou will want to discuss the ramifications and make plans before he has to deal with Albert Garfield's use of this information."

"What happens next?"

"I'll be out this weekend to see you and the kids. Then you'll come in for the direct observation sessions next week. Then I'll do the same thing next week with Tom. You're in the home stretch, Mrs. Tully."

"God, this has been a long race. How am I doing, Dr. Reece?"

"I can't answer that, Mrs. Tully. Let's just say a lot better than when you came in here. It may not feel like it, but it's true."

"Thank you, Dr. Reece. Regardless of what you decide about custody, you've helped me a great deal and that has to be good for the kids."

"I hope so. I hope so."

CHAPTER SIXTY-THREE

Morgan Reece woke from a fitful sleep Saturday morning and inventoried his anxieties. Was it the Tully case? No more anxiety than any other case. Rock climbing on Sunday? That could be it. He hadn't thought about it since he'd talked to Lindsay at the beginning of the week. Interesting, he thought of her as Lindsay, not Ms. Brinkman.

He could not recall any dreams. He had had dreams about falling of such intensity that he awoke with his arms in front of his face expecting concrete to greet him.

Reece went into the kitchen and poured himself a cup of coffee. It was more than just anxiety. He went into his study and took Danielle's picture off his desk. It was her school picture. The last one taken of her. He wished he had some candid ones of her. Her mother took them all the night she left.

Reece sat in the breakfast nook and propped the picture up before him. Danielle's copper hair flashed its gold highlights. Reece saw all the places where she and her mother converged. The wave in the hair, the high forehead, upturned nose, their lips so dark against their pale skin. He could not find himself in her flesh.

He and Elaine had fulfilled their marriage vows: "Till death do us part." They just hadn't known whose death. Reece never got over Elaine having her cremated without asking him. He understood that she wanted Danielle with her forever and that was the forever she needed. He had needed a quiet grassy place under a tree, where he could talk to her, where he could cry alone. He always saw her sleeping in the ground. A place where she could always be found intact as he remembered. He could not find her in that urn.

Reece had thought about killing himself. When he did not, he felt guilty that he was betraying Danielle by staying behind. That life without her was worth living. So, he sentenced himself to life without forgiveness. He tried to atone by doing some good every day, but he had not expiated his guilt.

Reece picked up the picture and put his fingers to the glass, as cold and unfeeling as her skin after she died. He stroked the glass and wondered if he was ready to just live and not endure. There were no answers today.

CHAPTER SIXTY-FOUR

Morgan Reece pulled into the driveway, jotted down the driving time, checked his list of questions and cut off the engine. He took his notepad and pen, got out and surveyed the house. Azalea beds on each side of the front porch. A well-tended front lawn. He peeked around the side of the house and saw the edge of a play gym in the backyard. There were curtains in all the windows.

He walked up the steps and rang the bell. A hand pulled back the curtain side panel and he saw little Tommy. The curtain snapped back and a moment later the door opened. Reece stepped inside.

"Good morning, Tommy. Where's your Mommy?"

Serena Tully stepped around the corner from the living room. She was wearing a short red silk kimono and she was breathing very slowly through her mouth. The engraved barrel of the Colt .45 jammed under her jaw explained that.

Serena moved forward slowly, with short stiff-legged steps, as if her ankles were shackled. Tom Tully appeared next to her.

"Well, if it isn't Doctor Reece, here to evaluate us. Good morning, Doctor. How nice of you to join us. Glad you brought your notebook. See, I'm conducting my own evaluation. And then I'm going to reach a conclusion and make some recommendations. Isn't that how you do it, Doc?"

Reece nodded very slowly. He couldn't take his eyes off

the gun and his mind was tuned to a dead channel, all noise and snow.

"Let's go inside." Tully waved the gun towards the family room to the left of the entrance hall.

Reece saw Tommy, wide-eyed and somber, come alongside him and their eyes met momentarily. Reece resisted the impulse to reassure him. Any attempt to undercut Tully's desperate show of power would probably get him killed.

Reece entered the family room. On the kitchen pass-through was a nearly empty bottle of Jack Daniels. Not a good sign, he thought. Rage, alcohol and a gun. The holy trinity of pointless death. Even with all his faculties, Tully would have been hard to reason with. With his inhibitions anesthetized and the distance from wish to deed just a finger pull, the slightest mistake in word or action could be fatal. Tina sat on the floor in front of the television talking in a hushed voice to her dolls. She did not even look up as everyone entered the room.

Tully waved everyone to a seat, then grabbed the bottle. Reece, Tommy and Serena all sat on the sofa. Tully swigged from the bottle once, then twice. Seeing that it was empty, he set it down, went to the liquor cabinet and opened a bottle of Wild Turkey. Draining an inch from the bottle, he took a deep breath, looked at his wife and son and said, "Let's do this right. You sit over here."

Serena moved over to a recliner, set ninety degrees to the sofa.

"Good. You're the first witness. Reece, you're the court reporter. We're gonna try this case right here and now. I'm the lawyer and this . . ." He stared at the gun. "This is the judge."

Serena tried to adjust her robe, which had slipped open above her knee.

"That's good, you slut. Leave it where it is." Tully shrieked, pointing his gun at her head.

Serena winced and turned her head away. Reece tried to see if the safety was off. He couldn't tell. The hammer was cocked. That much he knew.

"Let's start. You swear to tell the truth, the whole truth and nothing but the truth?"

"Yes." Serena whispered.

"I can't hear you," Tully thundered.

"Yes."

"Good. See how easy that was. First question for the witness. Have you been fucking other men while you were married to me?"

"Daddy, I have to go to the bathroom," Tommy said.

"Not now. Hold it. This is important. This is the kind of woman your mother really is. You need to hear this, Junior. The truth will set you free."

Tommy began to squirm. Reece looked down at the dark stain spreading across his pajama legs and soaking the cushion between them.

"Please let him go, Tom. He hasn't done anything. Do what you want with me, but don't hurt the children."

"Oh that's sweet, you bitch. Don't hurt the children. You're the one who's hurt the children. You're the one who ruined everything. Now you're worried about the children. It's a little fucking late for that. Answer the fucking question."

Tears streamed down her twitching, trembling face. "Yes, I did."

"Good. Who was it?"

"Doctor Tepper."

Tully's mouth fell open. "Doctor Tepper, that old fart? Jesus, Serena, you are sick." Tully began to laugh and took another swig from the bottle. "Why? Why him?"

"I thought I was in love with him."

"In love with him? Objection. You were married to me. You were my wife. You took a vow of fidelity. To me."

"Tom, my lawyer told me that you were having affairs too. You cheated on me, too."

"I did not. Don't you ever say that again." Tully got right in front of her and raised the gun high to smash across her face. Serena cowered and crossed her arms in front of her to take the blow.

"Daddy, I wet my pants. I gotta go."

Tully spun around to face his son. "Shut up. You wet 'em. You sit in it. You aren't a baby anymore, Junior."

Across the room, Tina picked up one of her dolls and smacked it viciously across the face.

Tully turned back to Serena. "You can't cheat a cheater. I didn't go looking elsewhere until you stopped sleeping with me. What was I supposed to do? That was your job. You're my wife."

"Tom, I couldn't. I was miserable. We didn't talk. You just yelled at me all the time. I was dying inside. My feelings for you died."

Tully mocked her with a singsong voice. "We didn't talk."

Then he roared, "Bullshit. Talk. We talked all the time. All you ever did was complain. You never did anything I told you to. I got sick of listening, Serena. You were unhappy and you were always gonna be unhappy. I couldn't fix it and you wouldn't. Don't try to lay that shit off on me." Another swig and the mocking began again. "Sorry honey. Not tonight. We didn't talk enough. I'm not happy yet. Make me happy first, then we can fuck." Swig. Roar. "That's not the deal. You used to want to do it all the time. You never said your feelings changed. You just went into the deep freeze."

"That's not true, Tom. I told you how I felt. I said let's go to counseling. You said no."

"Fucking right, I did. I didn't need counseling. You did. So I said go. I fucking paid for it, Serena. I paid for that guy to dick you. Jesus, Serena, he's a fucking Jew. You were supposed to go there and get your head fixed so we could go on being married. No, you decided to start putting out for him. Nice work, Doc. You thawed out her deep freeze so you could play hide the salami. Take a note, Doctor Reece."

Reece didn't move. Tully pointed the gun at his head. "Take a note."

Reece picked up his pen.

"When I'm done here, remind me to go to Dr. Tepper and blow his fucking brains out."

Tully took another long pull and let the gun drop to his side. "Where was I? Oh yeah. I'm gonna grant the divorce to Mr. Tully on the grounds of adultery and terminal whining and bitching by his wife. Now we have to have a property settlement, right? You've done this before Reece, isn't that right?"

Morgan Reece looked at Tom Tully. How long had he been at this? Since last night or when Serena arrived this morning? Must have been since last night. He wouldn't let her leave, so she changed into something to sleep in. With Tully? Had he slept at all? How much booze had he had? Maybe if they kept this going, he'd drink enough to pass out or slow down enough for him to be overpowered. Sober, he was too young, too strong, and too quick for Reece to even try it.

"Hey Reece, isn't that right?"

"Yes, Mr. Tully. That's right."

"Good. Let's see what we have to divide. Well we used to have all this." Tully turned, his arms outstretched, and surveyed the house. "And I had a job and a pension. You know what we have now, Serena?" He bent over so that his face was inches from hers. "Nothing. Nothing. You fucking ruined everything, Serena." He sprayed her with saliva as he screamed out the words.

"Not only are you to blame for this divorce. But you've ruined my life, Serena. You tried to steal from me. These kids, this house, my job, my retirement. What were you gonna do? Set up house with your Jew, huh? Figure you'd live off good old Tom Tully. No fucking way, you cunt. No fucking way."

"Tom, I don't know what you're talking about. We haven't asked for anything. You can have the house. You can have your pension. I'll give it all to you. Just let the kids go, Tom. Write something up, I'll sign it. I'll give you anything you want."

"Like last time? We used lawyers then. You signed the paper. Then boom! You turned right around and changed your mind. Next thing I know I'm out on the street, and I'm paying you to live here with my children. This is my house, Serena. Not yours. I paid for this. All of it."

Another swig. "Besides it's too late. I know what your lawyer found out. My lawyer told me. You fucked up everything, Serena."

"What, Tom? I don't understand."

"Your lawyer found my girlfriend. She's no fat old Jew, Serena. I'll tell you what. She makes you look like a dog, Serena, a fucking dog." Tully smiled at that wound.

"That means he knows I lied about the money. That I've got more money than I let on. He knows I lied to the ball club. I took money for trips with her that I shouldn't have. They'll fire me. I'll be blackballed. I'll never work in the league again. What am I gonna do? Coach high school? Be a gym teacher?

This is all I've ever done. This is all I know how to do. No more one hundred thousand a year paychecks. A hundred thousand? Two hundred thousand with Vinnie. Once I'm out, all that money dries up. How'm I gonna live on a high school teacher's salary? What am I gonna do? Pay you alimony, child support? With what?"

"I'll do without it, Tom. I'll get a job."

"Right. You'll say anything here. If I let you go, you'll run straight to that fucker Carlson. No thanks. Take a note, Reece. Kill Carlson."

Reece wrote the message very slowly. When would his name appear?

"You get custody of the kids, that fucker'll argue you should get the house. So they don't get stressed out having to move. Stressed out. I'll show you stressed out. Any money I've got, I'll have to give to the lawyer, especially if the league sues me. What's that leave me, Serena? You tell me? Huh?"

"It's just money, Tom. You make it. You lose it. You can make more. Maybe not as much. But you can. We've still got the kids. They need you, Tom. They need a father."

"Oh yes, the kids. Well let's ask the doctor here. So glad to have you with us today. Do I have kids or is this a shut-out?"

"Mr. Tully, this isn't a football game. There aren't winners and losers."

"Don't tell me that, you fucking sack of shit. There sure are winners and losers. That's what it's all about. Football. Life. Winning and losing. So what'll it be, Doc?"

Tully stood directly before Reece and pointed the gun right between his eyes. "The truth, Doc. If I think you're lying, you're dying."

Reece saw himself walking on a beach, his trousers were rolled up. Danielle was playing in the surf. Prufrock lied. The world would end with a bang. Not a whimper.

"Mr. Tully, I haven't made my mind up. I'm still collecting data."

"Bad answer, Doctor. I think you're lying." Tully slowly squeezed the trigger.

"I was going to recommend custody to your wife, Mr. Tully."

"Well fuck me with a chain saw, what a surprise. You laying pipe to her, too?"

Tully turned back to his wife. "Well that's that. This case is over. You get the kids, the house, and my money. I get to teach phys. ed. in west bumfuck. I don't think so."

Serena leaped from the chair as Tom turned. She reached for the gun with both hands. Tully pulled his arm free and ripped the pistol backhand across her temple. Serena collapsed like a dynamited building.

Reece swept Tommy behind him and took two steps before Tully turned the gun on him.

"Now where were we?" he said.

The doorbell rang.

CHAPTER SIXTY-FIVE

"Sit down," Tully barked.

Reece put his hands up and backed towards the sofa. Feeling the edge, he sat down. Tommy was on the near edge, looking down at his mother, who bled slowly onto the wood floor.

"Tina, come here . . . Sit on the sofa."

Tina walked past her mother. She had a doll hugged tight to her chest and her thumb in her mouth.

Tully pointed the gun at Reece's chest. "Don't move. I hear your lungs expand and I'll kill you. All the doors are dead-bolted and I've got the keys."

The doorbell rang again. Tully walked towards it. Reece scanned the room. If he threw a chair through the window, he could get out. Maybe he could scoop the children up in his arms and get them out. He'd never get Serena out. If he got out and whoever was out front got away, they could get the police here in minutes. It would be a hostage situation. They had trained negotiators. He couldn't save them all. Serena was the one he was most likely to kill. Maybe he should try to get her out. Leave the kids. She'd be the hardest to move with. He probably couldn't pick her up and carry her out in the time he'd have. No. This guy had put himself in a corner. He saw no options, no hope. This was exactly the situation where people killed themselves, their kids, everyone. If not in this world, they'd have custody in the next one.

Maybe getting out wasn't the answer. He should rush Tully at the door, when his back was turned. Hope it wasn't a neighbor kid over to play with Tommy. Together they might overpower him or at least disarm him. Reece decided to rush him if he had a chance; otherwise it was out the window with the kids.

Tully pulled back the curtain. He had the gun down at his side. The guy was some kind of deliveryman. He had a uniform on and there was a van in the driveway. Lost Arrow Deliveries. He had a box in his hands with a clipboard on top of it.

Tully stuck the gun in his waistband and opened the door.

"Tom Tully?" the man asked.

"Yeah."

"I got a delivery for you. Please sign here." The man turned the clipboard towards Tully and supported it with the box.

Tully looked for the line he had to sign on. The guy was an old geezer. Jesus, you live that long and you wind up a fucking deliveryman. Must have had a helluva divorce.

Tully reached for the pen. As he did, the old man pulled the silenced .22 from inside the box, put it against Tully's left eye and pulled the trigger. Phfft. Tully fell back dead and knocked the door open going down.

There were other people in the house. That idiot Colabucci told him that the guy lived alone. He was getting divorced. The wife had the kids. Fuck this.

Reece saw Tully fall back and the old man step across his body. What was going on? The man had a gun with a very long barrel in his hand. He closed the front door. Reece spun away and looked for Tommy. Tommy had run to the kitchen door and was turning the useless knob.

"Tommy let go. It's locked." Reece yelled.

The old man moved towards him, his gun arm fully extended. Reece swept Tina up in his arms and ran for the stairs. He looked back. The man was between him and Tommy.

Two long strides and the old man was behind Tommy. Christ, kids. He was going to have to talk to Vinnie about this one. He didn't get to this point by being careless. Prison was no place for a man of his years. Besides, a kid this unlucky was bound to die young.

He put the gun to the back of Tommy's head and pulled the trigger. The slow-moving bullet bounced around inside his tiny skull like a racquetball before it finally stopped. The old man lowered his body to the ground.

The woman on the floor was unconscious. Leave her for last? No. Easy enough to do it now. Who knows, she could come to any second. He pulled the trigger. Then again. Serena Tully jerked twice and died.

Okay. Up the stairs. One guy. One kid. Boom, boom and we're outta here. The old man had been doing this work for almost forty years. He prided himself that on only one hit had his name surfaced as a suspect. Ghost in, ghost out. Change m.o.'s. Use what was handy. This was not one he wanted to be tagged with. Killing kids. Not the reputation he'd worked so hard to build. A witness is a witness. Rule number one: no loose ends. No exceptions. He might just whack Vinnie when this was over for putting him in this situation.

Gliding up the stairs behind his gun, he found all the doors open. There were noises to his left. He pressed himself against the doorframe, then spun through it. The man was crouched in the far corner. He pointed the gun at him.

"Where's the kid?"

"She's in the bathroom. I locked her inside. She never saw you. I covered her eyes. Don't hurt her. She's only two years old. She's too young to talk."

The old man moved into the room. He saw the closed door to his left out of the corner of his eye.

"Hey, I'm sorry about this, but I got rules. You'd lie to save the kid. I understand that. I just can't take the chance. You all just ran into a shitload of bad luck. It happens."

The old man rapped on the bathroom door. "Open up honey. If you don't, I'll have to kill the nice man here. We don't want that to happen, do we?"

When the door didn't open, he tried the handle. It was locked. "What's her name?"

Reece shook his head. The old man pointed his gun at him. "What's her name?"

"Rebecca. We call her Becky."

"Okay Becky, honey. Come on, open up."

Reece knew that his life had come down to one single question and that he was seconds from answering it. When the old man turned his head to talk through the door, he shoved his hand under the mattress, found the grip and pulled the gun from the bed.

"Don't move," he croaked, his voice breaking with fear.

The old man looked at him. This was getting out of hand.

"Don't shoot. You don't want to shoot." He slowly slid down the door, until he was squatting, with his gun pointed halfway between Reece and the ceiling. "You know what you got there. That's a .44 magnum. You don't want to shoot me with that."

"Why is that?"

The old man rapped on the door.

Reece yelled, "Don't come out. It's not me."

"That's good. You got a code so the kid'll know when to open the door. I keep rapping. Maybe I'll get her to open up." He rapped again. "Hear that. You have a real problem. This is a hollow core door. That .44 is gonna go right through me, this door and that little kid. You shoot me and she's dead, too. Unless you're superman that is and can see through doors. No. You don't want to take that chance."

Even as he said that he began to draw down on Reece, who promised himself that if he was wrong, he would kill himself. He could not bear the weight of another life.

Reece fired. The recoil of the big gun surprised him and threw his arms towards the ceiling. He steadied himself to shoot again, but it was unnecessary.

An enormous hole had appeared in the old man's chest. He slumped over and fell away from the door. An even larger hole appeared behind him. Reece vaulted over the bed, and pushed the man out of the way.

"Tina," he yelled. "It's Doctor Reece. It's safe to come out now." He rapped twice very quickly, then waited a count and rapped once more.

Nothing. No noise. No turning handle. She'd told him she was scared as they ran up the stairs. He shoved her in the bathroom, turned the lock and told her to hide in her safe place. What if she hadn't? Reece closed his eyes and began to cry.

The lock turned and the door opened. Reece spread his arms and Tina Tully climbed inside. She buried her head in the crook of his neck and he rubbed her back trying to calm her. Danielle had always gone to sleep this way.

Reece stood up, stepped over the old man and walked to the top of the stairs. He looked over the railing and saw red stains flowing into the hall from two directions. He couldn't take her downstairs. Reece looked into the other rooms and found a phone in the guest bedroom. He called the police and then sat in the window, rocking the little girl until he heard sirens in the distance. Far, far away the hooves of fifty thousand horsemen came to a halt, in the space between the shrieking and the silence. Inside, in that very same place, Morgan Reece felt something move.

EPILOGUE

The following Sunday morning Morgan Reece drove out to Great Falls, parked his car and joined the others gathering in the parking lot.

He searched the crowd for Lindsay.

"Hi," she said, seeing him first, and broke away from two other women.

"Hi," Reece replied, wishing she'd take off her visor-style sunglasses.

"I'm surprised to see you. When you didn't show up last week, I figured you changed your mind."

"No. I didn't change my mind. Something came up at the last minute and I couldn't get away. But I'm ready now."

"Great. It's a beautiful day to go climbing," Lindsay said, and opened her arms to encompass the sun's warmth, the clear skies, the gentle breeze. She turned to head down the path to the cliffs that rose up from the river's shores.

Morgan Reece took one last look around, and hurried to catch up with her, glad to be alive.

ABOUT THE AUTHOR

Benjamin M. Schutz is the author of the novels and short stories about private eye Leo Haggerty. These works have been honored with a Shamus award as best P.I. Novel of the year for *A Tax in Blood* and both a Shamus and Edgar Allan Poe Award for the short story "Mary, Mary Shut the Door". Only one other short story has received both these awards. His non series short stories have appeared in such distinguished anthologies as *Crème de la Crime*, *A Century of Noir*, and *Mystery: The Best of 2002*. He is a forensic psychologist and lives in the Northern Virginia Suburbs of Washington, D.C.